The Winter
When Time Was Frozen

The Winter When Time Was Frozen

Els Pelgrom

Translation from the Dutch
by Maryka and Raphael Rudnik

William Morrow and Company ▪ Ne[illegible]

Printed in the United States of America.
1 2 3 4 5 6 7 8 9 10

Library of Congress Cataloging in Publication Data

Pelgrom, Els.
The winter when time was frozen.

Translation of De kinderen van het Achtste Woud.
Summary: In Holland during the last months of World War II a 12-year-old girl and her father find shelter with a farm family who courageously give sanctuary to all in need of it.
[1. Netherlands—History—German occupation, 1940-1945—Fiction. 2. World War, 1939-1945—Netherlands—Fiction. 3. Farm life—Fiction] I. Title.
PZ7.P363Wi [Fic] 80-21224
ISBN 0-688-22247-1 ISBN 0-688-32247-6 (lib. bdg.)

Contents

1 Sledding in the Dark *11*
2 Klaphek Farm *24*
3 The Furnace Pot and the Tobacco *31*
4 The Knapsack, the Coat, and the Bayonet *43*
5 The Wolthuis Family *52*
6 Fetching Bread *61*
7 The Billy Goat *71*
8 The Four Sows *80*
9 In the Night *87*
10 The Children of the Eighth Wood *94*
11 Munkie *104*
12 Sarah *111*
13 More About Sarah *118*
14 Broken Windows *125*
15 A Beautiful View *134*
16 No Need to Tell Sarah *141*
17 The Sick Horse *149*
18 Sarah Goes to the Doctor *157*
19 The Cows Go Out to Pasture *169*
20 Soldiers *179*
21 A Car With a Red Cross *191*
22 Hide-and-Seek *203*
23 The Boy Soldiers *217*
24 In the Cellar *227*
25 It Is Over *238*
26 Sissy's Death *246*

The Winter When Time Was Frozen

20

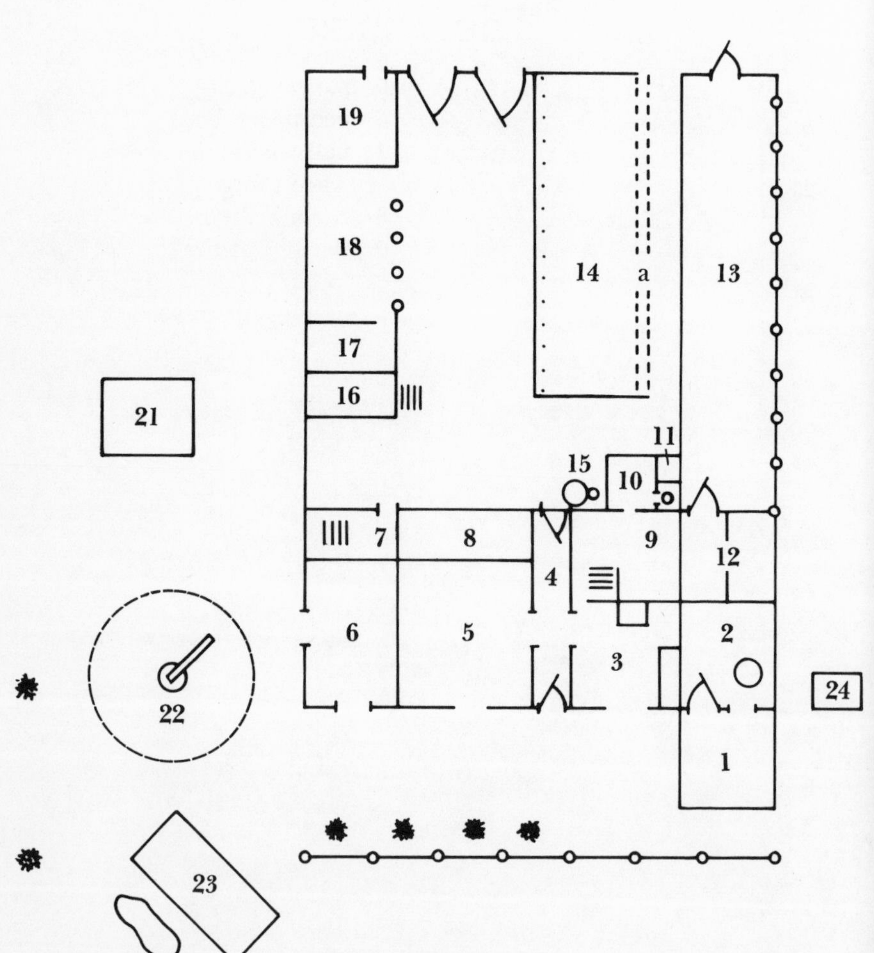

Klaphek Farm

1 pavement
2 scullery
3 kitchen
4 passageway
5 parlor
6 bedroom
7 hall with stairs to Theo's room
8 closet beds
9 sleeping alcove (cellar underneath)
10 inner courtyard
11 toilet
12 pigsty
13 open pigsty
14 cow area
a. drainage ditch
15 pump
16 room where feed cakes are kept
17 harness room
18 stalls for calves
19 horse stalls
20 the barn
21 well house
22 circular pavement for the pumping of water
23 summerhouse used for sawing wood
24 dog kennel
25 straw pile/grain stack
26 piece of a V-1
27 fruit trees

▪1▪
Sledding in the Dark

It had been snowing for days on end, and now the snow was freezing hard. The fir trees bowed their branches deep toward the ground under the heavy load they had to carry. On the small open pieces of land between the woods, snow lay as if on a frozen lake; the winter wheat slept in furrows that the harrow had drawn through the earth in autumn.

Evert Everingen and Noortje Vanderhook together had lifted the sled over the gate of the Calves' Meadow. On the other side, a narrow path ran down through the woods that grew up against the hill.

"Hang on tight! Here we go!" Evert yelled, and they shot off downward at high speed. The snow flew up and sent its powder swirling about and into their faces. Noortje held her breath, her cheeks tingling. She hung on, arms clasped tight around Evert. He was a year older, true, but so little taller that she could see over his shoulder.

Evert steered the sled with his feet. The rain had worn away the muddy path, and there were steep edges left on both sides. Noortje helped navigate the sled a few times, digging the heel of her clog into the ground.

A thick tree stood in the middle of the path. It left only a very narrow opening, which didn't seem wide enough for a sled with two children on it.

"Watch out!" Noortje cried.

Evert swung the sled past the tree, swerving a little up the banked sides of the path. Their arms scraped against the bark, they went bouncing slam-bang over a few gnarly roots, and then they rode on down a little more slowly. The slope was less steep now. The fir trees pressed closer together here, and the ground under the snow layer wasn't as hard and slippery. There were lots of fallen branches and dead ferns. So there was no need to put on the brakes when they got to the road, that wide asphalt road zigzagging from the village up through the forest all the way to the top of Heuven Hill and then continuing farther across the heath. With a last elegant flourish Evert steered the sled along the edge of the road and let it come to a stop with its nose tilted upward. On the other side of the road the slope continued downward and became thick with trees. Through the trees they could make out the shepherd's fields.

"Wow! That was some ride," he said.

Evert rarely spoke up like that. Usually he only mumbled a few words when Noortje would ask him something. That didn't bother her. She understood him very well, and she herself talked enough so it was never very silent between them.

They walked back and forth for a while, stamping their feet on the ground to chase the stiffness and cold out of their knees and legs. Evert was swinging his arms across each other, trying to slap his own back. Then he stamped his feet again, pacing about, and blew on his red fingers. Noortje was hopping up and down on both feet at the same time.

"Are you cold?" she asked.

"No."

"Why are you doing that then?"

"I just do."

"Does it help?"

"Yeah, sort of."

She tried it too, walking up and down just like Evert, taking big steps and hitting her back. Her hands stung. "It hurts," she said, "but it does make you warm, sort of. . . ."

Meanwhile, Evert had loosened the rope on the sled. Before they went downhill he had it tied around the slats on top, so it wouldn't get tangled in the iron runners.

"We've got to hurry," he muttered. "It's almost dark."

Noortje didn't say anything. She wanted to get warm all through before they went on, or else she'd be chilled to her bones in a little while. Evert couldn't be really cold, she thought. He was wearing a warm sweater underneath his jacket and had a cap with earmuffs on and long pants. And then he also had overalls, worn over the pants and sweater.

Now that winter had truly come she was almost always cold. Her legs were bare, and there was a hole in one of her clogs. Before they left she had stuffed some new straw into the clog, but the straw had gotten wet and her sock was already soaked through with melted snow. Before long that sock would be stuck to her foot, frozen stiff. That was something to think about: could a wet sock freeze onto your foot? Or would the warmth of your foot, no matter how cold it got, make the sock stay wet and not stiffen with ice . . . ? Actually a struggle was going on between the icy cold snow and the warm foot. While helping pull the sled upward, Noortje kept saying to herself, "Come on, foot! You can do it. Stay warm, please. Hup! One, two. Hup!"

It was getting dark fast. The forest was very dense here, and you could see only a small piece of the sky when you looked straight up. The sky was no longer blue as before, but gray. Was the sun already setting, or was there a new fall of snow coming? It was very still now. Not a single bird was rummaging around among the trees; they must have been safely hidden away in their nests. And the rabbits didn't show their faces either. They had nice warm holes, deep underneath the frozen ground. Only the crows were flying, passing high above the trees on their way to the birches scattered in clumps on the heath. But they weren't screeching as they usually did.

They didn't find it at all dreary or scary to be there in those woods, just the two of them. The silence gave them a nice safe feeling. They could hear their own breathing and the scrunchy snow under their wooden clogs. The sled was gliding so smoothly that you had to listen very carefully to hear the silken sound it made.

Suddenly they heard another sound. They immediately knew what was making it: a horse and wagon approaching up the hill. Because there were so many bends in the road, they couldn't see them yet. But the softly stepping sound of the horses' feet was already quite close.

"They're coming by on this side," Evert mumbled.

"Yes, we should get out of the way," whispered Noortje.

Who could that be, coming up behind them so close with his horse and wagon? They had better make themselves as invisible as possible. So they pulled the sled up onto the shoulder of the road and stood right against the trunk of a fat beech tree. It was so dark now that they could hardly make out one another's faces.

And yet they could tell at once who was coming around the bend there. It was Browny, pulling the milk wagon, and Henk, the hired man, at the reins. He didn't see the children and their sled till he was almost by them.

"Whoah, whoah!" he called out, and Browny stopped. The horse pawed with his left foot, scraping the hard-frozen crust of snow, blowing enormous clouds of steam out of his big, wide nostrils. Somebody else was sitting there across from Henk, a German soldier with his hands between his knees, bent over as if asleep.

"What are you doing here so late?" Henk asked. "It's almost dark. You should be milking, Evert."

"We've been sledding," Noortje said. "We found a nice steep little hill to go down."

"It's much too late to be outside," Henk said.

And Evert asked, "Can we tie the sled to the wagon, Henk, so you can pull us back?"

"All right, all right. But hurry it up. Your father is waiting, and we're still a long way from home."

The milk wagon was just a cart on two large wheels, and along its sides were two narrow benches. Evert tied the rope to the back of the cart and sat down on the sled, signaling to Noortje that she should come too.

"C'mon," he said. They felt a little jerk as Browny stepped forward, pulling the rope taut.

On the bottom of the milk wagon lay a few bulging sacks, potatoes probably. The soldier and Henk sat looking at the two children. The crunching of the wheels on dry snow sounded loud in the silence of the woods. Henk got out his small copper tobacco box, getting ready to roll a cigarette. But the German took a package of real cigarettes out of the pocket of his wide, grayish-green overcoat and offered one to Henk. The German gave him a light, and then cupped the flame of the match to his own cigarette.

"Thanks," Henk said.

Noortje sat watching the two men. She could only see their faces clearly when they took a drag on the cigarettes. For a second, the glowing ends would light up their faces, mouths, eyes, and lines of their cheeks. She couldn't see Henk's eyes, though, for they were under the shadow of his cap. His cheeks seemed less round than usual, and the little holes in his face, pockmarks they were, now looked like black splotches. The German had a very ordinary face, already a little oldish, and with something worrying in it, like a father who had sick children. If he weren't wearing that uniform, Noortje thought, you wouldn't be able to see that he's a German. You even might like him then.

Indeed he was sort of nice, for he said, "Bye!" and waved his hand when they came to the top of the hill and the children loosened the sled. They turned right, onto the cart tracks that ran alongside the heather field to Second Beech Lane. Henk drove his cargo on into the night, across the wide hilly landscape toward the Imbos, where a company of Germans were stationed. That's where he had to take the potatoes and the soldier. It was going to be very late before he'd be back at the farm.

Dark. They couldn't see if they were setting their feet in a hole or on a bump in the road. The sled bounced along behind them. Evert was in a hurry, and he didn't want to wait for Noortje when she stopped to shake the snow out of her clogs. At Second Beech Lane they could start a little jogging, for a path ran next to the wheel ruts there. The wind rustled the trees, rushing away through their tops, and under the canopied roof of the branches it was dark as a tunnel. Surely a change in the weather was on the way.

At the end of Beech Lane it seemed a little brighter. Klaphek Farm lay on a hill, surrounded by a sloping meadow and fields, which were closed in by the woods on all sides. The children were now walking on the path toward the house, and the wind blew straight into their faces. Where the house stood they could vaguely distinguish a dark spot; the barn with its pointed roof was another dark blotch. There were no lights anywhere.

While Evert set the sled upright against the wall, Noortje started opening the big door to the shed, which constituted the back part of the farmhouse. She let it turn inward slowly on its large hinges, and the upper part, unlatched, swung free. Evert pushed her inside and made the heavy iron latch fall into place. Only one small carbide lamp was burning in the shed; it was hung up behind the drainage ditch for the cows. But the space was so familiar to Noortje that she could see everything quite clearly, just as if it had been fully lit.

The cows turned their heads toward them when they came in. A few started lowing. And the third cow in the row, the one with the infected horn, banged its head against a pole. Noortje also saw that the rack for the horses had already been filled with fragrant, fresh hay and that only the Fox stood over it, her slender head beautiful there. The animal was slowly pulling bits out of the hay with its soft, warm mouth, swallowing them with great quiet dignity.

Pzzzt . . . Pzzzt . . . she heard. The farmer was already milking.

Evert threw off his jacket and quickly walked with a bucket behind the row of animals. "Which one for me, Dad?" he asked.

Farmer Everingen sat on a low, one-legged stool, his cap pulled all the way over his nose, a bucket squeezed between his knees, and pressed against the cow's flank. He hadn't looked up once, not even when the door banged. His hands let the warm milk stream into the bucket in steady, even squirts.

"Right here, boy. Next to mine."

Evert was sitting already. *Psssh . . . psssh . . .* the thin jets spouted into the empty bucket. The sound became fuller a little later as the jets became thicker.

Noortje stood alone in the center of the shed. She wasn't allowed to milk. Farmer Everingen didn't want her to learn how, because, he had said, a strange milker wasn't so good for the cow and in these times they needed every single drop of milk.

"Can I do anything?" Noor asked. No answer. "OK. Then I'll be back for the feeding soon," she said. She walked into the corridor leading to the farmhouse in front. It was pitch-dark there. She could hear Baby Sis.

She was used to walking through that pitch-dark corridor. She needn't hold her hands out in front of her for fear of bumping into something. At exactly the right spot, she took a step to the left to reach the kitchen door. The kitchen was all lit up and very warm. It seemed as if a warm cloud filled the small room.

Aunt Janna lifted a kettle off the fire and poured the boiling water into the coffeepot. Then she put the kettle on the back of the cooking range, away from the heat. The stove was the old-fashioned wood-burning kind, with concentric iron rings over the fire part. The bigger the pot the more rings you took out, and when you finished cooking you were supposed to cover the fire again, shoving the rings back into place. Aunt Janna did it all with one quick movement.

"Hello, Noor," she said. "Have you two been outside all this time? You know it's much too late, don't you?"

"Evert is doing the milking already," Noortje said.

"Uh! Uh! Uh!" cried Baby Sis.

Little Gerrit sat at the table eating a piece of bread. Aunt Janna was the mother of Evert Everingen, and Little Gerrit was his younger brother. He had beautiful blond curls and dark brown eyes, and he was only five years old. Sometimes he could be really naughty. Baby Sis was seven, and her actual name was Wilhelmina. But everyone called her Sis or Baby Sis. You couldn't tell that she was already seven. She was small and fat and couldn't walk. She sat the whole day in a crib pushed against one of the walls of the kitchen. In the evenings, after supper, Farmer Everingen and Aunt Janna carried the crib up to the sleeping alcove. That was a very small room above the cellar, where the whole family slept. There was a door in the kitchen, and behind that door was a trapdoor, which lifted up so that when it was open you could see the staircase going down to the cellar. Above that trapdoor there were a few steps, so when it was closed there was a tiny staircase leading up to the sleeping alcove.

Baby Sis had round, red cheeks and a small pug nose. Her little blue eyes were always filled with tears, and she was always drooling. She had thin, fine hair, cut off straight in front. Baby Sis made her noises all day long. "Uh! Uh! Ugg! Ugg!" she cried, and "prr*rrllll*!" Then she would bubble and splutter with her lips so that the saliva splattered all around.

Noortje's father had explained to her what was wrong with Baby Sis.

"She cannot grow as fast as a normal child and can't learn very much either," he had said. "That is because her little brains aren't working quite right. People call a child like that a 'mongoloid.' "

Noortje also knew that Aunt Janna's hair had turned so white because of Baby Sis. When Sis was born, Aunt Janna first thought she was a normal little child. But after a while she knew that Sis would never be normal, and then Aunt Janna's hair turned white in a week. Noortje often thought of that when she looked at Aunt Janna. She had the hair of an old woman, but her face was not old.

Aunt Janna had put some warm porridge on a plate.

"If you set the table now, I can feed Baby Sis," she said.

"Shall I feed her?" Noortje asked.

"No, no, I'll do that myself," said Aunt Janna, and she smiled. "Here we go, my little one. Come. We're going to have a nice little something," she said, bending over the crib and lifting the heavy child.

Sis was not toilet-trained, and there was always the smell of wet diapers near her crib. It wasn't a nice smell, but Noortje got used to it just as everyone else did. The smell of urine simply was part of the kitchen, just like the warmth of the stove and Sis's little noises.

Noor put the plates on the table. A small dish with homemade butter stood on the sink. The bread was there too. But she didn't have to cut the bread. "Anything else?" she asked.

"The cups and the spoons, and knives too," Aunt Janna said. "How else would you have us eat and drink, dear? And will you push the milk to the back of the stove, for it's already hot enough for the coffee? And then, please, get me another pitcher of water, and fill up the kettle."

Noortje did everything she was told. She took the white enamel pitcher and walked to the shed. The pump was right there, behind the door. While she worked the handle up and down so that the water poured into the pitcher in a few thick splurts, she thought that never in her life had she been in a house like this one where every little corner possessed its own smell.

For example, near the pump it smelled of dirty water, wet wood, and synthetic soap. Underneath the pump stood a large wooden tub to catch the water that still kept coming out when the bucket or pitcher was already filled. The tub was almost up to the top with dirty water. And on the iron bars of the pump handle lay a piece of clay soap. When the men had finished thier work, before they went in to eat, they washed their hands with it. When you were there at the pump, you had only to take two steps forward to smell something quite different. There, nearer the cows, you smelled their fodder, their feed cakes, and hay. But if you took three steps to the right of the pump you smelled the toilet, which was the worst smell of the whole house. The toilet was an old-fashioned one with a cesspit underneath. Just a wooden plank on a low brick wall, and in that plank was cut a round hole, which was covered with a wooden lid. You had to sit on that hole and got your bottom cold for there was a terrific draft from down below. Two steps to the left of the toilet you would be near the drainage ditch, and there it smelled of cow dung. Noortje sort of liked that smell. It was much nicer than the people's toilet, and also much better than the stink of pigs.

Noortje poured the water carefully from the pitcher into the kettle. Then she took a small poker, lifted a ring off the top of the cooking stove, and put the kettle on the fire. The fire was glowing hot! She had to squeeze her eyes shut. How did Aunt Janna manage to lift those rings with her bare hands? But of course, she had done it so often her hands had gotten a fireproof layer.

Baby Sis had finished her porridge. Aunt Janna gently cradled the child in her arms, rocking her back and forth, softly humming a song. You could see Baby Sis liked that. She sat very still and made no noises. Suddenly Aunt Janna sat up straight. "Yes, oh, yes," she said, and sighed a few times. "Are they almost finished with the milking?"

"I think so. Shall I go and help them feed the cattle?"

"Yes, why don't you? That's a good girl."

While Noortje walked again through the dark corridor, somebody knocked on the outside door. She opened it. First, she couldn't see a thing. But slowly her eyes got used to the dark, and she saw someone standing there, a man or a woman.

"Who is it?" she asked.

A strange man's voice answered, "I've come from Zemst to ask if I could get some milk here. We have a small child."

"Will you wait a minute?" Noortje closed the door again. She went to the kitchen and said, "There's a man asking for milk. I don't think he's been here before."

"You can let him in," Aunt Janna said.

No, they hadn't seen this man before at Klaphek. He was still young and very thin, and he looked like a real gentleman, even though he was wearing an old rag of a raincoat. Aunt Janna had put Baby Sis back into her crib; standing up straight in her small kitchen she looked very tall and large as she sized up the stranger.

"It's all right," she said. "Did you bring anything to put the milk in?"

The man had a bag with him. Out of it he took a bottle with a cork in it.

"Noor, will you go over and ask the men for a quart of milk?" Aunt Janna said. Soon Noortje was back with the bottle filled. It felt warm, because the milk was still warm. She heard the man saying, "We're from Arnhem, and now we are staying in Zemst. My wife is very weak. I still have two watches and a pair of good shoes. Would you accept those in exchange for more milk? What if I come by here regularly, for about four weeks, to get some milk . . . ?"

Aunt Janna's thinking line appeared just above her nose. Noortje had sat down on a chair near Sis's bed, looking at the grown-ups. She saw how Aunt Janna took the red cookie tin off the mantelpiece and set it on the table.

"We don't do that sort of thing," she said. "You can come here twice a week for four weeks, to fetch a quart of milk. It's eleven cents per quart. Before the war milk cost nine cents, but everything is more expensive now."

The stranger looked at Aunt Janna, amazed. "My, you don't find that anymore," he said. "Most farmers want to get something valuable in exchange for food. Eleven cents for a quart of milk, well . . . I'm happy with that!"

"I know there are farmers who take advantage, but not us. It's bad enough when people are hungry. We don't want to get rich from it."

Aunt Janna paused a moment. "Of course, we've had our bad times too," she said. "Before the war, things were very bad for farmers. But there's always something to eat on a farm. Now then, why don't you come back the day after tomorrow, and you get your two quarts."

The man had taken out his purse; he put eleven cents in Aunt Janna's hand. She dropped the money into the cookie tin and set it back on the mantelpiece. The tin was almost filled with small change.

Noortje opened the outside door for the man. "Good-bye!" he said. "And thanks a lot!"

She heard him walk across the meadow through the snow, wheeling his bike, to the gate of First Beech Lane. Oh, how cold it was! She was glad she didn't have to make that trip over the dark heath.

▪2▪
Klaphek Farm

Klaphek Farm lay hidden by woods, not far from Heuven Hill. When you walked down to the end of First Beech Lane, you could take a narrow winding path to the right across the heath to Klinger Wood, and then you were in Zemst. But when you stood there at the end of Beech Lane and took the path that led straight ahead through the heath, you came to the village of Ulsten. But, if you walked all the way down Second Beech Lane, the heath lay big and wide all the way to the hills in the north, as far as one could see.

Till September, 1944, Noortje and her father had been living in the center of Arnhem, just the two of them in an apartment. Noortje's mother had died several years before the war broke out. Noortje was still very small then.

She had always liked living with her father in the city. True, she'd been alone a lot, and it also became more and more difficult to find enough food because of the war.

When the British lost the battle of Arnhem, all the Arnhemers had to leave the city. Noortje and her father threw some clothes, a few blankets, and some books into bags and suitcases, tied them onto their bicycles, and pedaled out into the big moving stream of refugees.

All those people who were forced to leave their houses were not a very pretty sight. They saw a man and woman pushing a handcart on which someone sick lay. And old people, gray with fatigue, shuffling along, only a small bundle of clothes in their hands, because they weren't strong enough to carry heavy suitcases. One mother pushed a carriage with three small children in it. The people walked with set faces, staring straight ahead. They each had enough trouble of their own and didn't pay much attention to the others. There had also been many Germans on the road, trucks going up and down and troops of singing soldiers marching in the direction of the city.

Soon the farms situated on the sides of the roads, and also the barns belonging to them, were filled up with evacuees. That's what the people who were chased out of their city were called. Noortje bicycled north with her father; they were looking for a good spot to stay for a few days. But there were lots of people all over already, and together with twenty others they'd slept in an empty schoolroom.

There were refugees not only in the farms they passed, but also in the houses of the towns and villages they came through. They couldn't stop anywhere longer than a few days. And food got scarcer and scarcer. There was very little to be gotten with their rationing cards, and the Germans confiscated the farmers' supplies. Noortje and her father both got even thinner than they already were; there wasn't a single day when they really had enough to eat.

"We're straying much too far away from home," Father said one day in November. "We should be turning back. And if they still don't allow us to enter the city, we'll stay near it. The war can't last much longer!"

They rode back and a few days later arrived at the first houses of the city. There they ran into a guard station and had to get off their bikes. The Germans searched their bags and suitcases and found the half roll, all the food they had. They took it. Then they were told to turn around and get out of there fast. No one was allowed in the city.

"We should be glad they didn't grab our bikes," Father said, after they rode side by side in silence for a while. They both were tired, from the long journey, from hunger, and especially from the disappointment.

There were lots of soldiers on the road, but no civilians to be seen anywhere. They hadn't gone far when Father said, "I've had enough cobblestones and singing Germans for today. Come on, Noortje, let's go left here, into these beautiful woods. Then we'll forget all this misery and just pretend we're on a vacation."

Noortje was so tired she couldn't even laugh. They took a sandy path and came through a beautiful wood and then to the heath. It was wonderfully quiet there, not a single human being. You could see that autumn was already far along, and it was getting dark early. The sun set behind the hills, and the small, naked birch trees caught its last rays. They looked as if there were no such thing as a war going on, and as if all the terrible things of the last years hadn't really happened.

And so Noortje and her father first came to Beech Lane with its wagon ruts running between the thick, smooth tree trunks. A layer of gleaming wet leaves lay on the moss that grew on the ground.

"Let's go in here," Noortje called out. "It's lovely here, and who knows where it will lead to!" And so they found Klaphek.

Past the bend in Beech Lane, they suddenly saw the farm lying there. They hadn't expected to find a house so far away from the world of people, and Father said, "Maybe they'll let us sleep in the hay there for a night. And then we'll see what's next in the morning."

They ended up in the small kitchen, eating bread and

bacon, as much of it as they wanted. That same evening Farmer Everingen said to Mr. Vanderhook, "The wife and I have been thinking. If you would like, the two of you can stay here. It cannot last very much longer now, and if we all move ourselves a little closer together, there'll be space enough."

Everingen and his wife went to sleep with their children in the small sleeping alcove, so that Mr. Vanderhook and Noortje could have their own bedroom.

There was already one other guest at the farm when they came there—Theo. They didn't see him till the next morning. Sometimes, when the sun shone, he walked outside for a while, but he never came into the kitchen. He slept in the maid's room, which was called that because the maid used to live there. For the last few years now, there hadn't been a maid at Klaphek and all the work was done by Everingen, Aunt Janna, and Henk, the farmhand. When Noortje was awake during the night, she could hear Theo coughing in the room above. Theo was sick.

The first days at Klaphek, Noortje had the feeling she was in a dream. And when she woke up she would be back on her bike trekking from one village to the next. Or she would be in their apartment in the city, where she'd been alone so often. There was nobody to talk with there when she got home from school. She had to remember the events of the whole day, so she could tell them to her father when he came home from work.

Here at Klaphek she didn't have to go up a long staircase first to be at home. And aside from having her own father, there was another father, and a mother, and two brothers, and a sister. And then there were horses and cows, chickens and geese, pigs, and a nanny goat and a billy goat, a dog, and a whole bunch of cats.

The feeling that she was dreaming hadn't lasted very long. No, now it was just the other way around; her former life seemed very long ago, as if it hadn't really been hers, but the life of a different girl she'd once been told about.

The autumn went by and winter had begun, and they still couldn't go back home. Arnhem was an empty city, and they didn't know what it looked like there.

The Germans still occupied the greater part of the Netherlands. Life became very difficult for the Dutch people; the German armies had to eat too, and they took whatever they could use. There was hardly anything left for the Dutch.

Not a day passed without someone knocking at the door asking for something to eat. At each midday meal there were always strangers at the table sharing the food. These were people on a food-foraging trip who were lucky enough to arrive at Klaphek just at dinnertime. For Aunt Janna cooked at least twice as much as they needed for themselves, because she didn't want to send anyone away with an empty stomach.

On New Year's Day it started snowing. It snowed and froze almost every day. A thick layer of frozen snow covered the world, making everything around them beautiful and mysterious, as in an old tale.

The evening they'd been outside so late with the sled, Noortje and Evert, sleepy from the warmth of the kitchen, were sitting with the others around the table. There wasn't much talk. Aunt Janna was mending a sock.

"I wonder how Henk is doing," said Mr. Vanderhook. "What time will he be back?"

"Yes, who knows. . . . I would have gone myself, but

he felt he had to do it. They just order you around, the Germans. Bring this here, take that there!" Farmer Everingen said.

"Yes, Chris, but if one doesn't do it, they would make it even worse," Aunt Janna put in.

And Everingen said, "If I say 'no' I'll be taken away. And then who would see to the work here and look after the cattle? And quite a few people wouldn't be eating then."

"Still, it's very risky for Henk," Mr. Vanderhook said. "He's a healthy young fellow. They may very well send him off to Germany."

"That's exactly the point. They already know he's here. And now they use him in this way."

"Well, I won't get a wink of sleep till I hear him coming in," Aunt Janna said. "He's a good boy. You don't get many like him anymore these days."

"Yeah, he's strong as a horse. Come, we might as well get ready for bed." Everingen rose from his creaking wicker chair.

They said good night to each other. In the shed, it was ever so dark now. Noortje and her father had to grope their way past the wooden partition to the toilet. There they waited for each other.

Noortje could hear the cows chewing. Something rustled above her head in the hay. Now it was her turn to go to the toilet. "You'll wait for me, won't you?" she said to her father.

The toilet plank was cold. She finished as fast as she could. When they walked through the dark shed, they took each other's hand. Close to the pump stood a beet cutter. You had to watch out for it.

"Mind the cutting machine," Noor whispered. "Ow! I hit myself on that bar again."

The bedroom had become very cold. The stove must have been dead for hours, and the wind was rattling the shutters. She undressed quickly. The sheets in the old wooden bed were clammy and cold. Noortje crept close against her father. She fell asleep immediately.

But Mr. Vanderhook did not sleep. He lay listening to his daughter's quiet breathing, thinking that she was a real child of the war. Almost twelve years old, he thought, and what things she'd gone through already! What would she have been like if these had been normal times? Would she have been less serious and more childlike then?

He heard Theo's coughing in the room above. He sounded badly congested, and the coughing lasted a long time. And then finally, hours later, there was the sound of the big door rattling. Rachel, the old sheepdog, softly whimpered. The horse was taken to its stall where the Fox greeted him with one quiet snort. Henk kicked off his clogs at the bottom of the ladder, before climbing up to his little loft room.

In the alcove room Aunt Janna turned herself over. The farmer was snoring and the children slept quietly. Now she could close her eyes too.

▪3▪
The Furnace Pot and the Tobacco

The next morning Noortje was to help Aunt Janna in the scullery. Aunt Janna had started the furnace pot there. The furnace pot was a sort of very large kettle under which twigs were burned. When this big pot wasn't being used, it was terribly cold in the scullery, but now it was nice and warm. A heap of dirty laundry lay on the floor, sheets and undershirts and Sissie's diapers and kitchen towels. A funny sour smell came from all that dirty laundry.

Aunt Janna walked back and forth with two zinc pails, fetching water from the stone cistern near the well. She poured the water into the caldron, and Noortje took care of the fire. With a long poker she pushed the twigs and branches over the grate, adding new ones from time to time. The fire crackled and sparked, and it smelled nice. Some smoke escaped from the pipe that ran up into the chimney, and therefore they left the outside door standing open. The scullery filled up with blue smoke and steam, which made Noortje cough. Tears filled her eyes. And yet she felt good.

"Keep the fire going strong, Noortje. We still have the pigs' food to cook after we're finished with boiling the laundry," Aunt Janna said.

Noortje squatted in front of the stove, tending the fire.

When her legs ached from all that squatting, she got up and walked around a bit.

"Kssht, kssht, kssht!" she called out at the geese, who had flocked onto the little pavement in front of the door, stretching their long necks inside curiously. "You don't belong in here. You go and mess things up outside, but not in the house!"

She poked the ashes through the grate and broke a few branches into smaller pieces. Now she could push a whole bunch into the stove, for it was almost burned out. The branches were still sticking out quite a bit, and before they began to glow a streak of gray-blue smoke slid out and crept along them. . . .

Behind the scullery was the pigsty. There were four sows, and it was almost dark in there. Noortje opened the door to the pigsty. The beasts instantly started squealing and squeaking, pushing the lid of the trough up with their snouts. Pigs were always hungry.

"You've got to have some patience," Noortje said to them. "First the laundry and then it's your turn. Take it easy, will you!"

She looked down at their long, pink backs and their slack, hanging ears. The pigs looked at her with their small, yellowish eyes that gave her an eerie feeling. The stiff white hairs that stuck out of their skin made her think of those slices of boiled bacon they ate here at Klaphek. They were sort of glazed, and sometimes there were still a few hairs on them. She didn't really like that stuff, but she simply had to eat it. When so many people go hungry, you cannot say, I don't like that.

Evert was helping his father in the potato pit that morning. They kept their entire supply of potatoes in there. It had to last them until the next potato harvest.

"You can take these away," Farmer Everingen said, and

stretched his back. There was a deep worry line in his forehead. Evert lifted the full basket into the wheelbarrow and pushed it back into the farmyard. Every week they replenished the supply of potatoes in the cellar. More and more often now, it happened that the week wasn't over and yet the amount stored in the cellar was finished. It was going fast this winter. They wouldn't make it to the summer that way. Every day people came asking for food. They came all the way from Amsterdam or from The Hague, some on bicycles with wooden wheels, others on foot. Those people were thin as skeletons, and yet they were the stronger ones. Those who stayed at home were in even worse shape. It was said that some people had already died of hunger.

Farmer Everingen looked at the potatoes in the pit and sighed. "Well, we'll just have to see," he said to himself loudly, and he started covering the pit again with straw and sand, so that the potatoes would be protected against the frost.

Evert shoved the basket across the kitchen floor toward the stairs to the cellar. In the cellar there were rows of preserve jars, bottled pears and applesauce, standing on the shelf. A few bunches of onions were hanging from a beam, and in a corner stood a small barrel with sauerkraut. It was still half-full. On top of the sauerkraut lay a cloth, and on top of it a wooden lid with a heavy stone on it. On the bottom shelf stood a long row of empty preserve jars. The peas were already finished, and also the carrots and the endives too.

After he had taken the potatoes into the cellar, Evert joined Noortje in the scullery. They took turns shoving new branches into the furnace. The laundry was almost boiling now. They weren't talking, but it was nice sitting together like that and watching the fire.

Noortje looked outside. It was beautiful. The snow that glittered in the sun looked almost made of gold. Thick icicles hung down off the eaves, and in the warm rays of the sun drops were gliding down them and splashing onto the paving. Whenever a cloud came across the sun, it got chilly and somber for a minute.

Noortje thought of something she had seen the winter before, when she was still living at home in the city. She often found herself thinking of that—almost every day. One morning on her way to school, she was passing the railroad station just as she always did. There, on the square in front of the station, German soldiers stopped her. She was not allowed to walk on. She was not the only one. There were already a great many people standing at the edge of the sidewalk who were not allowed to go farther either. Not a word was spoken. At least a few hundred people were standing there on the square, and yet it was dead still.

A long row of people walked in the middle of the road. They had suitcases in their hands. German soldiers with helmets stood on both sides, pointing their guns. They didn't say anything and they didn't do anything. The trolleys too had stopped, and the people inside the trolleys looked out through the windows.

The men and the women with the suitcases walked on in silence toward the station. They all had a yellow star on their coats, so you could see they were Jews. Noortje knew that many Jewish people were picked up and shoved into trains and taken away. She did not know where to. It was called "deportation." There was a long row of them walking there now. And suddenly she was very startled. There was a man among them she knew.

This man worked in a furniture-repair shop in their neighborhood. He had said hello to her a few times, smiling, and one time she'd also talked with him. He had given her a few pieces of wood then, and she had made a string puppet of the wood at home.

The man held a little girl by the hand; the child walked very quietly alongside him. She was also wearing a yellow star on her coat. In his other hand he carried a large suitcase.

They had to wait there for a very long time. She got to school much too late. But the teacher didn't mind, for she knew all about the delay already. That whole morning in class Noor had felt the strange silence in her head, the silence of the station square, which had been so odd because so many people were there.

She was also thinking again of the days in September when they were fighting for the city of Arnhem. For the first time in her life she'd been afraid, really terribly scared. One day Noortje and her father had to flee inside with strange people. There were bombs falling nearby. The thudding of the bombs sounded right above their heads. It lasted a very long time. Yes, there seemed no end to it.

Because it was so crowded there, Noortje got separated from her father. She huddled close against a strange lady, a lady with lots of red curls. She put her arms around Noortje, pressing her firmly. Now and then pieces of plaster fell from the ceiling, and then someone muttered, "That one was close."

One woman kept saying, "Oh my, oh my, oh my, oh my!" But most people sat waiting quietly for the raid to be over. A small bulb that dangled from the ceiling kept flashing on and off.

Noortje was glad that she could sit so close to the lady with red hair. When the bombs came very near, she pushed her face against the lady's breast. She could feel her own heart jump in her throat. It was beating very fast.

And every time she pressed her head against the lady she would hear another sound. *Boom, boom, boom, boom,* she heard, and at first she didn't know what the sound was. Soon she understood; it was that woman's heart. She was afraid too and perhaps also glad that Noortje was so close to her.

She found herself thinking of all those things now, while looking out at that fairy-tale world of snow and glistening icicles and the dark woods in the distance.

"The war is a funny thing," she said to Evert. "Sometimes it's so horrible, and then sometimes it's so nice and cozy."

"Yeah, awfully nice. . . ." Evert said.

The burning twigs crackled and smoked. Old Rachel shambled in and lay in front of the fire, head on front paws, blinking at the flickering red glow.

Noortje thought it was wonderful at night in the kitchen, when they had finished eating and cleared away the dishes. This was Saturday night, and Henk was making tobacco.

The farmer and Henk had planted some tobacco the summer before, a small plot of it to the side of the barn. In autumn, they'd strung the large green leaves, threaded them on a line hung in the attic for drying. Every Saturday night Henk went up to get a small stack of tobacco leaves and brought them down to the kitchen.

One by one he smoothed the browned leaves out on the oilcloth and made them into neat little stacks. Noortje and Evert sat on each side of him and watched. Tobacco making was the most wonderful thing Henk did. He was really good at it. He took his time, pausing briefly after each step.

"What do you do next, Henk, roll it up, right?" Noortje said impatiently.

Henk said nothing. Very slowly he began to roll up the small pile, starting at the pointed ends and going to the stems. The leaves were dry, and yet they didn't break; it was good home-grown stuff and gave off a musty smell. When he had finished rolling, Henk had in his hand a fat, dark-brown roll of tobacco leaves that looked like a much-too-sloppy cigar. Now came the most exciting moment. Henk opened the door to the dark corridor and stuffed the roll between doorpost and door. Very slowly he began to push the door shut. It didn't close, of course; the roll was too thick, and the door groaned.

"If he keeps pushing, the hinges will pop out!" Evert whispered into Noortje's ear. Then Henk, the door, and everything would fall to the floor!

That never happened. Henk squeezed the roll a few times more, till he figured it was enough. The tobacco roll looked like a not-so-sloppy cigar, but it was still very big and fat.

"So, that's done," Henk said, "and now my coffee." Henk probably liked the business with the door best of all too, for after it he always enjoyed his coffee in slow, contented sips.

Now the tobacco needed only to be cut, and then he could roll cigarettes from it. With his large, razor-sharp jackknife Henk cut thin slivers off the roll on Aunt Janna's vegetable board. He put the tobacco in a tin; he had finished preparing his weekly supply.

"I'm going to have me a real nice cigarette now," he said, filling the copper box that he always kept in his jacket. Then he started rolling the cigarette.

Noortje's father did not smoke, and Evert's father chewed. His short teeth were all brown, and usually there was some brown tobacco juice in one of the corners of his mouth. Noortje and Evert once tried it too, to see if chewing was nice. They'd taken a tobacco leaf from the attic and twisted pieces of it up into a ball. Then each tore off a wad and put it in their mouth. Ugh! How awful! It was sharp, and it burned your tongue. They both flushed a hot red, and it made them cough and spit.

A cigarette like Henk's seemed much nicer. It smelled very good, and blowing a cloud of smoke out of your mouth must be fun. Even when he didn't have a cigarette in his mouth, there was always that nice smell of smoke and tobacco around Henk. It must have penetrated his clothes too.

The next day was Sunday. After their midday meal they saw Henk go off to the village on his bike. The house was very quiet. The farmer was having his afternoon nap, leaning all the way back in his own chair in the kitchen and snoring with his mouth open. Mr. Vanderhook was reading in the bedroom. The stove burned and the sun shone in. All over the house it was warm and quiet. Baby Sis and Gerrit were sleeping, and Aunt Janna was nowhere to be seen. Evert and Noortje were in the shed.

"Don't say a word. I'm going to do something. You'll see," Evert said. He started climbing up the ladder to Henk's little room. "You stay here," he whispered. "And whistle if you hear someone coming."

Noortje waited till Evert disappeared up over the top of the ladder. Then she kicked off her clogs and climbed up too. Henk's little room was a real farmhand's room. It was made of wood, on top of the loft, and there was very little space. Even Noortje had to bend down to get through the door. A table and a chair were pushed underneath the dormer window.

There were two closet beds in the room. One wasn't

being used. There was an old straw mattress in it. The other was Henk's.

"You were supposed to stay down there. What did you do with your clogs?" Evert asked.

"I took them off. That way I could climb up the ladder better."

"Stupid. What if someone comes into the shed and sees them standing there? Then they'll know where we are."

"But everyone is asleep. Anyway, what are you doing?"

Evert was poking around, looking in all the corners of the little room. Now he pulled a tuft of tobacco out of his pants pocket and showed it to Noortje. "I wouldn't mind smoking a cigarette myself," he said, "but I can't find the paper. Where did that damned Henk hide his cigarette paper?"

Maybe they're finished; maybe he's got the last ones with him, Noor thought.

They took another good look around the room. One thing was sure; the paper was not in the tin with the tobacco. Inside Henk's closet bed was a shelf on which stood a small kerosene lamp. It also held a few books and a wallet. But no paper.

"It's a very small bed for such a big man," said Noor.

"Oh, but he doesn't fit in it."

"What?"

"No. Look at what he's done." Evert lifted the blankets at the bottom end and pushed the bag of straw to the side a little, so that Noortje could see how Henk had solved the problem of the short closet bed. He had cut a square out of the wooden partition, and in that spot he had constructed a small box.

"You see," Evert said. "That's where he puts his big feet."

"Oh, yeah, but won't they get cold that way?"

"No, not Henk's feet. He always keeps his socks on. Come on now. If he finds us up here. . . ."

Noortje quickly straightened out the blankets and followed Evert down the ladder.

"How can I get hold of some paper now?" Evert said.

"Let me go and have a look at my father's."

"Your father doesn't even smoke."

"No, but he does have lots of paper." And very soon she returned wtih a sheet torn out of a writing pad.

At the back of the barn was a little corner where nobody ever came. There were all sorts of parts from old machines lying helter-skelter in a heap there. A thick layer of dust lay on top of all the junk. There were wide chinks in the walls, and the wind could blow through them freely. They sat down next to each other on an old plow.

Evert tore off a piece of paper and rolled it into a cigarette. It didn't really look much like a cigarette, and it wasn't much more than a tiny white pouch with some tobacco in it. He held a burning match near it, and the paper caught fire. He sucked in on the cigarette, the paper burned halfway, but nothing happened to the tobacco. The cigarette had gone out.

"It won't work with this paper," he said.

"Let me try."

"It's just not going to work. This paper is no good."

Noortje lit the cigarette. The paper burned and then it died out, and she didn't taste any smoke. They sat thinking quietly for a while. Noortje was thinking about paper. There must be a way to get hold of those small, thin, white sheets. They were so thin, so almost transparent, and they whispered between your fingers. There was something that looked just like that kind of thin paper . . . thin pages in a book. . . . And suddenly she knew where she had seen it.

"Stay here and wait for me," she said.

The kitchen was very quiet. Baby Sis lay on her back half asleep. Her eyes opened and closed without seeing Noortje. She heard Aunt Janna in the scullery, talking to Gerrit. And Farmer Everingen still snored in his chair, his brown hands folded over his stomach.

Above Sissy's crib in a corner near the window was a triangular shelf. Every day after the midday meal Everingen said to Evert, "Go and get it for me, boy."

And then Evert got up and took the Bible off the shelf. Everingen read a passage from the Bible, while the others sat very still. The pages of the Bible were made of very thin paper, just like cigarette paper.

It was a small, thick book, and the black linen cover was worn. There was a purple ribbon attached to the back, which lay between the pages Farmer Everingen had read from last. Noortje leafed through the book. Could she rip out a page? Would she dare do that? What if they noticed it?

But what use is tobacco if you can't smoke it? And see, all the way in the back of the book was an empty page with only the name of the printer on it in very tiny letters. Quickly Noortje tore out that page. You couldn't see it was missing at all.

Farmer Everingen groaned and his chair creaked. Startled, Noortje looked behind her. He had only moved in his sleep. His eyes stayed shut. In the corridor she put the page to her nose. A real Bible smell, she thought.

Evert gave her a rather strange look when she handed him the thin paper. He didn't ask where she had gotten it. With a solemn expression on his face, he tore off a straight strip and carefully rolled a cigarette. And yes, it really looked like the genuine article. He struck the match and lit it. The tobacco began to glow.

"Eh-huh, eh-huh, eh-huh," Evert said. He blew out enormous smoke clouds. The smoke didn't just come out of his mouth but out of his nose too.

"You're taking too much all at once," Noor said. "Let me try."

Noortje also took a puff, but only a little one. The paper lit up briefly with a real flame. It tasted like ash and fire. Slowly she blew a thin stream of smoke out of her mouth.

"Hmmm. Good," she said.

They took turns puffing the cigarette. Their cold little corner became nice and cozy. Before the cigarette was altogether finished it went out by itself.

"Tomorrow we'll have another one," Evert said.

He folded the page from the Bible neatly and knotted it into his handkerchief together with the tobacco. And then he hid it in a secret spot there in the junk shed.

▪4▪
The Knapsack, the Coat, and the Bayonet

When you climbed on the beams above the horse stalls, you got onto the hayloft. The hay was smooth and warm and fragrant. In the middle of the loft was a hole, through which Henk and Evert pitched hay every evening, but otherwise you had to be careful not to come too near the edge of it. It was nice to be in the hayloft to talk a little or just dream away. When you lay in the hay you were never cold. Evert and Noortje were lying there next to each other now, chewing on some pieces of hay. Noortje tried to imagine what the hay looked like when it wasn't cut and dried yet. There were also thistles in it, and they were prickly.

Evert walked with big steps over the lumpy hay all the way to the other side of the house. There was a narrow space between the hay and the roof, and there suddenly he let himself go sliding down. Noortje was startled. Evert sat more than six feet down, looking up at her.

"You coming too?" he called.

Noortje let herself go. Sitting almost straight up, she followed her feet down fast. And there she was next to Evert, pressed into a little hay hollow. Right before their eyes was a roof tile made of glass. They could see through it to the outside. What a wonderful spot, a perfect lookout post! They could see what lay beyond the tops of the trees of Beech Lane: the outlines of the fields against the hill, the squares and rectangles of plowed-over land, the woods around. When they looked left, they saw the cart ruts running from the gate to the house and in the distance the trees of Second Beech Lane sticking out above everything else.

Bunches of straw had been stuffed in between the roof tiles to keep out the wind. Noortje took some hay and wiped the glass roof tile clean. Now they could see even better. In the snow on the meadow, black spots had appeared.

"Oh, look, there are the geese!" Noortje pointed. How ragged they looked in the wind. Their feathers didn't seem so white anymore, and their orange feet were funny against the white snow. It blew so hard that a few of the feathers on their backs were standing up. Here so high and tucked under the roof they could hear the wind roar.

"You see, there in the distance, somebody's walking," Evert said.

"Where?"

"There, on the field, at the edge of the wood."

"I don't see anything."

"But I'm pointing to it. There, just a little past the corner. It's a man."

"Oh, yes, now I see him. That looks like Theo. He's always wearing something white around his neck."

"It is Theo. Funny that he goes out in this weather."

"Why? You can't always sit inside, can you? And I haven't seen Theo this whole week."

Evert said, "But this isn't his kind of weather. He's not supposed to go out."

"Is Theo very sick?" Noor asked. "Why doesn't he ever come into the kitchen?" Evert gave no answer.

"I think it's really a funny kind of illness. He goes outside, but joining us in the evening nice and cozy . . . ? Oh, no!" Noortje said.

"But you don't know everything," Evert said. "Theo's sickness is contagious. That's why he only talks with us when we're outside."

"Oh! Does he know that?"

"Of course he knows, silly. And he doesn't want us to get sick because of him. It's nice of him not to come into the kitchen."

"Shall we go see him?"

"All right."

They climbed down along the beams and ran to the field behind Beech Lane.

Theo was a man of twenty. He had been in the Resistance, and he had done some dangerous things. There were not many people who knew of his activities, and of those few most had been taken prisoner. Theo could have been picked up too. The Everingens understood very well that it wasn't only because of his illness that Theo appeared so rarely among them. Here at Klaphek he would be safe from the Germans as long as he didn't show his face too often.

Most of the day Theo stayed in his own little room with its slanted, boarded roof. There he lay in bed underneath five woolen blankets. His bed was the only spot where he could get a little warmth. There was no stove burning in this room, and the window was usually open. Theo was a tuberculosis patient, and a stove wasn't good for him. Fresh air was the only thing that could make him better.

If he had to, he could get out into the attic through a trapdoor at the back of the closet in his room, and things would really have to be bad if he couldn't escape through there. That day he came to the farm asking for a roof over his head, Farmer Everingen pointed out the trapdoor without any questions.

Lately Theo was more absorbed by his illness. The coughing fits were getting worse and worse. Often he couldn't sleep at all during the night. Aunt Janna had already asked him once if she shouldn't call the doctor in, but Theo didn't want that. "No," he had said, "that isn't necessary at all. I know what's best for me."

Evert and Noortje caught up with Theo. "Hello!" was the most they could say. They'd been running all the way up the hill, and now they stood there flushed and panting.

"So," said Theo, "you two look like twins."

Noortje and Evert said nothing. They were still out of breath.

"You're both as red as boiled beets," Theo said, "my favorite dish."

"Theo, aren't you cold?" Noortje asked. "And where are you going?" She had caught her breath a little.

"First," Theo answered, "I am not cold, although you may find that hard to imagine. For you, of course, think of nothing else but the question: am I cold, or am I warm? But, my dear child, cold like everything else is relative. When a man doesn't want it to be cold, it isn't cold."

"Ah, shut up," Noortje said. "You've got a thick sweater on."

That was true. Theo was wearing a thick sweater, and he had a towel around his throat. Whenever you saw Theo, you always saw the towel around his throat.

"You haven't told us yet where you're going," Evert said.

"Oh, I'm just walking about a little, enjoying nature. And I found something I want to show you two. . . ."

"What is it? What is it?" Noortje cried.

"Patience, madam. We'll be there shortly."

As always, Theo was in a good mood. He joked and he laughed just as he always did. And yet for the whole week he had been shut inside and not spoken to a single soul. Perhaps that illness of his wasn't so bad after all, Noortje thought. And she asked, "Theo, don't you ever get bored?"

Theo didn't answer.

The edge of the wood made a square corner here. Behind it was yet another piece of the field. You could still see that at one time, years ago, someone had cut away the trees that grew up against the hill to turn it into arable land, and then that person must have thought, well now, this seems good enough to me with a few trees left here, and on that piece I can grow some barley or turnips.

At the far corner of the field it became difficult to walk between the trees. Bramble bushes were growing low to the ground, and they had spread from one tree to the next, blocking the entrance to the wood. But the ploughing had made a narrow ditch there, and that's what they walked through now, Theo leading. After a few more steps he halted.

"It's somewhere around here," he said, and he pushed aside some of the dead branches full of tiny thorns. "There's a hollow underneath this bush . . . wait a second . . . was it here or over there? I discovered it last week, but it was already too dark to investigate any further then."

Evert bent aside some branches too, grabbing them firmly and not caring whether he got pricked or not.

"Here!" he said. "There's a hole here. I can't see it very well, because it's so black."

"I think there's something in it," said Theo. "Perhaps it's something we can use. I'm glad you two have come along. That hole must have been made by some crazy Kraut. Once in a while there's one who's smart enough to run away from the army. I'm sure a few of them are hiding out in these woods."

Noortje was on her knees. She looked in between the bramble bushes, then gazed up into the dark forest of firs and shivered. Bending down again, she saw the hole, a black rectangle in the earth.

"Let me feel," she said. "You keep those nasty branches away. . . ." She stuck out her hand all the way down.

"I feel something soft," she said. "Clothes. A coat or something."

"Get up," Theo said, and his voice suddenly sounded angry. "You better let me feel. Here, grab that branch, Noor." And he quickly squatted down, pushing her aside.

Sometimes, it's just as if he doesn't want you to be with him, Noortje thought sadly.

But she couldn't know that all of a sudden Theo had been afraid. He'd thought, Who knows what's in that hole? It could be a dead Kraut; it could be anything. . . . And like an idiot, I let that child reach in there.

He too felt something soft. Yes, it was a piece of clothing. He got it out and threw it on the snow-covered ground. It was a coat, a German soldier's coat.

"Hold on, kids, there's more!" he cried, and then a second later a bag flew through the air and landed in the snow. Out of sheer excitement Noortje let go of the branch she was supposed to hold back. It was such a beautiful bag, actually a knapsack. All three of them had seen German soldiers wearing such knapsacks on their backs when they were on the march. The flap of the bag was made of fur, a pretty, light-brown, rough kind of fur. Too bad, there was only a small cake of soap and a ball of wool inside.

"What kind of animal would this fur be from?" Noortje asked Evert.

But he wasn't listening. He was looking at Theo who'd gotten up with yet another thing in his hand. Theo was holding a big sort of knife, a gleaming silver-colored bayonet. He stood all hunched over, with his hand at his chest. Suddenly he turned around, took a few steps away from them, and began to cough terribly.

The coughing fit lasted a long time. There seemed no end to it, and it sounded awful and all choked up. They saw Theo's shoulders shaking. He kept his head bent over. The arm holding the bayonet hung slack against his side. Finally the coughing was over. Theo wiped his face with his towel. Slowly he turned around and came back toward the children. Noortje had gotten up. She looked at him with big eyes.

"Theo," she whispered, "you've cut yourself!"

There was blood on the towel around Theo's neck. Theo saw what she was looking at and quickly turned the towel over so that the red stain was no longer visible. But the children both kept staring at him. His face was very white, and drops of sweat stood out on his forehead.

"Oh, no, I didn't, silly girl," he said, whispering hoarsely. "It's just the coughing. Eh, what a dumb ox I am. Look here, Evert, for your collection."

"For my collection?" Evert said. "How do you. . . ."

And Noortje said, "For your collection? What? Have you . . . why can't I . . . ?"

Theo smiled. "No quarrels, kids," he said. "I've known for a long time that Evert has a collection. Up in the attic, right above my head."

They went slowly back home. Evert and Noortje walked ahead.

"May I please see your collection?" Noortje asked. She

couldn't stand Evert having something she knew nothing about.

"OK, OK," Evert said. "Since you know about it now anyway. But you mustn't talk about it with anybody. My father mustn't know. I've got a helmet and a rifle and a few other little things. Found them last summer on the heath."

"A rifle?"

"Well, it's not all that complete. You'll see. Tomorrow. It's already too dark up in the attic now."

Theo walked silently behind them. And when they came home, he went straight up to his room.

In the kitchen Mr. Vanderhook inspected the soldier's coat and said, "It's good warm material. Noortje, it wouldn't be such a bad idea if you had a nice warm coat of that stuff. Perhaps Aunt Janna will make something out of it . . . ?"

But Noortje cried, "Oh, no, never in my life will I walk around in a German Kraut coat! I'd rather freeze to death!"

The others all laughed, and the farmer said, "Well now, Noortje, if you don't want it, I'll take it. But I'll wait till the Germans have gone before I put it on. Otherwise, they'll think I'm one of them, and they'll send me to the front after all."

"And when the Americans are here, will you put it on then?" Mr. Vanderhook asked. "They'll take you for a German, and what will they do with you then?"

"No, Chris. Oh, no," Aunt Janna cried. "I don't want you to wear that coat, ever!"

They all laughed again, and Noortje gathered they'd only been teasing her, sort of. But Aunt Janna was glad for the piece of soap. And that same evening she mended a pair of the farmer's socks with the wool out of the knapsack.

"Real wool," she said. "How strong it is. It's a pleasure mending socks with it. That imitation stuff wears right through in one day."

"And beautiful," Noortje said. "The blue with the black, how well they go together!"

▪5▪ The Wolthuis Family

One evening, when they were gathered around the kitchen table, there was a knocking on the window shutter outside. They all stayed quiet, listening. Farmer Everingen called out, "Who's there?"

"Wolthuis!" a man's heavy voice sounded.

"Oh," Aunt Janna said, "the family Wolthuis."

A tall, stooping man came in. He had a sharply hooked nose and a ring of silver-white hair around his otherwise bald head. What was most striking about his face were his eyes. They bulged out so much that you wondered how they could possibly stay in their sockets.

"The time has come," the man said, after sitting down in a chair next to Henk's and rolling himself a cigarette out of Henk's tobacco box. "We no longer can stay there. So if that offer of yours is still good. . . ."

"That goes without saying," Everingen replied. "A promise is a promise. We'll have to do some pinching and scraping. . . ."

"I'll come tomorrow then, with the wife and children. There's also a neighbor with us, an old woman who has neither kith nor kin in the world to take care of her."

"If you keep her with you, that's fine. Right, Mother?" Everingen said.

"Yes, well, we can't leave a poor old soul all alone," Aunt Janna agreed.

The man with the strange eyes got up. He was so tall

that he had to bend his head to get through the door. "We'll come tomorrow then," he said. "I'm going to go back right away now. It's a long trip. But first I wanted to make sure. . . . All right then, good-night to all of you." And off he went.

Farmer Everingen explained to Mr. Vanderhook who the man was. "An old acquaintance of ours," he said. "He was here once before, to ask if they could come in case of emergency. Up till now, they've been able to stay in their own place."

"Are they from Arnhem?" Mr. Vanderhook asked in some amazement.

"Yes, they are. They live at the edge of the city, in one of the suburbs. It's called Geitenkamp, I think. Could that be right?"

"Oh, yes, that's right."

"They've lived in their own basement all this time, and apparently that neighbor woman has stayed with them too. They're solid people, and they won't give us any trouble."

"Where are you going to have them sleep?"

"Yes, well, that is a problem all right. But you two are in a big room together, and now that the apples are finished, I was thinking. . . ."

Aunt Janna was used to keeping her supply of winter apples in the closet bed of the rarely used parlor room. Hundreds of golden rennet apples had been lying there on the shelves, and every day everyone had gotten an apple after dinner. A few days ago they'd eaten the last of the apples.

The parlor was not only the most beautiful, but also the largest room in the whole house. There was a table with a tablecloth in it, and the chairs had green plush seats. The fancy dinner service in the cupboard was very old, and it was never used. An old-fashioned clock hung on the wall next to the mantelpiece. It struck the hours and half hours with big bongs. But it wasn't very cozy in the fancy room. It was damp and chilly—there hadn't been a fire in the stove all winter—and it smelled of old furniture and empty closets. It had only one small window, and the apple tree standing outside it let very little light in. The corners were always in a sort of twilight.

Aunt Janna looked at Noortje and smiled. "Mr. Vanderhook, would you mind sleeping in the closet bed in the parlor room?" she asked. "I've been thinking. Evert can sleep in the spare bed in Henk's room. Then Noortje can take Evert's place with Gerrit on the large straw mattress on the floor. Gerrit won't be any bother at all. He always sleeps like a log. Then the bedroom will be free for the Wolthuis family."

That night it froze hard again, and the following morning the snow glittered in the sunlight. The icicles hanging from the eaves had gotten smaller and smaller the last few weeks, but now they'd grown new sharp points and thick bubbles where the melting water had frozen again. Noortje and Evert both broke off icicles and were licking at them. They were clear as glass and tasted of iron and snow. The two children stayed in front of the house, watching the gate at the bottom of the meadow, for they wanted to be the first ones to see the Wolthuis family arrive.

"Are they nice kids?" Noortje asked Evert. She was afraid that it would be less fun now with other children in the house. She had a good time playing with Evert. Suppose there was a boy his age coming. Then Evert would probably want to have nothing to do with her anymore; he would want to do everything with the strange new boy. And she knew only too well that girls could be a nuisance also. It would have been much nicer if everything could have stayed just as it was.

Evert chuckled a little. He looked at her, and she saw he was tickled by something. "You'll see for yourself," he said. "They're very ordinary kids, I think."

"But you've seen them, haven't you?"

"Oh, yeah, I liked them OK."

"Are they boys or girls?"

"They're two girls."

"Oh!"

They didn't speak for a while.

Then Noor said, "How dreadful that they had to live in a cellar for so long." She tried to feel pity for those strange children but wasn't succeeding very well. Now everything depended on what sort of girls they would be.

"Come on," Evert said. "You want to have a look at the bayonet?"

First they went to the harness room, which was a small, bricked-up part of the shed where the horse harnesses were kept. Reins and collars and bellybands were hung on the walls. Evert took a jar of leather wax off one of the shelves.

"Keeps the rust away," he said.

Then they climbed the tall ladder up to the attic. The smell of tobacco leaves prickled their noses. Evert showed Noor how to get up to the eaves. There was no ladder against the wall, which was the back of Theo's room. They had to go climbing up along a slanted beam. At the very top of the house they couldn't stand up straight, and even when they sat on the floor they bumped their heads against the slant of the roof, for it was only a small triangular space. Luckily some of the roof tiles were made of glass. Otherwise it would have been pitch-dark there.

Between the floor of the garret and the roof itself was

a narrow opening. There, atop the beams, Evert kept his rifle, which he now took out to show to Noortje.

"Jiminy," Noortje said, "does it still work?"

"Of course not," Evert said. "Look, this is the barrel, and that's the trigger. But the butt is missing. I've got more things, over here in this crate." And he pushed a crate to the middle of the floor and showed her his other treasures. In the crate were a German helmet, a leather belt, a few cartridge belts, a tin plate, and a container of black boot wax. And now the bayonet too, the most beautiful of all.

"Feel how sharp," Evert whispered. "Do you know what the groove is for? That's for the blood to run off."

He put a big fat blob of yellow wax onto his finger and smeared it on the gleaming metal of the bayonet. "Look," he said, "it fits onto the rifle barrel. That's how they fight with it in man-to-man combat."

The bayonet fit into an iron ring on the barrel, and it locked in tight with a click.

"And then they shoot too, with the bayonet on it?" Noortje asked.

"Ah, silly, you don't know anything about it! Of course not. When the enemy comes very close, they stab them. Look, like this. . . ."

Evert lay on his belly on the floor, holding the rifle with two hands, and then he jabbed the bayonet with its sharp point straight ahead. He'd put the helmet on his head, and although it was a little too large for him, so he could barely see out from underneath it, he looked eager and fierce. Noortje shivered.

"Ah!" she said. "How mean! I'd rather have a bullet than get something like that. If I had to fight and was going to die anyway. . . . Bah! How can you like all that stuff?"

"I never said I liked it," Evert said. "Girls don't understand such things. When there's war you've got to fight. If you have to you have to. Shhh!"

They'd been whispering all that time so no one would find out about the secret hiding place. Now there was the sound of footsteps in the shed.

"Evert!" they heard someone call.

"Your father," Noortje whispered, even more softly than before.

"Evert, where are you, boy? You have to pump that water!" They heard Everingen muttering to himself in a low voice. "Where is that darn kid now. All those people. . . ." And then he was gone.

"Quick!" Evert said, and he put the rifle back in its place and the other things into the crate. The bayonet he hid between two roof tiles and covered it with a bunch of straw. Now there was no trace of it. They slid down, one behind the other, then quickly descended the ladder.

When they went outside, they saw that Everingen was harnessing Browny to a long, flat wagon. A sergeant and a soldier stood by, watching. The children both thought of the bayonet, the helmet, and the half rifle. What if those Germans had seen Evert a minute ago!

"Is that you finally?" boomed Everingen. "Quick, boy, you have to pump some water. I must take a trip with these gentlemen." Didn't Everingen sound just the slightest bit mocking as he said *gentlemen*?

"Yes, Dad. How long should I keep pumping?" Evert asked.

"There will be more of us later. So you pump three quarters of an hour. That should be enough. Tell them to be careful, and go easy on the water."

Everingen had finished the harnessing. Without saying another word, he went and sat at the front of the cart and clucked his tongue. "Here we go now, my little horse!" he cried. The Germans jumped into the back of the wagon, which was already moving. They bounced up and down, their legs dangling and swaying. They'd put their rifles next to them on the wagon floor. Evert ran to the kitchen.

"Where is Dad off to?" he asked his mother.

Aunt Janna had put a tub of warm water on the floor in front of the stove. Baby Sis sat on the table leaning against her. Aunt Janna was pulling a dirty, wet undershirt over her head. The fat child with her large baby body jerked back and forth and beat her hands. She grabbed a lock of her mother's hair and pulled it hard.

"Don't you bully, Sis, don't you bully me," said Aunt Janna. She loosened the strong little hand and, lifting Sis, carried her to the warm water. Sis changed completely as soon as she was in the bath, suddenly becoming all heavy and slow and sleepy. She sat very still and stared at her mother with those small, light-blue eyes. "Pr*rrr,* pr*rrr.*"

Aunt Janna was holding her so she couldn't fall over or touch the stove, and meanwhile she talked to Evert.

"He has to go to Spankeren for the Germans," she said. "They have to take the long way through the woods because there's shooting on the main road. And wagons and carts are big enough targets for the airplanes. It's a good thing they're taking that detour, but it will be much longer, of course. I don't know if he'll be home before dark."

With his hand Evert scooped little splashes of lukewarm water onto his sister's back. Sissy stayed very still, eyes closed.

Aunt Janna said, "And now you have to pump the water right away, for there will be many people later. And ask Noortje to come help me with the beds."

* * *

That morning everyone was hard at work. Mr. Vanderhook was at the straw-cutting machine, fixing fresh straw to fill mattresses with. Noortje cleaned out the closet bed in the parlor so her father would find it nice to sleep there that night. She wiped old cobwebs out of the corners and scrubbed the boards.

Evert harnessed the Fox to the pump and walked behind him, around and around, while Theo sat watching at the window of his room. Evert was so sunk in thought that he didn't look up once. He didn't know that Theo had been sitting at the window all that time.

To the side of the farm stood a small square structure with a slanted roof and two heavy bars on the door. It was strictly forbidden for anyone to open that door, for inside was a well, which was very, very deep. Outside, in the brick wall of the building, was a stone that had cut into it the words:

This well is 177½ feet deep
and was dug in the year
1847

The well was almost a hundred years old. Next to the small building was a stone reservoir, which held the water that had to be pumped up out of the well each day. The water was drawn up by means of a complicated system of iron wheels, and then it fell into that stone cistern. From there it ran through a pipe underneath the ground to the pump in the shed. In order to make those heavy wheels turn, a horse had to pull a wooden beam around. There was a narrow brick pavement laid in a circle around the wheel where the horse, tied to the beam, walked. Behind the beam walked Evert with a thin branch in his hand. Whenever he decided the Fox was going too slowly, he gave him a little rap on the behind. But the Fox was used to the monotonous work and kept stepping on quietly. He was wearing a halter with blinkers, to keep him from getting dizzy.

Evert thought, Has the three quarters of an hour gone by yet? He'd been so busy thinking that he'd forgotten all about time. It could just as well have been an hour or fifteen minutes that he had been walking around behind the horse. Suddenly his eye caught Theo. He waved at him, and Theo opened the window.

"They're gone, aren't they?" Theo called, but so softly that Evert could hardly hear him.

"Long ago!" he called back.

Theo nodded. "I heard you before, above my head," he said. "Did you really hide it well?"

Evert made the gesture of slitting his own throat. "They'll never find it," he said. "Have you heard yet that there'll be new people coming soon?"

"Yes, your mother told me. She said they can be trusted."

"Oh, yes. Whoah, whoah!" That last bit was meant for the Fox.

Evert decided he had pumped enough and untied the horse from the beam. The animal stood there clumsily against the wall of the house and had to be led backward to the stable door. "Ho . . . hup!" Evert cried, and hesitantly the Fox took another step backward. Handling the horse easily, Evert maneuvered him around the corner of the house.

▪6▪
Fetching Bread

Twice a week someone had to go and fetch their bread, on Tuesdays and on Fridays. And if nobody else was making the trip to Zemst or Ulsten, it was the children's task. The bakery stood a little outside the village, along the main road.

That afternoon Aunt Janna gave Evert the empty bags, and he called out to Noortje to come with him.

There were several routes to the bakery. If they crossed the heath at the end of First Beech Lane and took the path along the churchyard down to the main road, they would end up to the right of the bakery.

They could also follow the sand path over the hills and walk through the Deep Ditch, a gravel path that lay between two high embankments. That brought them out to the left of the bakery. Both routes were equally far.

Evert and Noortje decided to take the churchyard road on the way out. On the heath itself there was no real path to speak of; it was still covered with a thick layer of snow, and their feet kept sinking into holes. The top layer of snow had first melted and then frozen again, so it had turned into a hard crust. Noortje was wearing a pair of Evert's old pants, which were much too short for her. She lifted her feet up high, the hard snow crust hurting her bare ankles, for at every step she had to see whether her clog was still on her foot. They could only make slow headway.

A thick cover of leaden gray clouds blanketed the sky. They'd left home at half past two, and yet there was something of dusk in the air already. Out on the heath you hardly ever met anyone. It was nice to see the wide hills all around, with a few low small trees here and there. During the summer a herd of sheep roamed the heath, and the trees didn't get a chance to grow big. Sheep eat every little leaf and every young branch. Evert had explained to Noor that the heath would have become a wood long ago if it hadn't been for those sheep.

Near the main road it was a lot less pleasant than on the solitary heath. A truck with German soldiers rode past. A large number of the thick trees that had stood along the road had been cut down. Pieces of those trees lay on the ground beside the bicycle path. And in between, in neat rows, lay artillery shells, their silver-colored points placed toward the road. A few Dutch sentinels were walking up and down guarding the shells, and in the middle of the road stood soldiers keeping an eye on the guards.

At the baker's, they found the front door locked. They went around the back to get inside. There were already about ten customers, staring ahead with somber faces. It was very uncomfortable in that cold, bare space. The people weren't saying a word to each other, and you could see that no one trusted anyone anymore. Noortje and Evert stood quietly among them, waiting their turn.

The wife of the baker sat at a little table near the wall and wrote down the name of Everingen in her book. "Four and a rye," she said, and then she marked it. "It's already been paid for. It'll be your turn soon."

A thin man in a white shirt stood bent over a bathtub kneading dough. His arms and hands were red with cold. They got four loaves of the standard water bread and a large black rye that had been baked from their own Klaphek flour. The other customers looked at it with angry faces. Noortje was glad when they were outside again.

"Shall we take the other way back?" she said.

They decided to, and for a while they walked on without speaking. Since they weren't going by the graveyard, they had to keep on the main road much longer. A horse and wagon came by. The horse was in a nervous trot, its hooves clattering loudly on the cobblestones. The wheels of the wagon rattled.

"What a big hurry he's in!" Noortje said, laughing.

Suddenly they heard the drone of an airplane, coming closer. "Come on, off the road! Quick!" Evert yelled, and he started running.

He didn't look where he was going. If only they could get far enough away from those horrible artillery shells in time, for that's what the plane was aiming at, of course. They ran across a farmyard and dropped down behind a haystack. There they lay, faces pressed into the hay and the bags with bread in their arms. The shooting had started already.

The plane went into a dive, droning. Machine guns rattled. *Rat-a-tat-tat!* They heard the bullets skipping on the road surface. The sky was full of noise . . . and then it was still again . . . so still they could hear the hay rustling in the wind above their heads.

"Will they come back again?" Noortje whispered.

"I don't know," Evert said. "We've got to wait."

He pinched off a piece of bread and stuffed it in his mouth. The loaves were still warm, and Noortje had her cheek against them. She was also plucking at the bread. She rather liked those warm crusts, but not the inside; it was like a soggy gray mush.

"There it is again!" Evert said. "Lie down flat!"

And again there was an attack, this time not so very close. This time it's not as bad, they thought. Suddenly there was a hard boom and a whistling sound came toward them. They were terrified. Their hearts seemed to stop for a moment, then started banging very fast. A piece of grenade whooshed over the path by the haystack. Dumbstruck with fear, they lay there looking at it and didn't know what to do. The grenade shrapnel had stopped less than a yard away from their feet.

"Oh!" Noortje said. "Oh!"

Evert got up, sticking a large chunk of bread in his mouth. His jaws were chewing, and with his face set toward the sky he listened.

"They're gone," he said. "Hear that?"

"They can come back, though."

"No, no, I don't hear a thing anymore."

"I don't dare go back to the road."

"We've got to, it's already getting late."

But they didn't move yet. They just kept standing there, looking at the shrapnel on the ground. It was in the form of a triangle, with one of its sharp points curled over. Noortje bent down and picked it up.

"Here," she said, "for your collection." And she ran her finger along the sharp edge of the shrapnel.

Evert smelled it before he put it in his pocket, and Noortje was glad she didn't have to look at it anymore. That thing didn't belong there, on the ground near the sand and the snow and the hay. It was too new looking and clean.

Evert peeked around the corner of the haystack. No one could be seen. Halfway down the path to the road they noticed a black spot in the snow. A larger piece of the grenade had landed there and struck a hole in the ground.

"Here comes someone," Noortje said.

A man emerged from the house. He ran toward the children with a pitchfork in his hands and started screaming from a distance.

"Don't say a word," Evert said. "He's a real nasty farmer and he's in with the Germans."

The man came closer. "Get out of here, fast!" he shouted. "What are you doing on my property? Get away from here!"

"We were looking for cover," Noortje told him, "from the shooting. It hit over there." And she pointed to the black spot in the snow.

"What shooting? Nothing shooting! Get going, get out of here! I don't want anything to do with you, you mean little beggars!" the man kept screaming, looking at them angrily.

"Come on, Noor," said Evert.

Then the farmer called out after them, "Hey, you, wait a minute! Aren't you one of Everingen's kids? Now tell me, what were you doing over here? You didn't come from Klaphek by any chance, did you? Oh, then, do give my regards to your father!"

They didn't look back, and they didn't feel at ease till they were walking safely in the Deep Ditch, far from the main road.

"Beggars!" Evert muttered. "What a mean bastard! Those people over there will choke on their own food one of these days. They never give away a thing. Calling us beggars . . . !"

Night was falling fast now. The moon and the stars weren't visible because of the heavy clouds. Fortunately, the snow on the path was so white against the black bushes at the sides that they could at least tell where they were walking.

"We'll go through the wood," Evert said. "That's shorter."

And they turned into a narrow path that ran through a very dense wood. It was much darker here than out on the heath. Noortje held Evert by the sleeve of his coat so as not to lose him.

"I don't know this wood," she said.

"Shhh! Don't talk so loud. We've never been here. I'm not allowed to come here."

"Why not?" Now they were both whispering.

"Because the gamekeeper shoots rabbits here."

That was an odd answer. Noortje walked on thinking about it for a while, and the longer she thought the surer she was that Evert had just said the first thing that came into his mind.

"Do you know why you're not allowed to come here?" she asked.

"Shut up now."

But Noortje wouldn't be quiet. She wanted to talk, even if ever so softly. When she didn't talk she heard all those rustlings among the leaves and the snow on the ground and the strange noises that came out of the darkness between the trees. In the branches above their heads were sounds of sighing and creaking, and sometimes it seemed as if people were whispering up there. It is the wind in the treetops, Noortje said to herself. And then she asked Evert, "What is this wood called?"

"Not all woods have a name. This one doesn't."

"Oh, yes, I'm sure it does. It must. A wood like this always has some name."

"During the day it's just an ordinary wood. Nothing special. I bet you're thinking of ghosts, because it's so dark."

Beside them, but much lower than their path, they

suddenly heard a noise. Someone walking. Who was it? Noortje stood still and stopped Evert. She held her breath but didn't hear anything anymore.

"What was that?" she finally dared whisper, very faintly.

"Some kind of animal."

"It came from there!" Noortje pointed. "From under the ground. Or maybe not?"

"There's a ditch down there, a game ditch. Quiet now. . . . It could have been a wild boar."

Now all was silence, and they walked on quickly.

"I think this wood is called the Eighth Wood. Have you ever heard of the Eighth Wood?"

"Of course not," Evert said. "If it were called that, I would know!"

"Children live in the Eighth Wood, in secret. Not *ordinary* children, you know. I made up a song about it. You want to hear it?"

Evert didn't answer. It was completely still when neither of them spoke, and then they heard so much creaking and rustling that Noortje decided to say the song's words for Evert anyway, whether he wanted to hear them or not. Noortje's voice came out sounding now louder, then more softly, as the wind cut across it, blowing its own tune to the words:

The children of the dark Eighth Wood
eat potatoes without salt,
they get their porridge without oats
and sleep under the starry vault,
yet they are never, never cold.

These children have a good warm fur
on belly, leg, and arm,
and so they're never cold or bare

but always nice and warm,
even when it's cold and late
in the dense dark Wood of Eight.

She'd only just finished the last line when they emerged from the wood. Noortje immediately recognized where they were: at the beginning of First Beech Lane, not far from the farm.

"What are you doing here so late?" they heard Henk saying.

"Oh, Henk! How did you get here? We took a shortcut. It was so late and they were shooting on the road. Farmer Everingen back yet?"

"Ho, ho, not so many words all at once, if you please," Henk grumbled. "Noortje, you stop your chattering for a moment. Evert, what were the two of you up to in that wood?"

"Well, it's just as Noor says," Evert replied. "Don't be so bossy, Henk! And tell us, what are you doing here?" Evert didn't want to be lectured to by Henk. "What's that basket for, and that bucket?" he asked.

"Come on," Henk said, "we'll see who can get home first. You, Noortje, or me."

Evert started to run. Henk stood still and spread his arms wide out. In one hand he held the basket, in the other an empty bucket. "Jump on my back, Noortje, and we'll win!" he said.

Noortje took a little run and jumped onto Henk's back. She threw her arms around his neck and put her chin atop his cap.

Evert had run ahead; he climbed over the fence by the meadow and slowed down as he approached the house. With a few giant steps Henk caught up with him and cried, "We've won!"

* * *

They blinked their eyes against the light when they came in. There were a lot of strange people in the kitchen. Everingen sat in his own chair, his face red from being outside. Aunt Janna gave a quick look at Henk as he came in. Noortje noticed it, and she wondered about it. She, too, quickly glanced at Henk and saw him squeeze his eyes shut briefly, giving Aunt Janna a reassuring nod. But Noortje had no time now to pay further attention to them, for Wolthuis had arrived: the tall, stooped man with the bulging eyes. Beside him sat a fat woman with a coarse face, and next to her a little old lady.

"That is Evert," Wolthuis said to his wife, "and the girl is called Noortje."

The woman nodded and said, "I'm Ma Wolthuis. And this old lady here is my neighbor, Granny. The two others you'll get to know soon enough."

She began to laugh, and her face was sort of friendly then. The old woman was sleepy, could hardly keep her eyes open, and her head hung to one side, chin on her breast. The others, the ones Ma Wolthuis had nodded toward, were two young women. One of them had Gerrit on her lap and was softly rocking him back and forth.

Now that there were so many people in the kitchen, there wasn't enough room for all of them to sit around the table, not even when both sides were pulled out. Evert and Noortje had to eat separately, at a small table placed near the door to the cellar. They sat in their own little corner, eating the soggy gray bread and a fat slice of that good-tasting rye bread, and they drank warm milk straight from the cow. There wasn't much talk going on while they all ate. Baby Sis cried out from her crib, "Broo broo broo! Grrr, grrr!"

Poor Sis, she could see only the dark backs of strange people. Perhaps they scared her, for she began to cry, and soon the crying changed into screaming.

"I can't squeeze through here," said Aunt Janna. She'd gotten up to pour some milk into a cup. "Noortje, will you give Sissy something to drink?"

Noortje climbed into the bed. She held the cup at Sissy's mouth and one hand underneath her chin, as Aunt Janna did so often, catching the milk that ran out of the little mouth down the sides. Sissy looked at her while she drank, but her eyes didn't say a thing. You couldn't see whether she was happy or angry. When the cup was almost empty, she turned her head away and, wildly waving her arms, said, "Prrrr, prrr."

"So she's all happy again. Give that to me, child," Aunt Janna said.

"Hey, Evert," Noortje said, when she was back in her seat, "what about those children?"

"Children? What children?"

"The Wolthuis children."

"But they're here!"

"Where? I haven't seen them yet."

"Then you don't have eyes in your head. Over there, those two women, they're his daughters!"

"But you said—"

"Oh, yes, of course! I had entirely forgotten. Well, it's just as I said, isn't it? Two girls!"

Evert got into such a terrible laughing fit that his milk went down the wrong way, and Henk had to slap him hard on the back to keep him from choking. Noortje thought it seemed wisest to join in and laugh too. Having your leg pulled wasn't the worst thing in the world, she decided.

•7•
The Billy Goat

Now it was very crowded in the house. Grown-up people take up a lot of space and make such a lot of fuss too.

There wasn't much for Noortje to do in the kitchen anymore. Ma Wolthius liked nothing better than housework. And her daughters had learned to do everything just like their mother. Even the old woman was on the lookout to see if there wasn't something she could work at. She'd straighten the chairs out around the table, or put away the dishes in the cupboard. And so, she made herself useful by doing all sorts of small jobs. The house always looked clean and tidy, from early morning on. The work would have been too much for Aunt Janna alone, but now there wasn't work enough to keep all those hands busy.

When Noortje, just as she always did, picked up a knife and sat down near the basket of potatoes to help with the peeling, she was shooed away. And when she wanted to help them with the dishes, Alie and Dinie Wolthuis would say, "Go off and play!" Or they would sneer, "Get out of our way!" On the very first day after they'd arrived, they pushed Noortje out of the kitchen, saying, "Now listen, we don't need any kids around here, OK?"

Noortje didn't like all those new people around Klaphek. She was glad to get a chance to do the midday dishes alone with Aunt Janna one afternoon, because Alie and Dinie had gone to the village on an errand.

"Yesterday there was a lot of stew left over, and yet we didn't get a hot snack with our bread in the evening. Did you feed it to the pigs?" Noortje asked Aunt Janna.

"To the pigs? Oh, no, of course not." Aunt Janna laughed. Noortje couldn't understand it at all.

That whole morning a big kettle of pea soup had been simmering away on the stove. It smelled so wonderful that her stomach started rumbling all by itself. When everyone got up from the dinner table to go back to work again, that kettle was still almost half full.

Just then there was a knock on the door, and two women and a man came in, asking if the farmer's wife might have something to eat. They had come a long way looking for food, and they'd eaten nothing for two whole days, except for a few crusts of old bread.

"Why don't you sit down?" Aunt Janna said, and she placed clean dishes in front of the strangers. They looked tired and worn, their eyes started tearing from the warmth of the kitchen and their noses were red. Their cheeks were pale and hollow. They fell to eating silently, while Aunt Janna and Noortje continued doing the dishes. You could see they liked the pea soup. They'd gone through two whole bowls of it already, and Aunt Janna asked if they wanted some more.

"There's plenty of it, don't worry," she said. "You're quite welcome to a third helping."

The two women shook their heads shyly. "I can't anymore," one of them said, laughing, "but it really was delicious."

Aunt Janna poured a big ladlefull of soup into the man's dish. He brought his spoon to his mouth again, but more slowly than before.

The kitchen was warm. Baby Sis lay sleeping, making her little snoring noises. Gerrit sat at the table drawing on his slate board; the chalk scratched and squeaked. The clock on the mantelpiece ticked loudly.

Noortje felt tired and sleepy. She heard the geese go by the window talking to each other softly, sounds coming from deep in their throats to the rhythm of their waggling gait. The strange people had finished their eating. They got up and thanked Aunt Janna.

The kettle of pea soup wasn't nearly empty. Aunt Janna poured the soup into a white enamel bucket and took it to the cellar.

Toward the end of the afternoon, when the sun started going down, Evert had lots to do. And Noortje helped.

"*Chick, here chick chick chick!*" They tried to see who could yell the loudest.

Then the hens and chickens came tripping along, and in a few minutes they pecked up all the grains. They kept on digging into the ground for a while, for they didn't want to leave one single grain. Meanwhile, Evert and Noortje got the eggs out of the hen house, and when that was done they chased the hens back inside and dropped the hatch, so that they were safely shut in for the night.

The geese went to their night quarters all by themselves. They always wanted to sleep as soon as it got dark.

Inside the barn was a small sectioned-off area where a nanny goat and a billy goat stood. In the evening they were fed hay and water. It had become the routine for Evert to feed the nanny goat and Noortje the billy goat.

"How that billy gobbles everything all up," Evert said. "Dammit! He shoves in more than the nanny. And he doesn't even make any little ones!"

Noortje started laughing. "But, without the billy goat the nanny can't possibly have any young ones," she said. "You know that just as well as I do."

"Yeah, all right. But he eats too much. Don't give him anything today for a change. Come over here, goatie, you're moving to another spot."

An old gate had been set in one corner of the barn, marking it off. Evert put the billy goat behind it. Bleating anxiously, the goat bumped its horns against the boards of the gate. Noortje stood looking at him, startled. The billy was still a small animal, not more than a year old. Sweet-natured, he always looked lively and cheerful. Why wasn't he allowed to eat now?

"I'm going to give him his food anyway," she said angrily.

"No, Noortje," Evert said, "you shouldn't. My father said not to."

"But why not?"

"I can't tell. . . . Well, OK, if you promise not to let on to anyone that you know, I'll tell you. You see, we're going to butcher him. Illegally. So nobody's supposed to know."

"Oh!"

"So you'll keep quiet about it?"

"Yes. But why can't he eat?"

"Because it's a waste of fodder. He wouldn't have the time to digest it, anyhow."

Even during that winter when there was so much hunger, a farmer couldn't butcher one of his own animals. It had to be done by a real butcher with an inspector attending. If you didn't do it that way, you were liable to punishment and the meat would be confiscated. And if the Germans heard about it, they'd take away the meat. That's why Everingen wanted to butcher the billy goat secretly, unofficially.

Noortje didn't dare look at the little creature. She was sure that he understood what was being said. And what they were doing was so mean! She could understand that the goat had to be butchered. But it was mean not to give him his food because of that.

She couldn't stand the thought any longer. She walked out and leaned against a wall, still thinking about it. Evert came out too a little later and went by on the way to the shed without seeming to notice her. There was no moon yet, and only a few stars. She heard the billy goat bleating in his stall. Running to the shed, she sneaked inside. The heap of hay for the cows already lay on the floor. The farmer and Henk and Evert were milking. She heard the swishing of the milk into the buckets and Everingen's voice muttering at the cow he was milking. The beast swished its tail caked with manure against the farmer's head! Noor quickly snatched up an armful of hay and went back to the barn.

Even though he had to be butchered, the billy goat shouldn't go hungry. She stood listening to him in the half dark, his jaws grinding. She scratched him between his horns and tickled him under the white goatee. He liked that. He sucked on her fingers and pushed his hard little head into her stomach, without hurting her. While he stood eating the nice hay, she squatted down next to him and put an arm around his neck. She looked into his yellow eye, which had a thin black stripe in it instead of a round dot like most other animals.

He looked back at Noortje with his strange eye, and he seemed to be thinking of things she had never heard of.

That night a great round moon stood out in the sky and there were millions of stars. Evert and Noortje were outside; they saw Henk standing in front of the house underneath the bare apple tree. The moon and stars gave off so much light that they could see the edge of the wood and the thick cherry tree at the bottom of the meadow. A black cat slunk silently past the wall of the house; it stood still and turned its head toward them. Its eyes were two bright green lights.

Evert went and stood next to Henk, who was leaning over the gate. "What are you waiting for, Henk? Looking to see if your girl friend is coming?" he asked teasingly.

First Henk didn't answer. When there were grown-ups around Henk usually held his tongue, and often it seemed he was alone even when with others. But now, standing outside in that strange light with Noortje and Evert, he didn't mind talking.

"I'm not just standing here waiting for any girl," he said after a pause. "I'm waiting for a princess. But I see the princess has already come! There are some blockheads, young man, who can't recognize a princess, even when she's standing there right under their noses."

Noortje blushed, glad that Evert and Henk had their backs to her.

The sound of barking came from the wood and then a few brief, excited yelps. "Rachel's over there." Henk pointed. "She's tracking something. I wonder what she'll come home with."

"Ah, that crazy Rachel! She's much too old for hunting," Evert said.

Then they saw Rachel coming across the field. She trotted calmly toward them, holding something in her mouth, a small dark thing that hung down slackly. At first they couldn't see what it was. Then Rachel reached them and laid a dead rabbit at their feet in the snow.

"A rabbit! Such a good dog, Rachel, old girl, how clever of you," Evert said, giving her some pats on the back.

Rachel looked from one to the other, as if saying,

"Well now, what do you think of that? Aren't I a good hunting dog?"

"Evert, why don't we clean the animal right now," Henk said. "Your mother can make something nice out of it. There won't be much on it, such a small thing, but even so. . . ."

"Yes," Noortje said, "we can eat it, and then the billy goat doesn't have to be—" She quickly covered her mouth, and the others pretended not to have heard her.

Evert grabbed it by its hind legs, and Henk opened his knife and took one of the front paws in his hand. With a few quick strokes he cut off the head and skinned the animal. Then he cut open the belly and removed the innards. He shoved the heap of messy stuff out of the way with his foot.

"The cats can eat that," he said.

Noortje climbed on top of the gate. The rabbit without its skin had turned into a thin, bluish little creature. She didn't mind seeing that. Everything seemed so strange tonight in the light of the moon and the stars; it was as if things weren't really happening. Henk handed Evert the skinned rabbit and said, "You can lay it on a dish and put it down in the cellar." And he cleaned his knife with some snow.

Evert came back soon. The three of them stood leaning on the gate, looking over the snowy meadow and up at the sky full of stars high above. Suddenly there was a dark figure beside them. They hadn't heard anyone walking through the snow. It was such a marvelous evening that Noortje didn't wonder or worry about anything. Probably the white radiance of the moon was what made everything seem so different from usual.

The figure who had just joined them so silently was none other than Aunt Janna. She had been somewhere out in the night. That was strange, but everything seemed strange this evening, and Noortje didn't ask her anything. Aunt Jenna was wearing her clogs and thick vest, and she had a black woolen shawl thrown over her head and shoulders. She was holding a burlap sack in her hand. Noortje thought it looked as though there was a bucket inside that sack. Aunt Janna seemed to have arrived from a different world.

"What are you all doing outside?" she asked, and her voice sounded quite normal. "It's much too cold out for the children, Henk."

"A princess doesn't get cold so easily," Henk said. "All well?"

"All's well," said Aunt Janna. And then Evert said, "Mama, Rachel caught a rabbit. It's only a small one. It's in the cellar."

"That's very clever of Rachel. Come, it's time for us to go to bed." And Aunt Janna led the way into the scullery.

The children had to go to bed immediately. It was nice and warm on the mattress, for Gerrit had been there already for a few hours. He slept very soundly and didn't notice Noortje snuggling up beside him. He's just like a small, warm animal, she thought.

A little later she heard Aunt Janna and Farmer Everingen go to bed. They lay talking softly together awhile. Little Gerrit had thrown his arm around Noortje's neck and pushed his warm head of curls into her face. She could hardly breathe. She couldn't make out a word of the whispering in the big bed. Loosening Gerrit's arm, she carefully turned the little boy onto his back. Gerrit gave a few very deep sighs and slept on quietly. Noortje could breathe again and she fell sound asleep.

The round moon moved slowly across the purple-blue

sky. An old table had been placed in the vegetable garden. There, that same night, Henk butchered the billy goat and Evert had to help him.

The following morning there were large red chunks of meat lying on the floor in the cellar, and at midday they had delicious roasted meat with their potatoes. It had an unfamiliar spicy taste.

While she ate the meat Noortje thought of that undigested hay. Well, she thought, he had a good life to the very end.

▪8▪
The Four Sows

It had been snowing again. Now there was a layer so thick you could hardly walk through it. Your feet sank into the snow, and not a bit of the black earth was to be seen anymore.

The two stoves in the house devoured piles of logs. Mr. Vanderhook had the job of taking care of all that wood. Noortje helped her father take a tree out of the forest. They selected a not-too-thick birch, which actually was standing too close to another tree anyway. Mr. Vanderhook cut the tree down with an axe, and together they sawed it into pieces so they could carry the wood to the house. One by one they lifted those logs over the Calves' Meadow fence and loaded them onto the wheelbarrow. The work was nice, and it kept them busy the whole morning. Noortje's father had turned the little summerhouse into a woodshed. There he had placed the sawhorse, and now he sawed the birch trees into lengths that would fit into the stove. When the logs were too thick, he split them a few times with the axe.

The following morning Noortje also wanted to help her father with the sawing inside the summerhouse. Pulling the saw through the wood all alone was heavy work. She grabbed the other end and said, "Come on, Dad, let me help you now. It'll go much faster with the two of us."

But it didn't go faster. Because she was so much smaller

than her father, the saw was pulled crooked through the wood and it got stuck. Mr. Vanderhook had to wriggle it free and start anew.

"Leave it, Noortje. It'll go better if I do it alone," he said. And Noortje walked away sadly, thinking, Nobody needs me. I can't do a thing. . . .

When she opened the door to the shed, she heard Wolthuis yelling at his daughters. He was really angry. Alie answered back insolently and then cursed at her father. Noortje also heard some soft crying, which was probably Dinie, but she didn't stay to listen and quickly closed the heavy door again. She walked around the pigsty to the kitchen. Aunt Janna lit up when she came in and asked, "Noortje, would you go play with Gerrit? The poor boy doesn't know what to do with himself."

Well, all right then. She would take Gerrit with her and go play house with him. And when he had had enough of that, she could tell him stories and recite some rhymes for him. Gerrit was still such a little fellow that Noortje almost always let him have his own way.

At least it was quiet in the shed when they got there. All they heard were the noises made by the horses and cows. But Gerrit didn't want to play in the shed. He wanted to go outside into the snow.

The freshly fallen snow was really good for packing. Noortje and Gerrit both made snowballs and rolled them over the meadow, making them bigger and bigger. They turned into two giant snowballs, which they left at the bottom of the meadow near the old cherry tree. And so they rolled a lot of them. Evert joined them a little later, and then the three of them made a big fortress of snowballs around the trunk of the tree. Evert stacked fresh snowballs on top of the other ones to make a thick, high wall.

They built a beautiful fortress, and the following day they went to work on it again to make it even more beautiful. Inside they formed benches and tables of snow. It was very cold and freezing all day, but they weren't bothered by the cold because they were working so hard. When their fortress was finished, they first played that they were English soldiers. They used bean poles for guns, and they shot at anyone who dared come near them.

Then they were father and mother, the fortress was their house, and Gerrit had to be the child. But Gerrit didn't want to be the child, and he started to leave, crying for his real mother.

"Come on, Gerrit, you can be a farmhand!" Noortje called out. "Won't that be nice?"

Gerrit liked being the farmhand all right. He went off to catch one of the wild cats that lived in the shed and never ventured into the house. The cat wasn't used to being picked up by people and stuck its claws into Gerrit. Being scratched by the cat didn't bother him at all. Then the cat hissed and snarled at him, and all its fur stood on end. Gerrit dropped the creature and it ran off as fast as it could, running through the snow with its thick tail straight up in the air.

Now Rachel the sheepdog wanted to join in the play. Rachel would go along with anything. She quietly lay down in the snow with her head on her front paws and squeezed one eye shut, then another. Gerrit stroked her and said, "My good little doggy. . . ."

"Why do you have to have an animal?" Noortje wanted to know. "Don't you find it nice enough with you and me and Evert together?"

Gerrit smiled very wisely and patiently. "But I'm the farmhand, aren't I?" he said. "Then I have to have a horse to work with, don't I?"

"Yes, but a horse isn't possible."

"Oh, yes, it is. Rachel's my horse."

Rachel was a sweet and patient horse and watchful too. Suddenly the horse began to bark, even before the children heard something. They peered over the wall of their snowhouse.

Around the bend of First Beech Lane came a military truck. It lurched along slowly in the deep, slippery ruts of the road and came to a stop before the gate to the meadow. Two soldiers jumped out to open the gate. The truck began to creep up toward the farm.

"Quick! We've got to warn everybody!" Evert said.

Rachel stood in the middle of the meadow, barking loudly. The truck rode on a little farther; then it stopped. The two Germans walked to the house, and another soldier and an officer followed them. Evert ran around the shed side, and Noortje went to the kitchen. "We've already seen them coming," Ma Wolthuis said. "Nothing to do now but wait."

"Will you run quickly up to Theo, Noortje?" Aunt Janna asked.

Noortje hurried and went up the stairs. Without knocking first, she opened the door to Theo's room. There were her father and Theo playing chess. The chessboard stood on a low table before the wide-open window. They both wore thick scarves, and their hands were blue with cold. Astonished, they looked up at Noortje when she came in.

"Theo, there are Germans," she said.

Theo got up slowly and stretched lazily. "How many?" he asked.

"Four, I think, with a truck."

"Damn."

"I'll stay here," Mr. Vanderhook said. "When they come searching, they'll think this is my room. Don't you disturb me now, and go away. I want to solve my chess problem."

"It's all right, Noortje. You go back down fast now," Theo said.

Before she pulled the door shut behind her, Noortje saw him disappearing into the deep closet in the wall. She came downstairs quickly, on her toes.

But the Germans hadn't come for Theo at all. The officer stood in the scullery asking Aunt Janna, "Do you have any pigs? Where are your pigs?"

Aunt Janna looked alarmed. She pulled the door to the kitchen shut so that she didn't have to hear the sound of Sissy's screaming, but she still held the latch in her hand as if she couldn't let go.

"No, oh, no!" she said.

The German didn't listen to her. He opened the door to the pig shed and cried, "Oo la la!"

There were the four beautiful pink sows on a thick layer of straw behind the wooden partition. As soon as they heard the door open, the animals, happily grunting, poked their snouts into the trough and pushed up the little swinging section. The soldiers came in too. They opened the little door in the wooden partition and drove the largest sow outside.

Evert saw the first pig standing in the door opening. Amazed, it blinked its small eyes at the glaring light reflected by the snow. One of the soldiers kicked its haunches, and with a loud squeal the pig jumped across the clean-scrubbed pavement. It ran back and forth through the snow, screaming as if it were already being slaughtered. It must surely have felt too cold outside, for it was jumping crazily on its short legs. That wasn't so surprising. The pigs were used to the warm shed with straw and manure.

The three soldiers ran after the pig and tried to grab it by the tail. One of them stumbled and fell flat in the snow. He got up again, cursing. Then the soldiers threw themselves on top of the pig, so that it fell onto its side, with its legs kicking in the air. That's how they finally captured it. The geese came waggling up all in a row and stood there, furiously snorting. The pig was lifted by the legs and thrown into the back of the truck.

All through this scene the children stood watching without a word and without laughing once. Aunt Janna waited outside in front of the scullery, her face white and lips drawn tight. Taking her pigs was bad. It was so bad that it made her furious. How would they get their meat and bacon now? And where could they find new piglets?

The Germans had learned their lesson from that first nuisance of a pig. They knew better now than to let the others run out that way. Two of the soldiers went inside with a thick piece of rope. They threw the second pig onto its back and tied all four legs. And so they dragged it by pulling the rope, over the stone floor outside, and threw it into the back of the truck too. Aunt Janna turned away. She could no longer watch. Tears had sprung into her eyes, tears of anger and impotence. As if she wanted to hit someone, she moved one of her hands, then grabbed her apron to wipe away the tear that trickled down her cheek.

The officer stood there, watching the pig being dragged away, then watching Aunt Janna. He walked up to her and said, "Ah, poor mother!"

Aunt Janna didn't look at him and again he said, "Don't cry, ma'am. I'm a farmer myself, and I know what it is. We'll let one stay here."

And after the third sow had disappeared into the truck, he gave a command to the soldiers, climbed into the seat next to the driver, and slammed the door shut with a hard bang. The others got in too, and the truck roared off bumping across the meadow and disappeared out of sight.

And so there was only one pig left in the pigsty. At Klaphek too they had to be careful with food. Nobody knew how long the war could keep going on.

9
In the Night

Noortje woke up. She heard noises in the kitchen. At first she thought it was morning already, even though it was still pitch-dark in the small sleeping room. But Aunt Janna always got up at six o'clock, long before sunrise.

In the kitchen the smoldering fire in the stove was being stirred. She heard the poker rattling over the grate and the door to the firebox closing. Then she heard the pump handle in the back, going up and down with its squeaking sound. Baby Sis and Gerrit were fast asleep. Not a single noise came out of the big bed. The farmer had probably gotten up too. And yet Noortje sensed, although she didn't know why, that it still must be night and not really time to wake up yet.

She looked for her clothes in the dark and started putting them on quietly. The room was bitterly cold, and the bed on the floor with little sleeping Gerrit between the blankets was a wonderfully warm spot. But curiosity is stronger than the longing for coziness, and Noortje always was curious about things. It would be unbearable to lie in bed and listen to the noises in the house without knowing what was happening.

A small lamp stood burning on the kitchen table, and after the deep darkness of the alcove the kitchen seemed all lit up. The great water kettle was standing with its bulging bottom in the fire of the stove, making its singing sound. No one was there.

Noortje quickly went through the corridor to the shed.

At the door her feet found their own clogs all by themselves. Behind the cows shone a light. People were busy there. She heard the mumblings of voices. The cows looked at her. She saw their gleaming eyes in the weak light. A few shook their heads so their chains rattled and gave a deep short "moo" as if they wanted to say: it's a good thing you came; something is happening here.

When Noortje walked past the wooden partition she stood still. There she saw Aunt Janna and Henk and the farmer. Evert too. In the middle of the row a cow was lying on the straw. Two legs and the head of a calf were sticking out of the rear of her body. She was sure the calf was dead. Its eyes were closed, and it was all covered with slime and blood.

Aunt Janna held the tail of the cow up high. The farmer and Henk both stood bent over, one leg set across the drain. They had each grasped one of the calf's legs and were pulling at it gently. Evert stood behind them and held up the lamp.

The cow lay very still, without making a sound. Then a big shiver went through her body, the skin over her round belly rippled, and she lowed softly a few times.

"You can do it, old girl. Just a little more, then it's over," Farmer Everingen said in his calm voice. "You can do it. Here we go again."

And suddenly the opening in the rear of the cow's body became bigger, and with a jolt the calf came out almost all the way. Then its hindquarters appeared, and Henk caught the little animal in his arms and carried it to a heap of straw behind the drainage ditch. He immediately started rubbing the calf dry with a tuft of straw.

"It's a male," he said. "That's too bad."

The farmer said, "The rest will come soon now. Mother, hold up that tail a little more."

Noortje saw a long, white membrane hanging out of the

body of the cow. Again a shiver went through the animal, and she lowed softly. A stream of blood gushed out, and then there came something else. She couldn't understand what it was: a thick, black thing, it looked something like a big piece of black bread. The thing dropped into the drain with the membrane, and there it stayed.

"The afterbirth has come too," the farmer said. "We'll give that to Rachel." And then he straightened up to take a look at the calf.

Noortje came a few steps closer. She could hardly believe her eyes. Was that really the same calf that had only just come out of the body of the cow and that had looked so dead and dirty then? Now it was standing up, tottering on its four legs. It had a beautiful, glossy fur with reddish brown and white spots, and it blinked with big eyes at the light. Its mouth was very soft, white and pink and velvety. The calf seemed a cheerful creature, glad that it had come into the world.

"A beautiful calf. Really a strong one," Henk said. "Too bad it's a bull."

"Well, Henk, we don't have any say in that. I'm going to make some coffee," Aunt Janna said. Then she walked past Noortje, but she didn't say anything.

Noortje stayed and watched how Henk lifted the calf and carried it to the other side of the shed. Earlier he'd already partitioned off a nice little nook there with straw, right next to the horse stalls. Evert stuck his finger into the calf's mouth. It started sucking hard at once. Noortje did the same; it was a very funny feeling.

They sat in the kitchen, slurping hot coffee and talking about the birth of the calf. Noortje was near the window and didn't say anything. She had a strange, excited feeling. Something important had happened, and yet it was nothing more than a calf being born.

The coffee was piping hot. She poured it onto the saucer, a little at a time, just the way the men did, and slurped it down in neat little gulps.

"What time is it?" Farmer Everingen asked.

"Almost two."

"Then we can still catch a few hours of sleep. Come on, Evert. Let's get moving."

"Yes, Dad."

Evert didn't look as if he felt like going back to bed. He was wide awake and stayed sitting in the kitchen. Aunt Janna threw a lump of peat into the stove. It would keep the fire glowing till it was time to get up again. She set the singing teakettle aside on the stove, out of the fire.

"All right, Evert, off you go," she said.

And Evert had no way not to, for now Henk rose up also, and tipping his cap he said, "Good night all."

But Aunt Janna and Farmer Everingen apparently didn't much feel like going to bed again either. They stayed sitting by the stove and now and then spoke a few more words about the calf. Nothing was said to Noortje; they seemed to have forgotten that she was still there. Then Noortje heard a noise. Someone was walking outside in front of the house. Who could that be, in the middle of the night? Or was she mistaken? She turned her head to the side, ear closer to the windowpane. The shutters on the outside were locked, so she couldn't see.

Farmer Everingen and Aunt Janna sat silent, eyes half closed. The grown-ups were dead tired and Noor wide awake. She heard a sound outside, as if someone were standing there at the door, trying to lift the latch very carefully. Of course, Noortje knew that the solid bolt on the inside of the door was pushed shut. No one could get in.

Everingen stood up. "Come, let's go get a little sleep,"

he said. Noortje walked out of the kitchen toward the toilet.

Groping her way, she found the lamp in the shed. She knew how to light it. It stood behind the cows in the small arched window, which had been blacked out by means of sacks. A box of matches lay next to it. It was silent in the shed. She only heard the sound of the cows chewing their cud, chomping and chewing away as they always did, never knowing a moment of rest. You would be exhausted if you did that all the time, she thought, laughing a little to herself at her strange thoughts. What if people also chewed that way? And she waggled her jaws around and around. Would it taste nice?

She stood in the corridor with the lamp. Now she had to open the outside door and shine the light into the eyes of the stranger who was standing there, to startle him. And if it was a thief or a German, she would immediately slam the door shut and scream. Then the others would come to help her at once.

She listened, with her head pressed against the door. She heard nothing.

Very slowly she pushed back the bolt. It made a soft, sliding noise. Would whoever was outside hear it? And what would he do? Lifting the lamp high, to where she figured the head of a grown-up to be, she flung the door open fast.

The light shone into the dark night. She must not have closed the lamp properly when she lit it; a gust of wind blew out the flame. But a clear half-moon still hung in the sky, giving off enough light.

She saw the apple trees and the little gate in front of the house and the white spots of frozen snow on the grass. She also could see the dark rim of the hawthorn hedge around the vegetable garden. And she saw the sky, which was very dark blue, with a glittering star here and there. Way up high she heard an airplane flying over.

And then she saw the man. He stood right next to her, pressed against the wall. Slowly he turned and looked at her. His face was strangely white in the moonlight. He had black, curly hair and was wearing a dark coat. And the strangest thing was that he was so small, hardly any taller than she. She couldn't see if he was old or young. There was nothing about him that frightened her. In whispery tones he asked, "Mrs. Everingen, is she still in there?"

"Yes," Noortje whispered back.

"And the others?"

"They've all gone back to bed. A calf has been born. . . ."

"Go and tell her that it's time. I'll wait here." And after those words the man leaned back against the wall again, quietly and patiently.

Aunt Janna hadn't gone to bed. She'd been waiting for Noortje.

"There's a man outside. I don't know what his name is. I forgot to ask. I'm supposed to tell you that it's time." With those words Noortje looked to Aunt Janna questioningly.

"Oh, my, now that too!" Aunt Janna exclaimed, hastily getting up. "That must be Mr. Meyer. Now you've seen him, child."

She went to the outside door, and Noortje stayed right by her. Aunt Janna spoke with the strange man briefly. Noortje could make out only a few of their words. "Every three minutes," she heard, and, "if everything is normal."

Aunt Janna pushed her inside and said, "Put on your coat fast, and bring that lamp with you."

She quickly threw a few things in a bag. Noortje saw towels and a piece of soap. It was the piece of soap from the soldier's knapsack that they'd found in the wood. Carefully Aunt Janna opened the door to the bedroom and took her old coat off the hook. Noortje's hung in the scullery. She put it on and ran tiptoe through the corridor to get her clogs. She didn't put those on till she was outside.

▪10▪ The Children of the Eighth Wood

The three of them went across the meadow to Beech Lane, Noortje following Aunt Janna and Aunt Janna behind the stranger. Their clogs made muffled scraping noises, but Mr. Meyer was wearing shoes, and at every step he took the snow crunched, sounding very loud in the still night. At Beech Lane they could walk side by side again.

Mr. Meyer whispered, "Why are you taking the child?"

"She can help us," Aunt Janna whispered back. "She's a big girl." They didn't say any more then.

Underneath the trees the moonlight couldn't penetrate well, and it was very dark. The two grown-ups walked on at a brisk pace, taking firm steps. They didn't hesitate a moment about where to set their feet on the uneven ground. After a while they turned left onto a narrow path between densely growing trees.

The branches hung low here. It was a neglected and wild forest with lots of dead wood lying on the ground. Noortje stayed close, right behind Aunt Janna's broad back. That way she wasn't bothered by the sharp branches snapping back into her face. A few times they had to clamber over fallen tree trunks. It seemed almost as if the man could see in the dark. Every time the going on the path was hard, he stopped to help them.

Noortje felt strangely calm. This wood was so very still

that above her head she heard only the sound of the wind, making the branches creak softly and rustling the dead leaves left over from autumn.

Despite her calm, her heart was thumping more loudly than usual. That will pass soon too, she thought. There is really nothing to be afraid of here. It is so still, and we are so far away from people.

Again, way up high in the dark, came the distant droning of an airplane. They heard that sound almost every night.

Which wood were they in, actually? If you walked all the way down Beech Lane, and then turned left. . . . Oh! They must be in the wood that Evert had said they were not allowed to enter! And they'd gone through it anyway, back then, when they'd been so late, after that air raid at the baker's. . . . Henk had been standing there, at the end of the path.

This was the wood Noortje had called The Eighth Wood.

She had no time now to wonder about anything or even think. Aunt Janna halted and grasped Noortje's hand. Aunt Janna's hand was firm and warm.

"Careful, and bend down," she whispered. Noortje let herself be pulled along. They crept underneath a fir tree whose branches hung very low to the ground. Mr. Meyer stopped and lifted up something; Aunt Janna got down on her knees and went into a dark hole, Noortje following her, face close against Aunt Janna's back. It was pitch-dark in there. She felt herself going through a short passageway, and then she came into a space.

A match was struck; Aunt Janna took the lamp out of Noortje's hand, and a moment later there was light. Then she saw that she was in a small room that had been dug out underground. The walls were covered by thin logs, and a few thick ones held up the roof. There was a smell of earth and wood. It was low here; Noortje could stand upright, but Aunt Janna had to bend down. In between the logs she could see the black earth.

On the packed-down ground were some crates. They were the furniture of the room, for they served as cupboards and tables. On a heap of straw on the floor lay a woman. She sat up halfway when she saw them enter; her head leaned against a few pillows. Noortje noticed the same checkered pillowcases that were used at Klaphek.

The woman seemed still very young, almost a girl. She was pale and her eyes were large and dark. Noortje thought she had never seen such a beautiful woman. Mr. Meyer had knelt down beside her and was stroking her cheek. He spoke in soft, reassuring tones to her. Suddenly the woman squeezed her eyes shut, breathing fast, and under the blankets her stomach, which looked like a big hill, moved up and down. Mr. Meyer kept stroking that large stomach with his hand. After a while, the woman opened her eyes again. She smiled and said, "That was another one."

"Yes," Aunt Janna said, "that was a really strong contraction. It's going well. I'm sure it won't last very much longer now."

"Daddy!" a little voice cried out from one of the dark corners of the room. Noortje was so startled that she almost dropped the lamp. Only now did she see another bed of straw over there. Two little boys sat up straight on it, their knees tucked under blankets. They were wearing sweaters and had scarves knotted around their necks. With big eyes they were looking at their mother and at the people around her.

"Daddy, I'm so cold."

Their father got up and, stooping a little, walked over toward them and squatted down next to them.

"That's your own fault, Simon. You promised you were going to sleep. Come, be a smart boy and lie under the blankets."

"I can't sleep either!"

"You too, Leon? Well, you'd both better try anyway. It's night now."

"Will our little baby brother be coming soon now?"

"Yes, very soon. If you go to sleep like good boys now, he'll be here when you wake up."

The children lay down, but they didn't close their eyes. The father pulled the blankets all the way up to their chins.

"What should I do, Aunt Janna?" Noortje whispered.

"Put the lamp on that crate there, child, and come help me here."

Aunt Janna pushed a towel into her hands. Together they lifted up a big iron skillet in which pieces of charcoal lay glowing. They set the pan as near to Mrs. Meyer's bed as possible. Above the fire was a grate. On it Aunt Janna placed a pan with water.

"Now," she said after they'd done that, "it seems best you stay with the boys. Try to get them to sleep. Perhaps I'll need you later to hold up the lamp and give me some light."

Noortje sat down next to the bed of the two little boys. They were still quite small, not older than four or five years for sure. She was getting very cold sitting still on the moist earth. "Move over a little," she said. "Then I'll lie next to you. I'm so cold."

The boys immediately made a place for her.

"What's your name?" asked the smaller one, who was called Simon.

"I'm Noortje."

"Will you tell us a story?"

"All right, if you promise to be very quiet."

She lay on her back looking at the low ceiling of tree trunks and sand. What story could she tell these children now? Her head seemed empty. It was just as if she'd forgotten all the stories she'd ever known.

"Begin then," Simon said.

And Leon said, "Yes, begin. A promise is a promise."

"Well, all right then. Listen."

Luckily there was one tale left in Noortje's head. She started telling it, whispering, "Once upon a time there was an old man who walked in the woods. His little dog went walking with him."

"Was it in this wood?" Leon asked. "Would he be able to find us?"

"No, it was not in this wood. It's a very long time ago and in a country far from here.

"Then the man lost a mitten. It lay in the snow on the path, and he didn't notice it at all. Along came a little mouse. It saw the mitten and thought, Ha, that is a wonderful house for me! And the mouse went to live in the mitten. But then very soon a frog came by, and he asked, 'Who lives in this mitten?'

"The mouse said, 'I am Mouse Hasty-Fast. And who are you?'

" 'I am Frog Leap-Leg. May I live with you in the mitten?'

" 'Well, all right, you can come in.'

"And then the mouse and the frog lived together in the mitten."

"Did they also have beds? And tables too . . . ?" Leon asked.

"Shhh! Quiet. No talking. That's what we said, right? Listen! Soon a hare came along, and he asked, 'Who lives in this mitten?'

" 'Mouse Hasty-Fast and Frog Leap-Leg live here. And who pray are you?'

"And the hare said, 'I am Rapid Rabbit. May I come live with you in the mitten?'

" 'Well, you can come in.' "

"That's impossible, huh?" Leon whispered.

"Be quiet now," Noor said. "I think Simon is already asleep."

"But you have to go on telling. What else did they do with that mitten?"

"Well now, they made a little window in it and a stove with a chimney. Shall I go on?"

"Yes, yes."

"Well, then a fox came along, and it saw the beautiful mitten lying there, and this fox said, 'Who lives in this mitten?'

" 'Mouse Hasty-Fast, Frog Leap-Leg, and Rapid Rabbit are living here. And who are you'

" 'I am Fox Golden-Coat. Let me come in too, please.' "

Leon giggled very softly.

"Shhh!" Noortje said.

"Yes, but what else did they make, when the fox had come in too . . . ?"

"They made another window, and also a veranda."

"What's that, a veranda?"

"That's something like a balcony, but then downstairs with some steps to the garden. Shall I go on? So they lived all four of them in the mitten, and it was very warm and cozy. Then the branches creaked in the forest. A big animal was coming along their way. It was a wild boar."

Noortje looked at the two little boys. Both had their eyes shut. They were breathing quietly. Were they really asleep? Little Leon fluttered his eyelids, and Noortje whispered, "The wild boar snorted and grunted, 'Who is living in this mitten?' "

She didn't have to go on further. The children were asleep. Actually, she was sorry to stop, for it was such a beautiful story. She wouldn't have minded telling them about the wolf and the big bear who came to live in the mitten. And what she liked best was the end of the story, so she decided to tell it to herself. Her lips moved but she made no sound:

Suddenly the old man noticed he had lost his mitten. He turned back and started looking for it. His dog ran ahead of him; he saw the mitten first, moving as if it were alive. The dog began to bark loudly. All the animals jumped out and disappeared into the woods. Then came the old man, and he picked up his mitten. And never, Noortje thought, did that poor man know all that had happened in those few minutes.

Had she been sleeping? Perhaps she had. She didn't know at all how much time had passed since she told the story. It could have been a few minutes, or had it lasted longer? She looked at Leon and Simon. They lay quite still with their eyes shut.

There were sounds near the other bed, and Aunt Janna's voice saying, "Easy now, easy. It's going very well."

Noortje saw dark shadows moving, making fantastic figures against the walls and ceiling. The blankets of the bed had been thrown aside. The woman had pulled up her knees. Her legs were thin and white, and her stomach was enormous. Aunt Janna looked back.

"Noortje," she whispered. "Come over here. You have to hold up the lamp."

Very carefully, without waking the children, Noortje slid from under the blankets onto the floor. She stood at the bottom end of the bed and held the lamp as high as she could. It didn't give very much light, and everything seemed unreal. Perhaps the sleep was still in her eyes, or was she dreaming? All that had happened this night seemed so strange.

Mrs. Meyer had lifted up her head, and Mr. Meyer was supporting her.

"Go on, that's the way. It's coming along," Aunt Janna said.

Mrs. Meyer sank back onto the cushions again. She smiled, and Mr. Meyer wiped her face with a towel.

"Fine," Aunt Janna said. "Now we go on."

The woman had pressed her foot against Aunt Janna; again she lifted up her head. Her lips were pressed together tightly.

Noortje's hand holding the lamp trembled. She couldn't allow it to fall. That would be truly terrible. And she grasped it more firmly and looked wide-eyed at what was happening there in front of her. Between the woman's legs was a dark, round spot, which became bigger and bigger.

"The head is almost there," Aunt Janna said. "A little more."

Now Noortje was really wide awake. The head! So that was what was coming out there, the head of a child! She could already see the little hairs on it. It got still bigger, and then the whole head stuck out like a dark ball.

Mrs. Meyer had to take a little rest. And then everything went very fast. Noortje wanted to laugh and cry at the same time; she'd never seen anything that was so wonderful and yet so funny too. For now a small thick shoulder appeared with an arm attached to it. The head turned a bit, so that she saw a little face with its swollen little eyes squeezed shut. Moments later followed a beautiful back, two fat little buttocks, and then there was the whole child. It lay on the stomach of the mother, and the umbilical cord, a sort of long string, was still attached to the tiny belly.

The mouth began to tremble, it opened wide, and the baby howled. Oh, how it howled . . . !

"It's a girl!" Aunt Janna cried.

And Mrs. Meyer said, "Oh, oh, a girl!"

The father of the little child just sat looking at it and didn't seem to know what he should do. Tears were running down his cheeks.

Aunt Janna was suddenly very busy. First she tied the umbilical cord with a piece of thread and cut it. She had already heated towels above the fire, and now she swaddled the child in them, for she mustn't get cold. She also wiped her little face clean. Mrs. Meyer was very happy; that was easy to see. "Little Sarah," she said. "We'll call her Sarah, just like my mother. Oh, God. . . ."

The baby was all hidden in a woolen blanket now and was already crying less loudly.

"Now you can put down that lamp," Aunt Janna said to Noortje. "And go sit on that crate near the fire. I have to go on with Mrs. Meyer." And she laid the baby in Noortje's arms. "Hold her snug. That's it, yes," she said.

So there Noortje sat, with that very tiny child in her lap. She rocked the newborn creature gently back and forth and whispered, "Are you a child of the Eighth Wood also? Oh, yes, Sarah, and how do you like it here? Hello, child of the Eighth Wood. Hi, sweet little Sarah!"

The baby girl still had her eyes tightly shut. She didn't cry anymore. On top of her smooth little head were a few sticky black hairs. She was already making sucking sounds with her lips too. That was so cute. She must be hungry already.

Suddenly Noortje thought of the two brothers in their bed in the corner. Were they still asleep? No. Both were wide awake, sitting upright, watching wide-eyed at everything that was happening.

Mr. Meyer took the child from her and went over to the boys and squatted down beside them. "Take a good look," he said. "Here is your new sister. Isn't she sweet?"

A basket stood all ready for the baby, with sheets and blankets and stones that had been warmed over the fire in it. "Now little Sarah must go and have a good long sleep," the father of the children said. "She must be very tired from her long journey into the world."

And very carefully, he laid Sarah in the cradle.

An hour later Noortje and Aunt Janna were walking home together along Beech Lane. Mr. Meyer had gone with them through the wood.

They didn't say anything, but before Aunt Janna opened the gate to the meadow, she looked at Noortje. The moon had disappeared. It was very dark, and yet Noortje knew that Aunt Janna was looking at her.

"All through your life, child, you will never forget what happened tonight," she said. "And that is as it should be. But mind you, you cannot talk about it with anybody now."

"No, Aunt Janna. But do Farmer Everingen and Evert know about it?"

"Only the farmer and Henk and I know about the Meyer family. Evert knows we bring food somewhere every day, but he doesn't know any more than that. You understand, of course, that these people are Jewish. So you'll also understand why we have to keep this very secret."

Noortje immediately crept into bed. Aunt Janna stayed up in the kitchen. The men were already out milking. The first milk from the cow that calved that night would be brought in soon now. That first milk was called "beastings." It was rich and thick as porridge. Aunt Janna planned to make a big stack of pancakes for breakfast from the beastings.

▪11▪ Munkie

The kitchen was very crowded since the Wolthuis family had come. Therefore Mr. Vanderhook lit the parlor stove in the afternoon. He could be by himself then, reading quietly. In the evenings, everyone gathered there, sitting around the big table. Carbide had become scarce, and kerosene was no longer available at all, so they had to make do with a very tiny light. They made one out of a cotton thread put in a glass of water, on top of which floated some oil. It burned with a small yellow flame that flickered, dancing back and forth in the draft.

Wolthuis was a real grouch. Almost every day he quarreled with his daughter Alie and also yelled at Dinie. Dinie didn't answer back much, but sometimes she started crying. Ma Wolthuis stayed out of it.

One evening they were all sitting in the parlor again. Noortje was looking at Aunt Janna's little book of verses. It was a very beautiful old-fashioned album, with a cover of red velvet and tiny copper lock. It was larger and thicker than her own album of verses back home.

Suddenly Wolthuis got up and noisily put his chair back in its place at the table. You'd almost think he wanted to break its legs, he banged it on the floor so hard.

"I'm going to bed," he said. His eyes bulged even more than usual, and he looked around so savagely that Noortje didn't dare look up at him. "I'm making an early start tomorrow morning. Tomorrow I'm leaving. I've had it here! Always that nagging and picking and pecking of those two stupid girls! I've got plenty of relatives up in Groningen, and I'm not too old to walk. Don't you think that!"

With big, stiff steps, Wolthuis left the room. They all sat staring at each other, a little dazed. Then someone knocked on the front door. Everingen went to answer it. They heard a strange man's voice and then the deeper bass of the farmer. He had taken the light with him, and they sat waiting in the dark.

"It almost sounds as if they're talking German," Aunt Janna said. "Who'll light a match so I can find the door?" Mr. Vanderhook struck a match, and Aunt Janna had already risen when the door opened and Everingen came back in. Behind him stood a German soldier.

A very odd German soldier. They'd never before seen one who looked so strange. Wearing the uniform of the *Wehrmacht,* he had a fatigue cap on his head. He took it off and holding it in his hand politely, clicked his heels, and making a sort of bow said, "Good evening."

He wore a knapsack on his back, a rifle was slung over his left shoulder, and there was another one over the right. Their barrels banged against each other just above his head. Three cartridge belts full of bullets hung aslant across his chest, and hand grenades were hanging from his belt. They looked like smooth wooden sticks.

The people and the children around the table stared at the odd German. And he stayed quietly at the door for a while, gazing back at them. Then he removed the rifles from his shoulders and leaned them against the wall. He lifted the cartridge belts over his head and put them down on the floor near the rifles. Finally he also unclasped the belt with the hand grenades clattering together on it and placed it near the cartridges.

Without all those weapons, he seemed a different man, an ordinary little man in a gray uniform with thin blond hair. His cheeks were a purplish blue color.

"I simply had to let him in," Everingen muttered. Then, pointing to the empty chair where Wolthuis had been sitting, he said, "Go and sit over there for a moment."

The German clicked his heels against each other again and made another bow. "Many thanks," he said.

"Mother, have you got some coffee left? This boy here is almost frozen and starved."

"What's all of this supposed to mean?" Ma Wolthuis cried out.

Aunt Janna had gotten up for some coffee, but now she hesitated, looking at Ma Wolthuis.

Everingen was a man who never said more than was strictly necessary. Nobody ever heard him tell a story, and he didn't like jokes. Usually he mumbled words inside his mouth when he was speaking to people or to the horses when he drove the flat cart or to the cows when he was milking them. But now he opened his mouth wider than usual and said clearly and firmly, "Ma Wolthuis, you're a good soul and haven't had an easy time of it. But you're in my house, and my guests are my guests. This man will tell you his story soon enough, but first he has to have something to eat and drink. I don't care whether you believe him or not, but I can tell very well when a man is starving. And this one here hasn't had a thing to eat or drink in five days, nothing but what he could find in the woods."

Aunt Janna hastened to the kitchen. They all sat looking at the stranger, who smiled shyly, though not too successfully, for the muscles of his face were frozen stiff.

A little later there was a plate in front of him with slices of brown bread and rye bread, bacon and cheese on it and a big mug full of piping hot coffee. The room was dead quiet while the German sat there eating. Clearly he was terribly hungry, and yet he didn't want to seem impolite by stuffing the food too hastily into his mouth. The coffee was so hot that he almost burned his tongue with it.

That starved man eating was a strange sight. In between getting down the big chunks of bread, he took little sips of the coffee. Meanwhile, he kept looking around the room with his light blue eyes. Soon the plate and mug were empty. The color of his face had slowly turned from purple to bright red.

"Now you ask me," he said.

They all wanted to ask the German something at the same time, but he couldn't understand them. Mr. Vanderhook had to act as interpreter, since he understood German very well and could also speak it. Whenever the soldier said something, most of them did sort of understand him. Mr. Vanderhook needed to explain only a very little. But he did have to keep translating when they put their questions to the German.

They heard how he'd run away from his army unit about ten days before, because he'd had enough of the war. "What we do is not good," he said, "stealing and robbing and killing without it being necessary."

"He's a deserter. If they get him, they'll give him a bullet," Henk said.

And Ma Wolthuis cried out loudly, "That's something you should've thought of before, my friend!"

"What does she say?" the German asked Mr. Vanderhook. Then, when he was told, he said, "Yes, true. You know, I always thought Hitler was right. We all were brought up that way. My father, my brother, my uncle, my mother's brother, they're all. . . . They're dead. Fallen in battle. For the Fatherland. Oh, yes, but not for me anymore."

It all sounded so good, so nice, and yet there was no one in the room who didn't have a feeling of revulsion toward that gray uniform they knew so well.

"Where is he from?" Alie wanted to know.

"From Stettin," the German said. "That's a harbor town on the Baltic. We used to be Poles before."

Dinie hadn't said anything yet. Now she put in, "Mr. Vanderhook, why don't you ask him his name?"

But the German didn't want to tell them. "It's better I have no name. Names are not good for anything."

"Then let's call him Munkie," Evert said.

"What made you think of that?" someone cried out.

"Munkie, that's a good name for him."

The German sat smiling through this discussion. He seemed to think it sort of funny that they'd made up a name for him just like that. They all sat talking for over an hour.

He told them about the battles he'd been through. He had fought in Belgium, in the Ardennes. His company then moved up north, first going through the southeast part of Holland and later crossing the river Ijssel and arriving in the Veluwe, the central wooded part of the country. They had also stopped in Arnhem, and he'd seen how the houses were being looted there. He told them that whole trainloads full of household goods and clothing were being sent off to Germany. He said he disapproved of this looting and that the German people were following the wrong path.

That's why he'd run away, shortly before his unit was to receive orders to move on again. And he'd been keeping himself out of sight, lying low in the woods. He no longer remembered how many miles he had walked. During the day he stayed hidden. The one thing he could be sure of was that he'd be shot if discovered. The first two days of hunger hadn't been so bad, he told them. But he'd been very cold. It was freezing at night! So he'd walked a lot in the dark. Yes, the days were much worse, for then he had to stay still. A few times his countrymen had walked right by him. Then he pressed himself flat to the ground and crept away under the low-hanging branches. And because he had been lying still so much he almost froze to death.

He hadn't had a single piece of bread left in his pocket for the last five days! He'd eaten some of the grease he used to polish his boots with. And he tried to eat tree bark and moss, but they gave him cramps. He'd eaten snow to quench his thirst, and it made him cold to the bones.

The previous night and all during that day he kept close to Klaphek, spying on the house and its people. By then he'd realized that he would surely die unless he could find some help. Not until that night did he feel brave enough to knock on their door.

Everingen looked at his wife. Their faces were very serious. Almost imperceptibly Aunt Janna shook her head in refusal.

"Well, well, well," said Everingen. He kept on looking at the German, then at his wife again. And once again Aunt Janna signaled No.

"We're Christian people, Mother," the farmer muttered.

"Surely, and so we are. It is our duty to think of others. One night, no more. And he can come for food whenever he wants to."

The German understood those words very well. While he sat telling his story, his face had gotten a sleepy, contented expression. Now he sat up straight again and looked all around tensely, as if danger were near.

Everingen had risen. He took the light off the table. "I'll show you a place where you can sleep, but tomorrow you'll have to go. That is safer, both for us and for you," he said.

That night the deserter slept in the hay. The following morning he was wearing some old pants and a jacket of Henk's and also a cap. You could no longer tell he was a German. He was still a little blue in the face. He left without taking his weapons. Evert searched all over, but they were nowhere to be found.

That same morning Wolthuis went off. He was up at four in the morning and, without one of his family hearing him, departed from Klaphek. At least so it seemed. His wife had heard him all right, but she'd pretended to be asleep. She had learned her lesson in the course of the years and knew there was no use arguing with her husband.

No one said a word about Wolthuis. And four days later he was back. The walk to Groningen hadn't worked out too well. No one asked him anything when he marched in again. Afterward, there weren't so many quarrels.

Wolthuis never was told who that strange German in civilian clothes was, now and then coming in and getting a dishful of food. Munkie always arrived before dark. After a while he also found a bike, and then he rode from one farm to the next, begging food. No one knew where he slept.

He came to Klaphek once or twice a week, no more. With a smiling face he stood there, unexpectedly in the kitchen. He asked nothing, and always when he entered he clicked his heels together and made that polite bow. When he got his plate of food, he said in Dutch, "*Dank u wel.*"

▪12▪ Sarah

Sometimes it seemed that everything in that winter of the war happened at night. But it wasn't really so.

In the mornings the eastern sky turned a very light gray, then the sun came up, and soon the world looked a bit more cheerful again. During those cold months, the mossy trunks of the old trees had a wonderful green color, the bills of the geese were bright orange, the air was all tingling and fresh. Whenever it was clear of clouds, the sky seemed endlessly high and very pale blue. And high also were the airplanes that flew over like small silver birds drawing their long, thin wake of white vapor through the blue space. Sometimes they were so high that you couldn't hear their motors and all you saw was that white trail.

At Klaphek, every day seemed the same as the one before. Sometimes Everingen and Henk and Mr. Vanderhook would be sitting together in the shed. Then they talked about the war and about politics and the years before the war. After the war everything would be better, they told each other. Then no one would want for anything. For surely they had learned something in these years, hadn't they? First the country would have to be rebuilt, and everything would be divided fairly. But they never agreed as to how that could be arranged.

Evert and Noortje sometimes sat with them, listening to their talk. They couldn't remember those years before the war very well. They knew that back then they'd eaten chocolate once in a while, but they'd forgotten the taste of it. And they didn't know what a banana looked like anymore either. They couldn't imagine what it would be like later, when the war was over. And yet perhaps the time would come very soon.

The women in the kitchen didn't talk about war very often. They were always busy, peeling potatoes, sweeping, washing. There was a lot of washing to be done because of all those people living together. The furnace pot was lighted every week, to boil the laundry. On those days Evert and Noortje had to walk around behind the horse for fifteen minutes longer, to pump up water.

When the laundry was done and the white underwear, towels, and pillowcases lay drying in the sun on top of the hawthorn hedge, where they couldn't blow away because the little thorns held onto the clothes, then the red bricks of the pavement glittered and gleamed. First they were wet down by dirty washwater, and then cleaned with clear rinsing water.

The women found it a nuisance that the pavement stayed clean for only a few minutes each time. For as soon as they disappeared inside the kitchen to warm their hands, red and tingling painfully with the wet cold, at the stove, the geese came. And geese do drop a lot, really an awful lot; wherever they walk they drop their thin, slimy, green blobs. That didn't matter as long as they stayed in the meadow. But as soon as the women had finished doing the laundry, the geese came to the door of the scullery and started screaming. First the two girls and Ma Wolthuis didn't notice anything. They were tired from the hard work outside. But Aunt Janna did hear the geese, and she immediately chased them away. Often it was already too late. The beautiful red bricks were covered with filth, and you slid on it with your clogs.

One afternoon Evert and Noortje climbed up Dassen

Mountain, together with Theo. The weather that day was raw, and the sky all hidden by gray clouds.

Actually, Dassen Mountain couldn't be called a real mountain, even though it stuck out way above the surrounding hills. In summer, it almost looked like semolina pudding with red currant sauce; it was covered with heather, and lots of narrow white paths ran up to the top. The paths were the white pudding you could see through the red sauce. Now, in winter, not much of that sauce was visible; everywhere the clumps of heather bushes still held spots of snow. At the top of Dassen Mountain stood a group of birch trees with their tall crowns exposed to the wind. They had become tough and supple.

A bee enthusiast from Zemst had set up his beehives there, in order to collect the good heather honey from them. This winter the beekeeper hadn't had sugar for his bees, and so he'd left the honey inside the hives; that way the bees could stay alive on it. But someone had taken away all the honey, and now the hives were full of dead bees. They were also outside at the entrance, clotted together. It was a sad sight. Evert maintained that German soldiers must have been the ones who stole the honey.

From Dassen Mountain you could see the water meadows in the distance and the serpentine river Ijssel winding itself through them. But when you turned the other way you looked out over the Eighth Wood.

Noortje stood underneath the birches, her hair flying, and gazed at the top of the trees down below moving to and fro in the wind. It wasn't easy not to tell the other two what she had experienced that night, only two weeks ago. But she had been closemouthed about it all that time, even to Evert.

"What are you looking at like that?" Theo asked.

"Nothing. Why?"

"You're making such a face, as if you're seeing spooks."

"If I want to see a spook I needn't look so far. You're just like one yourself."

Theo turned away with a sad face. He knew only too well that he looked awful. His face was very pale, his sleek blond hair hadn't been cut in a long time and was hanging over his ears, and his lips were almost as white as the towel around his throat.

Noortje instantly felt sorry that she'd been so mean. But what if her face had betrayed what she was thinking of while she stood looking at the Eighth Wood! How could she let Theo know that she didn't mean to hurt his feelings? They were walking single file down one of the narrow paths. When they got to the bottom of the hill, Noortje came up to walk beside Theo.

"Hey, Theo, will you teach me how to play chess?" she asked.

"Girls can't play chess," Theo said.

"What makes you think that? I can play very well. I even beat my father once!"

"Oh, so you already know how to play! Why did you ask me if I want to teach you then?"

Now Theo was even more hurt. He knew that she'd only asked him to teach her out of friendliness, to make up. Noortje didn't know what to say anymore. Sometimes she said things that made everything awful. And when she wanted to make up for it she said something that was all wrong, and then everything became even worse. She wanted to tell Theo that she really liked him, but how?

They walked on in silence for a while, side by side. Then Noortje felt Theo put his hand on her shoulder. He said, "Little girls who can play chess are often wiser than grown-ups. I'd very much like to have a game with you someday."

Noortje laughed again. "Theo," she asked, "are you really very ill? It isn't so bad, right?"

Theo made a funny jump in the air, and then he kicked a stone away with his foot. "Ow, dammit, that darned stone!" he cried. "You better watch it if you ever again talk about being sick. Don't you know that there's a witch living in this wood, and when she hears that I'm sick she'll come to get me?" And he walked ahead, taking a few big steps with his long, thin legs.

Noortje looked about her, a little frightened. For they'd come to First Beech Lane, and to their right was the Eighth Wood.

Past the bend in the lane Evert said, "Look, there goes my mother. Funny, the way she's walking."

And Noortje thought, I'm the only one who knows where Aunt Janna has been.

The children began to run. Soon they'd left Theo behind, but they didn't catch up with Aunt Janna till she was at the gate to the meadow.

Aunt Janna was carrying something. It was a small package, a thing rolled in a blanket, which she held carefully in one of her arms. With the other hand she carried a heavy bag. She walked toward the house with quick steps, not saying anything. Evert closed the gate.

In the kitchen Aunt Janna laid her package on the table. First she removed the scarf around her head; then she gave a few very deep sighs. And still she hadn't said one single word. Dinie and Alie and Granny were sitting at the table, Gerrit on Alie's lap. They looked wonderingly at Aunt Janna, who slowly took off her coat. Noortje couldn't keep her eyes off that rolled-up blanket. She thought she knew what was in it.

Aunt Janna hung up her coat. Then she picked up the package and started unrolling the blanket. Very carefully, and with a smile playing about her lips, she lifted out a very small child. The child was all wrapped in linens and pieces of cloth. Only a little red nose and a pair of tightly squeezed-shut eyes were visible. The sleeves of a little vest were pulled far over the clenched fists, and a little hat made of all sorts of wool remnants almost entirely covered the tiny head.

"Well, now," said Aunt Janna, "here you are."

"Ah, Oh, my, oh, my, oh, my! What did you bring home now!" Granny cried out.

And Alie and Dinie said simultaneously, "Oh, my goodness, a baby!"

"A little baby!"

Aunt Janna glanced at Noortje, and Noortje saw the laugh in Aunt Janna's eyes. Noortje nodded and said, "Little Sarah."

Suddenly the kitchen was full of people. Farmer Everingen and Henk had apparently sensed that something unusual was up, and they both came in to have a look. Mr. Vanderhook entered too, a book still in his hand. Theo stood outside, peering in through the window. Gerrit hung over the table with his face close to the child.

"A little baby! A little sister! Is it ours?" Gerrit cried out with his loud voice.

His mouth was so close to Sarah that it was almost on the hat. Sarah's lips began to tremble; her mouth opened wide. You could see a tiny tongue and also the gums, for she didn't have teeth yet. The head got all wrinkly, and inside the pieces of cloth two legs started kicking. Then the sound of screaming came out of that little throat. Goodness, how that child could scream! Where did it come from, all that force? Noortje solemnly nodded her head a few times, for she already knew how loud that baby could cry.

Gerrit was startled. He let himself slide off Alie's lap and crept away underneath the table. Then he fell into a crying fit, trying to howl even louder than the baby.

Baby Sis had clambered up in her crib, and because she didn't like all that noise, she started crying too.

"Hoo, hoo, hoo," Sis roared.

"Well, you've got yourself a nice choir going in your house, Mother," Everingen said.

Now Ma Wolthuis also stuck her head in at the door. She'd been up in the attic and till then hadn't noticed any of the hullabaloo. "Dear heavens, what have we got here?" she cried. "Is the world coming to an end?"

Aunt Janna had picked up the baby and held its face cuddled against her neck; she took a few steps up and down. It soon made Sarah quiet again.

"Gerrit, my boy, now you stop your bawling too," Aunt Janna said. "Nothing has happened, nothing at all. Don't worry. It's not your fault that the baby was crying. It's something little babies like to do."

Gerrit stopped, and a little later he dared stick his head above the table again. Only Sissy was still crying, but they were all so used to that, they didn't really hear her anymore. Aunt Janna sat down on the chair in front of the stove, Sarah on her lap. She removed the tiny woolen hat.

"Evert," she said, "will you go upstairs to the attic for Mama and take a look in the gray chest. There should be a baby bottle in it. Go on up and get it for me now, my boy."

Then they were all set to work, for Sarah had to have a cradle, hot-water bottles, and a whole lot more. The nursing bottle had to be sterilized before she could drink from it. A baby only a few weeks old in the house! There was much to be done.

13
More About Sarah

Aunt Janna didn't tell the people at Klaphek where Sarah came from. Nor did she explain that Sarah had screamed so loud she could be heard throughout the wood. And that the baby cried so much because she was hungry. Mrs. Meyer wasn't strong, and she hadn't milk enough for the child to drink. His face drawn with fear, Mr. Meyer had told Aunt Janna how he'd gone to the path through the wood the night before and could hear the crying all the way from there. Little Sarah would betray them in the end, the Germans would find them, and. . . . It wasn't necessary to say anything more. Aunt Janna and Mr. Meyer understood one another very well.

"The mother is a friend of mine, and she doesn't have enough milk," Aunt Janna said in the Klaphek kitchen, as if that explained why they were taking the child in.

"Huh!" Ma Wolthuis said. "I find that pretty odd! A little child belongs with its mother. She's the one who should be taking care of it."

"The mother is ill," Aunt Janna said. "And if the Germans ever stop here, asking where the child comes from. . . ." She looked hesitantly around, for she didn't quite know how to handle this problem without giving away the whole thing. The fewer the people who knew about that hiding place in the wood, the better. "Well, then," she said, "we'll tell the Germans that it's Mr. Vanderhook's baby and that his wife is still in the hospital. Yes, that's the best way." The big girls Dinie and Alie began to giggle. Even Granny had to laugh a bit, and Ma Wolthuis roared with laughter.

"Mr. Vanderhook!" she cried. "Who would have thought he had it in him! A baby! Woman, don't make me laugh so hard." And she wiped the tears from her eyes.

But Aunt Janna wouldn't budge an inch. "Perhaps it won't ever come to that," she said. "but if they ask, that's what we'll have to say. All of us. For the safety of the child. It can't lead to anything good, once they start finding out where she really comes from. I can't say any more about it."

"So Sarah is my little sister now," Noortje said.

"Yes, she's your sister. And you have to take care of her. You can give her bottle to her and change the diapers. I'll teach you how. You're clever enough. I'm already busy with Baby Sis."

Noortje turned a deep red. She was going to take care of little Sarah! Exactly what she wanted, only she hadn't known it before. To take care of a little child! And she could do it, too; she was sure of that.

But Alie and Dinie stuck their noses in the air indignantly. "Noortje, that little kid!" they cried. "Ridiculous, she can't possibly do it! No, you better leave the little one to us. We know all about taking care of babies."

How angry those two were! They thought of Noortje as a very small girl, not good for anything serious, while they themselves were actually all grown-up already. And they pushed their breasts forward proudly.

But Aunt Janna had decided. "One person has to take care of her. The child has to get used to one person only. Noortje can do it very well, and she's also the one who has the most time for it."

And so Noortje's father had now also become to some extent the father of the baby. Therefore, he had every right to know who her real parents were. Late that night Aunt Janna told him about the Meyer family in the wood. It almost made Mr. Vanderhook shy when he heard that his own young daughter, Noortje, had been present there at the birth of Sarah, and so late at night too. . . .

"May I please tell Evert also?" Noortje asked the following morning. "It isn't fair that we know everything and Evert doesn't. He's a whole year older than me!"

"I think she has a point there," Everingen decided. "And that Evert of ours can be silent as the grave. All right, Noor, you can tell him, but that's where it stops! You have to make him promise he won't let on to anyone else. The Wolthuis family doesn't have to know everything. Understand?"

"And Theo?"

"The fewer the people who know about it, the better. So why tell it to that young fellow? No, not Theo."

Noortje took Evert up to the hayloft with her. They let themselves slide down along the roof till they felt the floor of logs under their feet. It was their own secret spot. The hay supply had grown much smaller now that it was almost spring. The cows had eaten almost all of it, but there still was enough to hide in.

Whispering, Noortje told Evert the big secret. They looked out over the meadow and woods through the glass roof tile. Behind the tall trees of Beech Lane they could see the tops of the trees in that piece of the woods that hid the Meyer family. They also saw the field against the hill and the edge of the wood where, some time ago with Theo, they'd found the coat and the knapsack and the bayonet. That seemed a very long time ago.

"Was it there?" Evert asked. "In that part of the woods?"

"Yes, in the middle of the Eighth Wood."

"Oh, come on. That's not what it's called at all. That wood doesn't have any name. I did know for sure that they were taking food somewhere every day. I've got a pair of eyes in my head too."

"Do you still remember that rhyme, the one about the children of the Eighth Wood? Well, things really turned out that way. That's why I still call it the Eighth Wood. So now the wood does have a name."

Evert did sort of remember that Noortje had once recited something about children in some strange woods. But he didn't remember how the words went. Noortje liked to recite all sorts of rhymes, and he only half listened to them. Rhymes made him think of school, and Evert never particularly felt like being reminded of that. Yet he asked, "How did it go again?"

"The Children of The Eighth Wood," Noortje said, and she went on a little solemnly:

> eat potatoes without salt,
> they get their porridge without oats
> and sleep under the starry vault,
> yet they are never, never cold.

"You're crazy," Evert said. "It's exactly the opposite. They don't sleep out 'under the starry vault.' That wouldn't be possible in winter anyhow. And such little boys too. What did they look like?"

Again Noortje had to tell about Leon and Simon and the place in the hollowed-out earth, the beds of straw on the ground, and the pan with glowing charcoal that was their heating.

"My mother never gives anyone potatoes without salt," Evert said. "You and your crazy poem."

Ah well, Noortje could understand that Evert had to

talk like that. He couldn't easily swallow that he'd been sleeping while she had walked through the woods with his mother and Mr. Meyer.

"Perhaps they'll let us bring food to them sometime," she said. "I know the way now."

But that never happened. Henk and Aunt Janna quietly continued their missions through the dark evening to bring food to the people in the Eighth Wood. And when they stepped into the warm crowded kitchen afterward, nothing in their faces betrayed where they'd come from. Only Noortje noticed that Henk, when he came in alone from a trip, briefly looked at Aunt Janna and winked. That was the sign everything was all right.

They were all busy with little Sarah. A cradle was made out of a large basket. There were enough sheets and pillowcases but not enough diapers. So they cut a few old bed sheets in pieces and hemmed them. The cradle was placed on two chairs in the parlor room. It was quiet and sort of cozy now that the stove burned there all day.

There were two diaper children in the house now, and so they had to do the laundry every day. A few of those white things were always hanging above the stove to dry.

Noortje had plenty to do. Aunt Janna taught her how to hold the baby when she gave her the bottle. And she learned very fast how to put on a clean diaper. She did it carefully because she was afraid she might prick the baby in the stomach with the large safety pin.

The women set themselves to sewing and knitting. That poor child had almost no clothes. It was marvelous how many things they could do with a couple of men's worn undershirts! Dinie and Alie made beautiful vests and jerseys and bibs out of them. One of Everingen's old knitted sweaters was unraveled. It's true the wool was dark gray, but who would complain about that as long as the child stayed warm? Granny, too, crooked her fingers, all stiff and knobby with arthritis, around the knitting needles. And she managed all right too, although the work went slowly. She knitted a pair of socks and two woolen vests. And Ma Wolthuis, there was a fast knitter! In a few days she'd already finished a jacket and pants. Then Sarah was beautifully dressed in those white and gray clothes. They all were quite proud of her.

"Doesn't she look darling now," Dinie said.

And Granny tickled the baby under the chin, saying, "Hello there, my little one. Hello, my pet! Yes, now you look like a real baby."

Sarah kept crying a lot during those first days. Poor Mr. Vanderhook! He liked to sit reading quietly in the parlor after he had finished sawing and cutting a day's supply of wood. And that little child cried and cried and cried. Every five minutes or so Noortje came to take a look at the howling little monkey.

"She misses her mother and her little brothers so much," she said to her father.

He laughed a little mockingly. "Wouldn't she also miss her father a bit?" he asked. "Or are fathers not as important?"

"Of course they are," Noortje said, "but she's got a father here, doesn't she? You."

Half an hour passed without any baby cries, and she figured she'd better take another look in the parlor. When Sarah cried it wasn't very soothing, but now that she was quiet Noortje felt anxious too. Who knew, perhaps she had to be burped again and couldn't get any air? Or could she have burned herself on the hot-water bottle?

Noortje very quietly stuck her head around the parlor door. What she saw almost made her laugh aloud. With big, gliding steps her thin, serious father was walking up and down holding little Sarah in his arms! And was it possible he was singing? She didn't even know he could. She had never heard him before. And yet there he was, singing for little Sarah, and the baby lay listening to him very quietly. Noortje closed the door quickly, leaving it open a tiny crack. She didn't want her father to hear her laugh while he sang his lullaby:

Rockabye baby
Out on the farm,
When the wind blows
I'll keep you warm.
When the wind blows
Your cradle may fall,
But I'll catch little Sarah
Cradle and all.

That's what Mr. Vanderhook sang for little Sarah.

•14•
Broken Windows

In the evenings, when the small children were asleep, the grown-ups would often step outside for a while. Evert and Noortje too. They stood in front of the house looking up, though there was nothing to see. They heard the droning sound of airplanes way up in the sky. They flew from the west to the east; they were English and American bombers. Almost every night they went flying over on their way to Germany to bomb the big cities. There was no need to be afraid of those airplanes.

Toward the east big searchlights beamed through the skies, but the planes went too high for the German anti-aircraft guns. The droning lasted for hours. There must be an incredible number of them up there. And every evening the same conversation took place in front of Klaphek house.

"They're going to get what's coming to them," Wolthuis said. "Thousands of bombs up there, ticketed for Krautland, just what they deserve."

"But there are also people living over there, human beings," Aunt Janna said, "children too. . . ."

Wolthuis spat on the ground a few times emphatically.

"Come, it's time we went to bed," Everingen would say.

Noortje lay in her dark room listening to the planes for a long time. And once in a while, when she'd wake up early before it was time to go milking, she'd hear them again. The planes were coming back, flying from the east to the west. Noortje imagined they made a different noise then. Because they were rid of all those bombs, they sounded different.

Yes, those airplanes flew with their heavy load of bombs from west to east. But in those dark nights the Germans sent something back also: a mysterious invention that they thought could still win the war. The thing flew through the sky making a murderous din, though never as high as the airplanes. It had a tail of fire and looked like a slow-moving comet lost in space. They were called V-1's. The strangest thing about those V-1's was that there was no one inside to steer them.

The Germans planned that the V-1's would fly to England to cause fear and destruction there, and that winter many V-1's did come down on London, but the mechanics of the thing were anything but perfect yet. Often, after the rocket had been on its way for some time, the motor would begin to make a *put-put* sound. Then it went still and suddenly nosed downward toward the earth, the fire of its tail extinguished. It landed with a tremendous bang and exploded.

Some of them ended up in the North Sea. They couldn't really do much damage there. But reaching the North Sea was already quite an achievement for that marvel. A large number of them didn't get that far, and they would come down on the narrow piece of land that lies between the North Sea and Germany called Holland. The people who lived there had more than their share of troubles and grief, and then those hellish machines were added to the list!

Whoever woke up easily now had sleepless nights.

"They've been flying them again," they would say the next morning. "I didn't sleep a wink."

That was how it affected Granny. She suffered a lot from rheumatism and had trouble falling asleep on her hard mattress set upon the floor. She felt so lonely surrounded by all these people. Each little sound woke her, and then she lay there, eyes wide open, listening to the V-1's. From far in the distance, she heard them coming, closer and closer. Some flew by far to the north, their sound dying away slowly. There goes another; that one will get a lot farther, she would think.

But soon another one came, and now the thing seemed aimed straight at the farm. Right above her head, it thundered through the sky. She saw the light of its tail through a crack between the shutters, and pulling the blankets over her head she waited. Had the motor turned off? Was it making that strange *put-put* sound?

Ma Walthuis, too, often lay awake those nights when many V-1's came over. She counted them, and the following morning she'd say, "I heard ninety-two of them. It's a terrible thing, isn't it? I heard five of them crashing down. Fortunately for us, it was far from here." Granny counted them too. But she always got confused in her count, and then she'd have to take a guess. The next morning Ma Wolthuis and she would squabble about the number.

"Eighty," she'd say. "I'm positive. Woman, I wasn't able to go to sleep for one minute."

"Ninety-two," Ma Wolthuis would say indignantly. "You must have been sleeping some of the time, Granny. You sure missed a lot in your count."

"Me, asleep? At my age? Where did you get that idea? You know very well how lightly I sleep."

"Stupid old ninnies," Wolthuis grumbled. "Why don't you cut out all this nonsense. Who cares how many of the damned things were up there? Night is made for sleeping. Just be glad that when you wake up in the morning, you're still alive."

There was someone else at Klaphek who lay awake at night listening to the V-1's. That was Theo. He felt his illness making his body weaker and weaker. He had to stay in bed now for days in a row, too tired and exhausted from the coughing to get up. He would keep on dozing off briefly. When the sun shone into his room, he felt best. Then he could close his eyes and see a rosy light, which made him happy and sleepy.

But the nights were dreadful. In the dark, ghostlike thoughts came to him as he lay there in that big bed thinking about everything he'd gone through. He thought of his friends, of people he'd worked with in the Resistance. Some were dead. A few were in prison. He wondered and worried about them. If only he could be with them. Anything was better than lying here, so very much alone, in this room.

There were such grim thoughts going around in Theo's head. He knew he was on the wanted list. If the Germans should get him, what would happen to the Everingens then? And to the others? And now here was little Sarah too. Would they all be shot right away, or would they be sent to a concentration camp? Maybe it would have been better if he had been taken after all. Then his life would have ended quickly. Instead he was lying here sick and endangering others.

So Theo spent many of the nights, looking at the dark hole of his window, wide awake. He heard the V-1's come too, of course. Sometimes he saw their lights going by. Theo did not count those manless machines. He didn't care how many of them there were.

One night, which had been quieter than most, almost

still, a few V-1's had come roaring over first, then none at all. Even Granny was asleep. Suddenly an enormous bang woke up everyone in the house.

Aunt Janna jumped down the steps of the alcove and threw open the kitchen door. Noortje sat straight up in bed and shivered. She couldn't tell if she was asleep or dreaming. Had something really happened? Gerrit was crying, and Sissy started her howling.

Without saying a word, Everingen slid out of the high four-poster bed, stumbling downstairs barefooted.

"My God, Mother, what's going on here?" he said.

"Let's have some light," Aunt Janna said, "so we can see." She struck a match for the third time, but it blew out instantly.

"There's a draft," Everingen said. "Dammit, who opened that door?"

"Don't curse like that, Chris," said Aunt Janna.

At last she succeeded in lighting the oil wick. In the flickering brightness, they both looked around, aghast. The shutters had been blasted open and the windowpanes lay in splinters on the chairs and floor. Aunt Janna had to screen the little flame with her hand. Wind blew into the room through the broken windows. Aunt Janna shivered. "Mama," Gerrit screamed. "Mama, where are you?"

"Put something on your feet," Aunt Janna told her husband. "There's glass all over the place. Think of yourself too."

Noortje still wasn't really awake when Aunt Janna came in with the light. At first she didn't understand what she was seeing. In the small sleeping alcove was a tiny window that looked out on the inner courtyard. Pieces of glass were all over the blankets and pillow of the bed. Gerrit sat up next to Noortje, crying.

"Gerrit, oh my poor little Gerrit, what is it? Did you hurt yourself?" Aunt Janna asked.

It was almost incredible; neither Gerrit nor Noortje had a single scratch. The window above their heads had exploded inward because of the bang, and pieces of glass lay scattered all over their bed, but not one piece had touched them. Because it was so cold during the night, they'd probably slept hidden all the way under the covers. The shock was the worst of it.

Sissy's bed had a tall, wooden side. The shattered glass didn't reach that far, but Sissy was terribly frightened. She cried in howling gasps and almost choked in her tears. "There's nothing wrong with Sissy," Aunt Janna said, "thank God. Children, be careful of the glass. Find your clothes and get dressed. But get something on your feet first."

"Sarah!" cried Noortje, suddenly paralyzed with fear.

Then she jumped up, trembling, ashamed she hadn't thought of the baby sooner. She walked quickly to the parlor, without taking care about the glass. There she saw her father bending over the cradle. He held a glass with a wildly dancing flame in it above his head. The wind rattled the shutters, making the only sound. Noortje didn't dare ask anything. Her father slowly turned and looked at her.

"She's alright, Noor. She isn't even crying," Mr. Vanderhook said.

It was the same in the parlor as in the kitchen. The shutters stood wide open, and the floor was covered with pieces of broken glass. In front of the window stood a small table with a copper pot on it. That table had a gash in it almost an inch deep. A great shard of glass had cut into it. Behind the table, on two chairs, lay Sarah's basket. The blankets were pulled all the way up to her mouth. On top of the blanket lay a thick piece of glass!

Noortje looked at the glass. She took it in her hand and felt the sharp edge. She examined the cut in the table, together with her father. Then she pulled the blanket away from Sarah's face. The little girl's cheeks were already rounded out a bit. Her eyes were shut, and not a lash trembled. Only her lips moved, making smacking sounds, as if she were drinking out of a bottle in her dreams.

"No one's hurt," Mr. Vanderhook said. "It's a miracle."

And Noortje thought, Now actually I should cry, at least a little. . . . But I'm not crying, how strange.

Aunt Janna came into the parlor to have a look also. "Everything's all right in here," said Mr. Vanderhook. And Aunt Janna went off back to Gerrit and Sissy, who were still howling with fear and cold.

A little later they all gathered in the kitchen, with wild, disheveled faces, discussing what had happened. A V-1 must have come down, all agreed. That was it. And how were things in the rest of the house? The men went outside and to the shed to see the damage. The women started clearing the glass in the kitchen away as best they could.

If it all hadn't been so strange, you'd almost have to laugh for in the little light cast by that flame it looked as if they were acting in some play about ghosts. Ma Wolthuis bustled about in her white nightgown reaching to her feet, a stringy pigtail hanging down her back. Granny didn't know what to do and stood there on shaky legs in a pink gown with a black vest over it. And Dinie and Alie looked like dolls in their flowery pajamas.

Even though it was still dark, they got out the dusters and brooms to sweep away the mess. Wriggling the loose pieces of glass out of the window frame, Dinie cut one of her fingers badly.

"Ow, ow," she cried, and her mother calmly ripped off

a strip of one of the diapers hanging to dry over the stove and bandaged the bleeding finger with it.

Aunt Janna first dressed her children warmly, and then she stoked up the fire. Dry twigs were always lying ready to start a hot fire fast. A little later the water kettle was singing out, and she made a large pot of the ersatz coffee. The eastern skies slowly began to lighten to gray, and they could see what they were doing a little better.

The men came in again too. There wasn't a window left whole in the entire house, they reported, and on the southern side of the building lots of tiles had come loose on the roof. The cows were restless because the wind was blowing through the hayloft at them. They stood there lowing softly. The damage was great, but it could have been much worse. Where the V-1 had actually come down, they didn't know; there was no sign of it outside.

"Where has Evert gone?" someone asked.

Yes, where was Evert? He had quietly run up the stairs to take a look at Theo. None of the others had thought of Theo. They hadn't even missed him because he usually was in his room all by himself anyway. Evert was not afraid to go in to see Theo. He knew he was strong and healthy, and so he always just walked in.

Here, too, the windows had fallen in. The room was still dark, and the wind, which was on that side of the house, was blowing in. It was even colder there than in the kitchen. Theo was hidden under the covers. Only one tuft of his hair sticking out was visible. Evert sat down at the edge of the bed and started to talk. He told Theo what had happened and how everything looked downstairs. He described the pieces of glass on the beds and how, as if by a miracle, everyone had escaped without a single wound. He told of the tiles blown off the roof by the blast—the roof of the shed and that part of the front where Theo's room was.

"It must have been a V-1, don't you think so, Theo?" Evert asked.

Theo slid halfway out from under the covers. Evert gave him his sweater, and Theo flung it on. Neither of them saw much more than a dark blur where the other sat.

"Sure it was a V-1. I saw it myself."

"You saw it?"

"Yeah, I was still awake. It was really the quietest night, and then there it was! I heard it coming. I always hear them coming from far away. It's just as if the damned things start getting slower and slower. And then I saw its light through the window, almost right over our house. All of a sudden the sound cut off, and then I didn't see the light anymore either, and then came the big bang."

"If it had been really right above the house, you wouldn't have been able to see it."

"No, my boy, and then you and I wouldn't be sitting here so quietly discussing it, either. We have all had a very narrow escape."

For a while neither one spoke. Evert shivered.

"You shouldn't stay sitting in the cold like that," Theo said.

"Yes, and you get back down under the covers. When it's light, we'll come. We'll probably fix this window first."

▪15▪
A Beautiful View

The frost still held in the ground. Almost every night it froze a few degrees, and in the mornings you could stamp with your clogs over hardened bumps and ridges, the frozen tracks made in the mud by people and animals. The day after the V-1 had come down it was terribly cold. A strong wind blew, bringing wet snow with it. In the afternoon the temperature went to below freezing, and the world around Klaphek was white again. The windows were broken, and you didn't feel the heat of the stove. People walked about the house with their coats on and scarves tied around their heads. Sissy cried almost the whole day through and looked purple with cold.

Only Sarah didn't seem to be bothered by it. Noortje took care that she always had two hot-water bottles in her basket bed. She placed one against her back and one at her feet, in between the covers. That way Sarah wouldn't burn herself. And when she gave the baby her bottle she left her lying in the cradle so she would stay nice and warm.

Burlap sacks and pieces of brown paper were tacked over the windows. They kept out the wind to some extent, but the house stayed freezing cold the whole day long. And it was somber too, for very little light could come through.

Henk had gone to the village with a wagon to see if he could find some glass somewhere. Everingen and Mr. Vanderhook set ladders against the roof and were putting the tiles back into place. Most of the tiles had only slid over on one another. Few were broken or fallen off. In the harnessing room was an extra stack of roof tiles, kept there in case a storm should blow a few off the roof.

The work in the kitchen went on as usual. After each and every little splinter of glass had been swept up, the girls and Granny sat down to peel the potatoes. Oh, it gave them such stiff fingers! Noortje was glad she didn't have to help. Since her father was busy on the roof, she decided to take care of the wood. There still were plenty of thick logs, already cut to size. She only needed to split them once or twice with the axe so they would fit into the stove. She liked the work, and it made her warm too.

Meanwhile, Evert was hauling roof tiles to the rain gutter, bringing them up the ladder stacked on his shoulder four at a time. When the grown-ups stopped for a coffee break, he came to fetch Noortje.

"Want to bet that I dare go up on the roof?" he said.

"Sure you can," Noortje answered. "There's nothing to it with a ladder."

"You stay down here, and you'll see."

Evert climbed up the ladder very fast, as far as the rain gutter. He'd already done that more than twenty times this morning, and loaded with a few roof tiles too! Then he clambered onto the room over the laths, where no tiles had been set yet. Noortje stood next to the well house, watching. The higher Evert climbed the higher the roof seemed to become. She really hadn't ever noticed that it was such a high roof. How strange, for it wasn't any different at all.

Evert climbed on calmly, and the higher he got the smaller he seemed. Finally he sat all the way up on the ridge, above the shed. And only then did he look down, waving at her.

"Hey!" he called out. "It's fantastic up here!"

Noortje didn't give it a moment's thought. She was

crazy to stay standing down there. Who'd ever get the chance to go climb on top of a roof, just like that, and be able to look out far away over the world? She grabbed the ladder firmly and started up. It was only a small distance to the rain gutter, for the walls of the shed weren't very high. That darn ladder, though, did slide from side to side a little, and she was glad when she stood on the top rung and could step into the gutter with one big step sideways. She let herself fall forward against the roof at once. There, that felt better.

"What are you doing?" Evert cried.

"I'm coming too!"

"Well, it's up to you! But I'd take off my clogs if I were you!" Oh, that was it. Yes. Evert had left his clogs down below on the ground. Well then, Noortje could leave hers in the gutter. And she began to climb up in her socks, calmly and quickly.

Actually, it wasn't so scary. The roof slanted up so gradually that it seemed as if she were crawling up a hill on hands and feet, and there wasn't much of a chance she would slide off those tile laths with her socks on. But now, as she clambered up, the roof seemed to get bigger and higher, to the left and to the right and upward. That ridge was really quite far.

Finally she reached Evert, all the way on top. Was that frightening! When she looked over the edge she got dizzy. . . . on the other side was an endless drop. Evert grabbed her arm.

"Come and sit on it like me. This way," he said. "Nothing can happen then."

They sat behind one another, one leg out on each side, as if on a huge, gigantic gray horse. Noortje looked all around. How far one could see from the top of a roof! A lot farther even than from their spot with the glass roof tile in the hayloft. They could see the heath behind the woods, hill after hill, covered with small, dark stains. Those were the juniper bushes, and the paths across the heath were thin white lines.

The clouds seemed farther away here than on the ground. There was so much sky around them. And it blew much harder here too. The wind whipped Noortje's hair into her eyes. Wet snowflakes were flying about and stuck onto her coat. They formed wet spots on the roof tiles.

"Look, the Eighth Wood, over there." Evert pointed. Yes, there it lay behind the beech trees, the Eighth Wood. From up here you couldn't see any trace of people. A good thing. . . .

"Do you see the shepherd's field over there?"

Ah, how tiny the sheep pen seemed now. How could such a large flock ever fit in there? And the white house next to it seemed even smaller.

"It's just like a painting," Noortje said. She sat behind Evert holding onto him by his shoulders, while he pointed to the left and to the right.

"Now you have to let go of me," he said, "and stay here. I'm going to have a look on the roof of the house. I'll tell you what's to see there." And Evert started to crawl over the thick, rounded tiles of the ridge toward the house part up front.

That looked pretty scary, but he went across quickly and steadily, as if he did it every day. Again Noortje got that same feeling she had before, when she stood on the ground watching him. Whatever he could do, she could do too. And if she didn't follow him over the roof right now, she'd feel ridiculous all her life, even if she were to live to be a hundred years old. So Noortje also crawled over the round, smooth ridge toward the roof of the front house. Where the two roofs came together they formed a capital *T*. Actually, the whole house was sort of one big *T* when you looked down on it from up there.

Evert didn't say anything when she sat next to him, straddling the ridge. They looked down at the house and the yard around it.

"See that little space?" Noortje pointed. "The inner courtyard. Funny, huh?"

"Yes, and see, there goes Rachel. What is she doing near the gate?"

"Shall I call her?"

"No, no, don't call out." Evert whistled a few times. Rachel did not look up. The sound was blown away by the wind.

It should have been scary to be sitting on top of the world in a stiff wind. And yet the longer they sat there the more natural it seemed. Noortje wouldn't have wanted to miss it for anything. To be able to see so far was wonderful. They could gaze way beyond the village, to the watery marshes near the Ijssel. The farms lay along the main road like tiny squares. And all the way in the distance where the world seemed to end, far beyond the flat land, they could make out some hills. They were little more than a dark-gray wavy line at the end of the gray land.

"That's Germany over there," said Evert.

"Huh? Really? Are you sure. . . ?"

That couldn't be Germany, Noortje thought. Germany was a different country. It must be much farther away.

"Yes, really. Didn't you know you can see Germany from here? On a clear day like this you can see very far."

"But were you ever up here on the roof before?"

"Oh, no. But sometimes you can see Germany from Dassen Mountain also. When we were there the other day, it wasn't clear enough. Over there, see, where those hills are."

Yes, Noortje did see it. Germany actually looked beautiful, she thought. And suddenly she saw something else.

"Hey, look, Evert, in the woods there. An open spot. What could that be?"

In the new wood behind the Calves' Meadow they saw a bare, bald spot; it seemed as if trees had been ripped out of the ground. Perhaps it was where the V-1 had come down.

"We'll go have a look later," Evert said. "Now we have to climb down. They'll be back from their coffee break soon!"

Before Noortje came down off the roof she looked all around one more time. Germany had disappeared. The clouds suddenly hung low on the land, and more and more big wet snowflakes blew into her face. The world seemed to have gotten much smaller. Ijssel still lay there, like a black ribbon that had fallen into the grass.

It was an odd feeling to be back on the flat and firm ground again. The wind didn't amount to anything here.

None of the grown-ups ever knew that the day after the V-1 came down Noortje and Evert sat on top of the roof.

In the afternoon they went to investigate the hole out in the woods. A big bald spot had appeared; a great pit had been made. The young trees around it were snapped off in the middle. A big thing lay in the hole. A curiously crumpled thing of steel. It was strangely quiet there. Nothing was going on.

That same afternoon they discovered something else, closer to the house. Evert had to pee, and he wanted to do it against a young apple tree behind the woodshed. "Come have a look!" he called out to Noortje. And while he was busy near the tree, he pointed behind at what he had found. There, in the fresh, wet snow, lay a chunk of metal; it looked like a tube ripped in the middle and bent. It had to be a piece of the V-1, flung all the way here when it exploded.

The fragment wasn't made of iron, but of copper or

brass. The piece of the V-1 remained in that spot, always. And when Evert had to pee he no longer used the apple tree but that broken tube instead. Noortje did it there too once in a while, and perhaps some of the grown-ups as well. Soon the copper turned a different color, a splendid green!

A few days passed before a man from the village came to put new glass in the windows. Then the cold wind could no longer get inside, and it was warm and cozy in the house again.

•16•
No Need to Tell Sarah

Noortje gave Sarah her bottle five times a day, and Aunt Janna did so one time late in the evening. At first the baby didn't want to have anything to do with that large rubber nipple, but quite soon she got the idea that the nice warm milk filled and warmed her stomach. Then she emptied the bottle fast in greedy little gulps.

While Noortje gave Sarah the bottle, she was allowed to sit in Farmer Everingen's wicker chair with the knitted cushion, her feet resting atop Aunt Janna's little footstool. She could put her arm on the armrest of the chair, which made it much easier. For even though Sarah was very small and didn't weigh much, Noortje still got tired when she had to hold her in her lap for any length of time. She always had to support her head very carefully, and the head was heaviest of all.

"Look, isn't that funny, the way she's lying there?" Noortje said to Aunt Janna. Sarah was drinking. She had her eyes tightly shut, and her hands balled into tiny little fists held next to her head. Now and then one of her feet kicked impatiently.

"See that, Aunt Janna! It looks as if she wants to go running."

"That child has a healthy appetite. You'd better watch her, though. Take care she doesn't drink too fast. Let her rest now and then."

One morning after Sarah was washed and had finished

her bottle, she laughed at Noortje. "Oh, oh, do you see that? Sarah's laughing!" Noor cried out excitedly.

Alie was stirring a pan of porridge. With a contemptuous face she turned toward Noortje. "Oh, come on, don't be so silly," she said. "A baby a few weeks old doesn't laugh! Those are little spasms, that's all. A child like that doesn't even know who's helping her, you or someone else. It's all the same to those babies, for they can't even see yet."

Sad and angry, Noortje picked up the baby and walked into the parlor. She laid Sarah in the basket without saying a word. Her father was sitting at the table and looked up from his book somewhat astonished. It was unusual for Noortje to put little Sarah to bed without talking to her!

"Is something wrong?"

"No, nothing. Well, I thought she was smiling at me, but they are only 'spasms.' "

Her father came over and stood by the cradle. "That's funny," he said. "The other day I also thought she was trying to laugh. But then I could see it wasn't a real laugh after all. But of course, the first time she does, she'll do it for you. She knows you best."

"Yes, you do, don't you?" Noortje said, bending over the cradle and stroking Sarah's thin black hair. The dark blue eyes looked at her with a fixed stare, the tiny mouth opened wide, the lips trembled but no sound came out of Sarah's throat.

"See now!" Mr. Vanderhook said. "You were quite right. She *is* smiling at you."

That year spring didn't seem to want to arrive. It stayed cold and was often stormy. The buds on the trees and bushes were already quite swollen. They looked as if all they needed was one warm day and they would burst open. How much more friendly the earth would look if only the sun would shine a little more often.

The grassland still had its somber winter color, and there was some snow left here and there. Even the birds were later than normal that year. You couldn't hear the wood pigeon cooing in the wood yet, and the meadow birds, the lapwings and the herons, hadn't returned from the south. They knew quite well the cold hadn't been driven off and that it wasn't safe to go back to their old nests. In the woods, the woodpecker was hammering away for hours on the bark of the beech tree, looking for insects that also were later than usual. In that last winter of the war there was much suffering, much hunger and cold, both for the people and the animals.

From time to time they heard the latest war news, but they didn't know what to believe of all those stories. The people who came to the door to ask for some milk or potatoes told whatever they knew about the way the war was going. Those stories weren't very cheerful.

In the west of the country, the situation was getting worse and worse. If the war were to continue much longer, no one would survive it there. One boiled potato cost five dollars on the black market. The Allies were advancing very slowly. The south of the country had been liberated, but the area between the rivers was a kind of no-man's-land, and no one could live there anymore. All the bridges were blown up. How could the English and the Americans ever reach the Veluwe, where Klaphek was, and the northern part of the country? What if they forgot about that small piece of the Netherlands? Perhaps they would just turn their backs on it and go directly to fight in Germany.

At Klaphek, too, they were looking forward to the end

of the war impatiently. The grown-ups especially got a bit testy sometimes because of all the tension. It wasn't easy to live for so long in a few small rooms with so many people. And yet, comparatively, they didn't have such a difficult time of it. At least they had something to eat. Because there was nothing to do in the evenings, they went to bed earlier and earlier. Usually the Wolthuis family and Granny went first.

One evening Mr. Vanderhook and Noortje were sitting around talking with Everingen, Aunt Janna, and Evert. They were in the kitchen. Suddenly Henk stood in the doorway, eyes cast down, silent. They hadn't even heard the latch of the door when he came in. He held the sack with the panful of food, the bag with bread, and a bottle of milk in his hands. He stood there blinking, his hands trembling as he very slowly placed the bread on the table. Aunt Janna had risen from her chair and looked at him with a very tense face.

Then Henk took the bottle out of the bag and set it down next to the bread. The bottle was still full of milk. They all stared at it, no one saying anything. Henk sat down, took off his cap, and buried his face in his hands.

Noortje couldn't bear the silence any longer. "Henk," she said, "what's happened? Say something, Henk!"

Aunt Janna was the first to move again. She took the bread off the table and put it on the sink. She set the pan with food and the milk bottle next to it.

"Leave Henk alone for a moment, child," she said.

Then finally Henk began. As on any other evening, he had made the trip to the wood. With most of the snow melted, he didn't have to fear leaving prints so much anymore, but the branches were creaking more loudly under his feet. It wasn't terribly dark, not as dark as on some other evenings. How else would he have been able to notice from a distance that the entrance to the hole was open? Branches had been broken off the thick fir tree and the dark-brown piece of cloth that hung before the entrance was gone. The earth around it was all rooted up as if many people or animals had trampled the soil there.

He'd thought that strange and careless, but didn't yet understand what had happened. Stopping in front of the hole, Henk called out softly. No answer came. Then he crawled in; it was dark down there and dead quiet. He had asked whispering, "Are you there?"

And then, because he heard nothing, Henk called out in a voice much too loud, "Say something! Where are you?"

And only then did he strike a match and light the lantern with shaky hands. That lantern had the very last bit of real kerosene, which they'd kept for these trips.

The hole was empty. The people were not there. The young woman, not yet very strong after the birth of her child, gone. Mr. Meyer, too, gone. And the two little boys were not there either. The crates and the beds were kicked all over the place. In one corner there still were some clothes. The fire in the cooking pot was out.

And suddenly Henk was afraid. As fast as he could he ran home through the wood, giving no thought at all to the noise he was making. Not until he was halfway down Beech Lane did he stop to listen for someone following him. But no one was. He heard nothing but the wind in the trees high above his head, rising and falling. There was no other sound. Rachel had come to meet him and stayed right with him. And even that had been strange, for Rachel knew very well that she wasn't allowed to come on those trips through the wood in the evening. She'd never done so before.

For a long time, no one in the kitchen spoke. The

farmer heaved a few sighs, and Aunt Janna wiped her eyes. Her mouth twisted very strangely as if she were going to cry, but she didn't. Noortje's father sat nervously drumming his fingers on the table, his eyebrows lifted high, and didn't look at anyone. He always did that when he felt at a loss. The silence became so oppressive that Noortje had to speak up, whether she wanted to or not.

"What could have happened?" she asked, her voice sounding strangely loud. "Shouldn't we go look for them?"

"Who would do such a crazy thing? Go look for them!" Everingen said curtly. "Come on, wife. We're going to bed."

Aunt Janna silently prepared Sarah's bottle and gave it to Noortje. "Noor, you'd better give it to her tonight," she said.

The others went to bed; Noortje and her father took the little oil light with them to the parlor. The stove was almost out there, and it was unpleasantly chilly. The flame in the glass spread a small circle of yellow light. Around its rim everything was darkness. Only the table and the chairs were visible. The room might well be quite large, with all sorts of bad things hiding in the corners. On other nights Noortje wasn't really bothered by that. She had never been afraid of the dark. But now she had the feeling that something in the room threatened her, something invisible that wanted to harm her and little Sarah.

Noortje's father had seized a chair and gone to sit in front of the stove close to Sarah's basket. He bent over the fire and threw a log on it. Soon the red and orange flames shone through the mica windows, making the big room a little cheerier. Sarah gurgled while she drank.

"Actually we ought to tell her what has happened," Noortje said. "Only she can't understand it yet. So there's no need to tell Sarah."

Her father didn't answer. He cleared his throat a few times. The room was quiet. Noortje wanted to know exactly what had happened, and there was no one she could ask but her father. She cleared her throat a few times just like him. Then she asked, "What do you think happened?"

It was a difficult moment for Mr. Vanderhook. How does one tell one's daughter about the terrible things of the world? Who wouldn't much rather wish to keep them hidden from her? "I think you already know," he said, "for you've heard it talked about so often. You know that the Meyers are Jewish, don't you?"

Noortje couldn't say anything. She could hear the silence in the whole house. Sarah had fallen asleep on her lap.

After a while her father started again, "I'm afraid the worst has happened, the worst thing that could have happened to them. The Germans found them."

"That's impossible. No one could find them there."

"Maybe someone discovered them by accident and betrayed them to the Germans. That's happened before. Not everybody is like our Farmer Everingen and Aunt Janna."

"But who could have done it? Do you know? Not a soul ever came into that part of the woods! How is it possible?"

"I don't know, Noortje. I just don't know."

"What are the Germans going to do with them?"

"What they do with all the Jews, I think. Send them away to a sort of camp."

"You mean a prison?"

"Yes, something like that. I'm afraid it will be very bad."

Sarah's bottle was empty. Noortje held the baby upright with her warm head against her cheek, because she still had to be burped. She didn't burp.

"You know, Father," she said. "I wish I had a rifle. Oh, how I wish I had a rifle! And if one German soldier had the guts to come in here, you know what I'd do? I'd shoot him right in the head."

"Ah, my child," her father said, "you'd better give Sarah a clean diaper. There's nothing else we can do now."

▪17▪
The Sick Horse

After that evening everything seemed changed.

There was no real cheerfulness in the house. Noortje and Evert didn't quite know how to play anymore. They would romp and chase each another and then all at once stop and stand still, staring straight ahead, not laughing anymore. Something had happened, something they never talked about that made them a little like the grown-ups.

It was a good thing Noortje had the baby to be busy with. That little thing dirtied many diapers, and sometimes she wet her whole bed. Noortje would simply hang the wet sheets in front of the stove, for there was already much to be washed and they had no soap. . . . It did make the room rather smelly, of course.

Not long after the Meyer family had been taken away, soldiers came riding into the yard with carts and horses. They needed shelter for the night they said, and one of their horses was sick. The farmer led them to the barn where they could bed down on the straw. The Germans were satisfied with that for themselves, but they wanted their sick horse to spend the night in the shed.

It was a small, lovely, brown animal, which looked around with big eyes full of wonder and pain. The horse was very restless and twitched its ears back and forth in order to catch each sound inside the strange house. The cows lowed companionably, as if they wanted to say, "You needn't be afraid. This is a good place."

A few soldiers stayed with the horse all the time. They let it drink some water and then forced the animal to eat something. And so the Germans discovered the hayloft, which still held some of the best and most fragrant hay from the water meadow. They wanted that beautiful hay; it would be better for their horses than the bales of pressed hay they'd brought with them. The farmer could have those in exchange for the hay from the hayloft. One of the soldiers climbed up and threw down a big pile.

Everingen was angry, but he didn't say anything. What could one do against those fellows with their rifles and their boots and their loud shrill voices? He had to be careful. Wasn't it a miracle that no German had ever come to question them after the Meyers had been discovered? Hadn't they understood that those people must have had helpers? Who else could they suspect but the farmers living nearby? And consider little Sarah. Would the Germans really believe that story about Mr. Vanderhook being the baby's father and the mother being in the hospital? Imagine if they started searching the house and questioning everybody. They also had to think of Theo. He was a sick boy, but that was not the whole story. The Germans had him on their lists, so he had to stay hidden. Everingen had no choice: he grunted a bit, but in the end he let them have their way.

That whole night some of the soldiers stayed with the sick horse. The animal stood trembling on shaky, thin legs. You could easily see these soldiers weren't used to handling horses. They just let it stand there in a draft, right by the doors of the shed, which kept opening whenever anybody came in. They pushed its head into a bucket of water, forcing it to drink. They yelled at it and stuffed hay into its mouth because the horse didn't want to eat.

The small horse neighed anxiously. It tried to get away

from their hard hands and pawed the earthen floor of the shed. One soldier kept hold of the halter, another of its tail. They were cursing all the time.

Henk was getting riled. Before he went to bed he looked in on the shed again. He tried to explain to the soldiers that it would be much better for the horse if they let it lie on some dry straw and covered it with blankets. They also shouldn't give it so much cold water. The animal was running a high fever. But the Germans didn't listen to him at all.

That night Henk couldn't get to sleep. Sometimes he'd doze off for a while, but then all of a sudden he'd be wide awake again sitting up straight in his bed. All his life he'd worked with horses. If something was wrong, he was the one who was called in. And this was such a lovely young creature, sleek, with a fine nose and beautiful color. If it were treated in the right way, it would surely recover in a few days at most.

The horse was standing in the shed all trembling with fever, and he, Henk, wasn't allowed to take care of it or even come near it! No, the job was for those stupid Krauts down there; they thought they knew everything but did it all wrong. Henk clambered out of bed a few times and peeked around the door. He saw the Germans squatting around an oil lamp playing cards. The horse seemed quieter now. Those pigs, he thought, they just sit there playing cards, while that poor creature. . . . But there was nothing to be done about it; he'd better go back to bed. Such a handsome horse. . . . He would like to have such a horse himself sometime, Henk lay thinking. He'd wanted one like that for ages. It was still a young animal. You could teach it anything. It could pull a not-too-heavy load . . . or he'd ride it himself . . . buy a big, beautiful saddle . . . Henk yawned. If the Germans left tomorrow and the horse was still sick . . . maybe they'd leave it behind . . . Henk fell asleep.

He woke up with a start. He didn't know what time it was. The cocks were already crowing, but they crowed in the middle of the night sometimes, long before the sun was up. Henk quickly slid out of his closet bed and opened the low door of his room. It was dark in the shed, not a soul to be seen. Where had they gone with the little horse? He had to know, and quickly too. Henk began putting on his pants and shirt, trying to make no noise. Evert woke up anyway.

"Henk, what are you doing?"

"Shh. I'm getting dressed."

"Is it time to get up?"

"No."

Evert sat up straight in bed. "How's the horse doing?"

"That's just it. It's not there anymore."

"Oh! So what are you going to do now?"

"Don't speak so loud. They mustn't hear us. I want to know what they've done with the little thing, the stupid bastards."

Evert leaped out of bed even faster than Henk and put on his socks. "Wait for me, Henk."

"OK."

They took their clogs in their hands, then looked around by the light of a burning match. Yes, the little horse was indeed gone, and the soldiers too. The Fox and Browny were nervously stepping back and forth, restless in the small space of their stalls. A cow lowed plaintively, shaking her chain. Henk and Evert were outside in a moment. The sheep dog came running up to them.

"Rachel, where are they?" Henk whispered. "Tell me, old friend."

Rachel whimpered softly once. She sniffed Henk's hand and walked ahead of them, stopping at the pigsty. They saw a weak light flickering between the trees. Evert grabbed Henk's arm.

"Over there, Henk."

Henk had already seen it. Again a cock crowed. It made such a racket that it must have awakened all the animals on the farm. They heard a few geese making their hoarse sounds; the goat bleated and a cow lowed. Something had definitely happened. Henk and Evert stood pressed against the shed, watching that light swaying now under the beech trees.

People sometimes sense when something awful is going to happen to someone they love very much. Even before they know the cause, they feel somber and nervous. Was the same thing possible for animals? For wasn't it strange, that they all were awake and nervous tonight? And there were three cats stealthily stalking through the grass, their bellies pressed against the ground! But of course, cats are usually outside at night, hunting for frogs and mice.

As quietly as they could, Henk and Evert walked down the meadow and then stopped near the gate, standing quite a distance from that light. The soldiers were busy digging a hole in the woods next to Beech Lane. The horse lay on the path, its legs sticking out straight. The horse was dead. They could see that immediately, even in the dark. It lay there stiff and still.

The soldiers had finished their digging; then they began to pull at the horse's legs. It was heavy, heavier than they thought, and one of them started pushing from behind. When that didn't work he braced himself, planting his boot on the back of the dead animal. So they moved it, inch by inch, closer to the pit. Not a word was said. The whistling of a thrush already sounded somewhere in the branches of the trees. The sky to the east was getting lighter.

The Germans began to rush; they wanted to be finished before it was light out and they pushed and pulled even harder till finally the dead horse fell into the pit. For one long moment it seemed as if it were standing upright looking over the edge. Then it collapsed on its stiff legs, falling over to one side. The soldiers shoveled sand over it. Henk pulled Evert away by the arm. They returned to the shed unseen.

"You go and get some more sleep. I'm staying here. It's almost time for milking anyway," Henk said.

The Germans left toward midday, without telling anyone what had happened to the horse.

A day later, early in the morning, they saw a big mound of yellow earth on the place where the horse had been buried. Evert and Noortje went over to take a look. The grave had been opened and the pit was empty. The dead horse was gone.

"Yes, this was the spot all right," Evert said. "Look, the horse lay here. And then they shoved it in, like this." He pointed. There were footprints all over in the wet ground.

"What could have happened to it?" Noortje asked. "Do you think the Germans came back to get it?"

"No, it couldn't have been that."

Wolthuis also came to take a look at the empty pit. "Yes, yes, it's a strange business," he said, whistling through his teeth.

"Do you know what happened?" Evert asked him.

"Hmmm, yes. But who knows . . . whether I should let you two in on it. . . ?"

Noortje set her most stubborn face. She didn't believe that Wolthuis knew anything about it at all. He only said so to seem terribly important.

"You kids can sleep through anything, huh? But if you walked around outside during the night once in a while as I do when I feel like it, you get to see some strange things going on. . . ."

"Were you outside last night?" Evert asked.

"Certainly, yes."

"And Rachel, was she out too? And did the cock crow, just like it did the night before?"

No, Wolthius maintained, the dog hadn't shown herself. The hens and the geese too, were soundly asleep. It had been dead quiet around the farmyard. The horses were in their stalls, silently staring through half-shut eyes. Wolthuis had taken a look at the animals before he ventured out.

"I didn't hear you in the shed," Evert said.

"No, of course you didn't. Because I was careful to be quiet, and you were all tucked in, sleeping like a rose."

Wolthuis told them it had also been very still and quiet outside. He'd walked down the meadow toward the gate, and there he had seen something strange. Dark shadows moving among the trees. Without being seen himself, he'd come closer and seen men and women, at least twelve of them. They had knives and axes and spades! And they were cutting the horse into pieces and taking everything with them. Noortje and Evert had better not mention it to anyone. . . .

"That sick horse?"

"Yeah, well . . . sick! It was dead, wasn't it? So what's the difference?" Wolthuis laughed mockingly. "My boy, the people in this village are hungry. And he who is hungry likes to eat a piece of meat."

"But how could they know about it?"

Again Wolthuis intoned, "Whoever is hungry likes to eat a piece of meat. And will do anything he can to get it. People will sniff it out, wherever it can be found. . . .

Hey, you two won't tell anyone about this, right? It'll be much better all around if you don't, understand?" He looked menacingly at them.

Later Evert said to Noortje, "I would really like to know what Wolthuis was doing yesterday. Did he go off, down to the village?"

"I don't know."

"I'll bet you anything he was the one who told someone about there being a dead horse buried here!"

The pit was covered over again, and soon you could no longer see where the horse's grave had been. The wind blew leaves and threw branches down over the bare spot, and the rain drew its fine lines on the ground like tiny streams and rivers. But Evert and Noortje could never again walk past that place without briefly thinking of the little horse.

▪18▪
Sarah Goes to the Doctor

March had come and still it was winter. One night there was still another heavy snowfall. The following morning the sky was clear and blue, and the world looked like some picture on a Christmas card. It was beautiful all right, but oh, how long that winter was lasting! Even the children began to dislike the snow. It wasn't too pleasant when it came in through the holes in your clogs, and you had to walk around with your feet soaking wet.

The only sign that spring must be on its way was the change in the light. In the mornings the shutters could be opened after breakfast, for it was already light outside.

One such fine morning in the first week of March, Aunt Janna announced to Noortje, "I'm riding in with Henk to see the doctor this afternoon. The appointment was made a while back."

"Are you sick?"

"No, child, I have to go to the doctor every half year for a checkup. That's nothing unusual. But I've been thinking, this time you and the baby should come too."

"Little Sarah, to the doctor? Oh, no! That's much too dangerous. We can't do that, Aunt Janna!"

"No, it's all right, girl. We can trust the doctor. He knows all about it. And a baby needs to be looked at by a doctor once every so often. Sarah is already more than six weeks old."

Henk had to get a sack of rye ground by the miller in

the village. In the afternoon, right after dinner, he harnessed Browny to the milk wagon and put the sack inside. Noortje walked up and down nervously. She already had her coat on. Aunt Janna was still busy with Sarah. First she gave her an extra good washing, and then she dressed her in her very best clothes. Then Sarah was lifted onto the wagon, basket and all. There were two hot-water bottles in between the covers.

Henk held out a hand, helping Aunt Janna climb onto the wagon, and Noortje had to keep Sarah's basket from tipping or sliding. So there the three of them sat. Henk clacked his tongue and off they went. At the bottom of the meadow, Noortje jumped down off the wagon to open the gate. She saluted politely while Browny passed her at a walk, and then she closed the gate again.

"Henk! Henk! Wait for me!" she called.

Henk pretended not to hear. He calmly drove on, lighting up a cigarette in the meantime. Noortje ran after the wagon crying out, "Hey, stop! Come on, let me on."

"Whoah, whoah!" Henk said, and Browny stopped right away. "I beg your pardon, princess. I had no idea you wanted a ride. I thought you were the keeper of the gates!"

Sticking out his hand, Henk pulled her up onto the seat. But Noortje didn't want any help. She stuck out her tongue indignantly and quickly sat down.

"Let's go," she said, "and I am not a princess." She felt shy when Henk called her princess, so she pretended to be mad.

They rode on at an even pace. Sarah lay looking up with wide-open eyes; she was really sweet. It was nice that Sarah could come outside with them. Everything was new to her: the trees, the snow, the horse and wagon. She is seeing it all for the first time in her life, Noortje thought, sitting with her head tipped all the way back so that she could observe things as if through Sarah's eyes. On all the branches and twigs of the beech trees lay a fine layer of snow. High above the trees the sky was a light blue. Black lines and white against the blue—how beautiful that was when you rode underneath it.

"Wonderful, huh, Sarah?" Noortje said. "The world is really a nice place, you know. Take a good look. Soon the snow will be gone, and then it will be a long time before you'll see winter again."

She was sure Sarah thought it all very beautiful too, for she kept gazing up all the time. They came onto the heath, and now Sarah saw only the blue sky. She squeezed her eyes shut and twitched her little mouth as if she were going to cry. Fortunately, she didn't get into a bad mood easily, that brave little Sarah, and she didn't cry. She looked at the people around her, their heads and shoulders bobbing up and down above her. She looked at Aunt Janna, who sat deep in thought, looking straight ahead, her bare hands in her lap. She looked at Henk, who let the dead butt of his cigarette hang from a corner of his mouth and stared at the road running past the line of the horse's back. And then again she looked at Noortje, who looked at Sarah. The little round face remained earnest, and yet it was just as if she were laughing at Noor with her eyes.

Noortje felt very strange and joyous during that trip. She felt happy with little Sarah, and she was proud, too, for now they were going to show her to the doctor. The doctor was sure to say, "I've never seen such a beautiful, healthy baby before. You have taken excellent care of her!" And then perhaps Aunt Janna would say, "Yes, that's Noortje's work, for I have no time to do it myself." And then the doctor would look at Noortje for the first time, a little astonished, with his eyebrows pulled up high, just like her father. And he would probably say something silly, as grown-ups usually did, but she wouldn't let that bother her. "Well, well, what a good little mother," the doctor might say.

For a moment Noortje felt saddened because Sarah's own mother wasn't there; she couldn't see how pretty Sarah was getting and how well she was growing. The sad feeling didn't last very long, but it was so deep that Noortje's happiness felt changed by it.

While they were at the doctor's Henk was to drive to the miller's. He would come back to pick them up later. They had to wait in the waiting room. There were no other people. Soon the doctor came in, and they followed him back into his office. Aunt Janna immediately began to undress Sarah.

Meanwhile, Noortje took a good look at the doctor. He was a big man with a brown suit and vest on. The room was gloomy. She saw cupboards with glass doors, filled with all sorts of odd things inside: small white dishes, syringes, and scissors. The bookcases were full of thick books reaching all the way up to the ceiling. She was pretty sure that little Sarah didn't like it here, lying naked on top of the table. But Sarah was very brave and didn't make a peep, and she kept moving her arms and legs as she always did.

"Well, well," said the doctor, "let's start off by weighing her." And then that big, strange man lifted Sarah and put her on the scale. The doctor moved the indicator back and forth until he thought it was at the right number.

"Nine pounds and eight ounces," he read. "Fine."

Noortje felt she was getting angry but wisely kept her mouth shut. That man didn't even know how to weigh! What funny-looking scales he had anyway. They would weigh her again at home on the scale in the shed. You could weigh things, potatoes and grain, very exactly with that. Sarah was much heavier, of course, with that round tummy of hers and those little legs that were so fat they had creases in them.

The doctor was still busy examining Sarah. He listened to her back and chest with the stethoscope, tapped her stomach with his fingers, and examined her eyes and ears and legs. Just as he was finishing, Sarah wet on the clean cloth underneath, soaking it. Noortje pretended a yawn, so the doctor wouldn't see she was laughing.

"You can put her clothes on again," the doctor said, and he went to wash his hands. Noortje felt more and more dislike for the man. Why did he have to wash his hands now? Wasn't Sarah clean enough for him or something? And he kept talking and talking.

"Everything is fine with her. She is in perfect health. I'll give you something, and she should have half a teaspoonful of it each time you feed her. And in a month or so you can come back with her."

Sarah was dressed again. "Now, Noor, you go into the waiting room with her. I'll be with you soon," said Aunt Janna.

Aunt Janna stayed with the doctor a long time. Noortje was sitting with the baby on her lap, playing with Sarah's fingers. The door opened, and a woman and a girl entered. They sat down opposite Noortje, looking at her inquisitively. The girl was little. She couldn't be more than nine. Noortje shifted around on the wooden bench. She pulled her coat down further over her knees. That coat was much too short for her, and it looked so childish. Sarah kept gazing at her with big, earnest eyes, tightly holding onto Noortje's finger.

Those people must be thinking that Sarah was her child.

Such a young girl, and already a baby, they were perhaps thinking. I hope they won't start talking to me, Noor thought, and luckily they didn't. They didn't say anything at all, just kept staring at her. Finally Aunt Janna came back. She went outside to see if Henk was there yet.

"Come," she said, sticking her head back in the doorway, "Henk is here."

Sarah was tucked into her warm basket again, and she fell asleep instantly. The swaying movement of the milk wagon gently rocked her.

"Where are we going now?" Noortje asked.

"To the mill," Henk said. "The miller hasn't taken me yet. I had to wait so long I decided I'd better come and pick you all up first."

Their sack of flour was ready, waiting for them at the mill. Hugging it against the front of his dusty, whitened overalls, the miller carried the bag out and set it in the wagon.

"See you," he said, and went back inside his mill. You could hear the din made by all those wooden wheels and millstones. And outside the great sails were turning around and around, making a wooshing sound every time they passed the ground, something like, *zoof! zoof! zoof! zoof!*

"It's a nice breeze for the miller," said Aunt Janna, "but not for us." And she shivered in her coat, pulling her scarf a bit tighter around her ears.

The mill was past the village, where the water meadows began. They were driving over the winter dike, and in the distance they could see the summer dike. Behind it was the river, which they couldn't see. A siren began to wail in the village.

Air-raid alarm! The drone of airplanes sounded right

above them, and there was nowhere to take cover, no houses around.

"Look, there they are!" Henk pointed.

Two small airplanes were chasing each other, like two birds at play. But this wasn't a game. It was serious. They were shooting at each other, a dull, thudding sound, and little white puffs drifted into the blue.

Quickly they all three jumped off the wagon and lifted Sarah's basket to the ground. Then they lay down at the side of the road in the snow-covered grass. Aunt Janna was bent over Sarah, and she pressed Noortje close to her. Henk sat on the ground beside Browny, holding the reins. He could see the air battle going on from under the horse's belly. The horse stood very still. You could only tell by his ears that he was scared. They twitched nervously.

"Good boy, good boy, easy now," Henk said to reassure Browny.

One of the planes was hit. It dove with a burning wing, straight down to the meadows. A white parachute with a black dot at the bottom slowly drifted away, farther and farther, getting smaller and smaller. They all got up to look at it.

"It's English," Henk said with regret in his voice. "Before that pilot comes down he'll be almost at the German border."

"Let's hope he'll land on the field of a farmer who will help him," Aunt Janna said.

"They're sure to look for him anyway."

"Let's move on. The wind is starting up." They put the basket back on the wagon and got in.

"Onward, here we go." Henk clacked with his tongue, and they continued on their way.

* * *

When they arrived home, Sissy was sitting screaming in her crib. Big tears were dripping down her cheeks, her chin was all covered with saliva, and she was banging her fists against her head. Gerrit lay on the floor drumming his feet against the baseboards. His screaming was almost worse than Sissy's.

First Aunt Janna put Gerrit back on his feet, wiped his nose, and said, "What's going on here? What's happened?"

"Oooooooh!" Gerrit yowled. "They never let me do anything! It's Alie's fault. She never lets me! Everyone can always do anything they want to except me!"

"Ah, my poor little Gerrit, what is it you're not allowed to do?"

"I can't go play outside. I always have to play in the kitchen. And I'm never allowed to go to the doctor either!"

Alie sniffed and laughed scornfully. "As if we all could get to go to the doctor every day," she said, glaring furiously at Noortje, who still had her coat on and was looking around, startled.

"So, my little boy," Aunt Janna said, again wiping Gerrit's nose, which had gotten all swollen and red, "is that it? No one ever lets you do anything? But that's not true. You can do lots of things. Now Mommy has to take care of Baby Sis. And you be her big boy and help me, all right? See? That's exactly what I thought: All wet and dirty."

Sissy quieted down as soon as her mother was near her. Aunt Janna stroked her head and took off the dirty diaper. Poor thing, she'd gotten all red. She'd had that dirty diaper on for much too long. Alie and Dinie, who figured they were so much better at taking care of a baby than Noortje, were squeamish about Baby Sis and didn't want to change her.

"Gerrit, will you hand me that diaper hanging over the stove?" Aunt Janna said. "You'll both get a big hot mug of milk and a sandwich in a little while. And Gerrit, if you give Noortje one of your very sweet looks, maybe she'll go and play with you."

Gerrit climbed on top of a chair to grab the diaper. He didn't want Noortje to help him. And Noortje just stood there, a little awkward and feeling a little ashamed. It was true; she wasn't too keen on playing with Gerrit. When she and Evert were together, they always tried to get rid of him as soon as possible or else they hid. And sometimes they would hear him cry in a small, sad voice, "Evert, Noortje, where are you? I want to play too."

Noortje and Gerrit walked to the shed. The men were already busy with the cows. Evert was helping his father, and Henk was taking Browny to his stall. Gerrit had grasped Noortje's hand.

"What shall we do?" he asked.

"Let's go look at the calf."

The calf was still in its small corner next to the stall for the horses. It was less than seven weeks old, just like Sarah, but it had grown fast. They let it suck on their fingers, and Noortje scratched its head between the bumps.

"They like that," she said to Gerrit. "You try it too."

"I want to play," Gerrit said.

"All right. What shall we play?"

"House."

Noortje actually felt she was too big for playing house, but she would do it this once, to please Gerrit. Next to the small nook for the calf was a cow stall that wasn't being used. They found a few poles and some burlap sacks in a corner, and Noortje also knew where there was a crate. They made a house of the poles and the sacks, and they used the crate for a table. Gerrit liked that. He sat in front of the house on an old wheel-barrow and watched Noortje gathering together their pots and pans. He loved everything she did. She brought a few rusty tins to the house and a piece of wood.

"This is to cook in," she said, "and that's to cut bread on."

"Nice, isn't it, without Evert?" Gerrit said. "He's no fun at all."

Noortje didn't say anything to that.

"You stay here, and I'll go and see if your mother has got something for us," she said after a while. A little later she returned with the two mugs of hot milk and two slices of bread and butter. And there was some real sugar sprinkled on the bread! That was a treat! Real sugar! They were careful not to spill a single grain.

"This is what the king always eats too," Gerrit said, with his mouth full.

"Yes, and he gets cream in his coffee every day. And applesauce."

"Mmmmmmm. And what does the prince eat?"

"The prince eats . . . uh . . . the prince eats chicken soup. And custard with cherries. And afterward he smokes a cigar."

"No, not the prince. He isn't allowed to smoke yet. It's the king who smokes."

"Oh, yes, of course."

"Hey, I want to be the the prince! And who does the prince play with? With a princess, right? Do you want to be the princess?"

"I don't know."

They drank their hot milk in small sips. Noortje was thinking about a rhyme she had learned in school long ago, and she said, "I know a rhyme about a prince. If you listen like a good boy, I'll say it for you. OK?"

Gerrit nodded.

"Listen:

"A little prince was seeking
a beautiful princess.
He was four or five or six
or seven, more or less.

"He spotted one or two
who were extraordinarily fine,
but oh, how sad, and what a shame,
they both were ninety-nine!

"He walked and walked
through wood and field
and waved his hat and stick:
Our hero would not yield.

"But where, oh where, to find
a beautiful princess
who's four or five or six
or seven, more or less?"

"What is a hero?" Gerrit asked. He had listened to Noortje very attentively.

"Well, if you're not afraid of anything, then you're a hero."

"Like the grown-ups?"

That set Noortje to thinking. Grown-ups are also afraid sometimes, she thought, but Gerrit couldn't know that yet. "A hero isn't afraid of anything or anybody," she said. "And you could become a hero too, you know."

"A hero wouldn't be afraid of Wolthuis either?" Gerrit whispered softly.

Noortje had to laugh. "Why are you afraid of Wolthuis?" she asked.

"Shall I say why? But if I say it, you'll be afraid of him too. You know, when he gets very angry? Then I'm afraid his eyes might roll out. And if you were having your bowl of soup just then, and they fell into it . . . and you didn't notice . . . then you'd think, oh, what nice little meatballs! Because you wouldn't know they were Wolthuis's eyes, right?"

"Yes, right, that's enough." Noortje laughed. "You and your crazy stories."

Dinie came in to call them for supper. Noortje washed her hands at the pump. "You go on ahead," she said to Gerrit.

It was already dark in the long corridor. Little Gerrit walked to the kitchen all by himself; Noortje held the door open a little and heard him stepping along over the stone floor on his socks. Such a brave little kid, she thought.

Gerrit's loud, high voice rang out in the dark. "How big I am! I'm a hero!" he called. Then he was at the kitchen door.

▪19▪ The Cows Go Out to Pasture

Rain was dripping and dropping from the roof gutters and eaves. The rain kept coming down, and the wind blew. The snow was almost gone, but there was still some ice. The wooden gates had slippery pieces of dirty ice on top. And there was ice on the hard ground that had been hidden underneath the snow. Now that it was thawing it could be slippery anywhere. When you were least expecting it, you could suddenly start slipping and sliding.

Dark clouds were driven across the sky at a furious speed. The sun kept breaking through the clouds briefly, and when it disappeared again everything on earth looked bleak and gray. Things had become dirty and black and wet all over. The rain stopped, then started again in thick, cold drops.

Granny complained that she didn't dare go outside. Her poor bent legs couldn't carry her so well anymore, and she was sure to fall and break something if she tried walking on that slippery surface. Alie laughed at her. "You never go outside anyway, so what are you whining about now?"

That was true. Granny had hardly gone outside the whole winter. But now it was thawing! The sun was giving more and more warmth, the grass was growing green again, and in a few days the buds would open. The woods first turned a very light green, and alongside the roads the small yellow stars of crowfoot, celandine, and lots of monkshood appeared. Spring was coming, and there wasn't a soul of them who hadn't intensely longed for it.

Granny wanted one more season in the sun, sitting in a chair feeling her blood slowly warm and run faster again. She was old and lonely and didn't see much point in living any longer. But she wanted to experience spring one more time and feel comfortably warm. Those girls shouldn't go on teasing her like that. She just couldn't bear it. She pursed her lips together and sat down near the window with half-closed eyes.

"The old sock is asleep again," Alie said.

"You can go out without your coat!" Noortje called to Evert. "It's really warm, almost like summer!" And outside they went to slide on the hard iciness beneath the gray slush of snow. In the meadow, they kept on finding even better stretches to slide on. Mud and snow spattered around them. The geese were getting excited too. They ran after the children and nipped at their legs.

"Back you, go back!" Evert yelled, kicking at them. The geese kept on coming, their stretched-out necks a few yards away from him, hissing.

Noortje discovered a nice, steep hump in the meadow where it was very slippery. She ran and slid . . . and then *splash!* She was sitting on the ground. Now it wasn't so easy to brush the snow off her clothes. Ice-cold water crept into her pants, and she felt herself getting wet through and through. *Uggh!*

Well, she was soaking wet already, so she might as well go all the way now. And she did. She slid and slid, watching the clouds chasing each other and looking at the patches of blue sky in between. The sun came out and shone in her eyes. She had to squeeze them shut and felt the warmth of the sunbeams on her cold cheeks. There was the rustling sound of feathers close by. "*Honk, honk, honk!*" the geese cried, rushing up to her.

"Help, Evert, help!" Noortje called.

Apparently the geese figured someone all laid out in the mud wasn't very impressive. They wanted to jump on top of her and investigate with their bills how such a creature was put together. "*Gah, gah, gah,*" the geese cried. One was already pulling at Noortje's sleeve with its hard mouth, and another was pecking at her naked toe, which stuck out through a hole in her sock. Evert just stood there laughing. When he saw that Noortje was getting anxious about those screaming beaks around her, he picked up his clog and threw it in the middle of the pack of geese, yelling and screaming at them, "Go away, get away!"

And off they went, Indian file, their heads indignantly stuck up in the air. They muttered and grumbled, waggling away, and then, when they'd gone quite a stretch, started pulling at the short grass, looking for grain kernels that had been left in the straw heap.

"Stupid things," Noortje said, wiping the wet mud off her clothes.

"Stupid girl." Evert laughed. "I never saw anything so funny in my whole life." And he stretched out his neck at her, hissing like a goose, as if that would frighten Noortje.

The thaw persisted, and it really began to become spring.

"Another five days or so," Farmer Everingen said one afternoon. "Then we can put the cows out to pasture."

"Already?" Aunt Janna said. "But couldn't it freeze again?"

"As soon as the frost is out of the ground and the grass begins to grow," Everingen said.

The winter had no business lasting much longer. For the last few weeks the cattle had been fed little else but chopped beets, and the milk tasted of it. Those beets! The feedcakes had been finished a long time ago, and they couldn't get new ones. When you looked up, standing in the shed, you could see all the way to the roof through the log floor of the hayloft. There was only a very small amount of hay left around the opening in the middle. Evert's father didn't allow him to get onto the hayloft anymore; now Henk had to throw the stuff down in the evenings. When you stood with your clogs on those round logs, it was difficult to keep your balance. You could easily take a wrong step and then fall all the way down.

In the afternoon the doors to the shed were wide open. The wind came in and blew up dust and rustled the straw. The cows blinked their eyes at the bright glare, turning their heads toward the semicircular opening of the doors and lowing. Their nostrils flared as they sniffed in the fresh air and banged their horns against the poles to which they were tied. Strange smells came floating in at them. The cows had had quite enough of standing still in the shed so long. Grass, sweet, juicy grass was what they were longing for.

When all the snow was gone, Everingen said one evening, "Tomorrow we'll go. We must be careful, of course, for I've heard that the main road is full of Germans. It seems that whole companies of them are moving to the north, and others are on their way south. Something is going on, that's for sure."

Wolthuis and Mr. Vanderhook were going to help take the cows out to the meadow. Noortje didn't understand at all. Why was it such a big job? And what did the main road have to do with it? All you had to do was open the doors, untie the cows, and let them out, right?

"What are they talking about?" she asked Evert.

"Tomorrow the cows are being put out to pasture, didn't you hear?" And Evert wouldn't say any more about it. "Papa, we can come too, can't we?" he cried.

"Yes, you can come," his father said.

The next morning they started milking half an hour earlier than usual. It was going to be a really beautiful bright day. Small, white clouds were floating in the morning sky. The rising sun shone on the barn and lit the edge of the wood behind the fields. Everything seemed golden then, and even the old wooden barn was more beautiful than Noortje had ever seen it before.

"First come the calves," Henk said. "Evert, you go and open the gate to the upper meadow."

In front of the house was a sloping meadow, marked off at the bottom by First Beech Lane. To the side of the house was another meadow, a square enclosed on three sides by forest. That was the Calves' Meadow.

Evert had opened the gate all the way, and Henk pulled the doors of the barn open. When the calves came out, one step at a time, they at first didn't understand what was happening. They'd never seen anything else but the dark shed. They'd been born there and had never been out of it. All that high blue sky made them dizzy, and the wind riffled the hair on their coats. The ground under their legs was soggy, soggy and wet and green, and full of humps and bumps. Suddenly all at the same time, the calves began to leap, their tails up. Evert and Noortje stood and watched, laughing.

"Move it, come on, let's move it!" Everingen and Henk cried, and they tapped the calves on their behinds with sticks to get them to walk in the right direction.

But the calves didn't undrestand at all. They hardly knew yet what it was to walk properly. They sprang with both hind legs in the air, so that they almost fell forward on their heads. A few started to trot behind each other, going around in a circle. Each sniffed at the one in front of it, and they sniffed at the ground. They poked their noses into the grass; it smelled nice and new, strong and fresh. They ought to take a few bites of it. It seemed to be there for them. And so the calves discovered that grass was there to be eaten, and they were very glad to do so.

Now they were all grazing underneath the apple tree at the side of the house. That was a good moment to drive them in the direction of the open gate. And five of the calves moved obediently, but the sixth was stubborn. He threw his head and tail into the air and galloped by the front of the house over the stone pavement and past the pigsty. There he bumped his nose against the straw heap and stopped still on stiff legs, full of fear and wonder. Evert and Noortje had run after the calf. They calmly walked up to him now. The calf was standing very still. He didn't dare move a leg. He looked back over his shoulder with big, amazed eyes.

"You get on that side, and I'll stay on this," Evert said. "And when he goes the wrong way, you call out 'Forward!' Or else give him a tap. Here's how you do it."

So Noortje learned how to drive out calves and cows. She had a long stick in her hand just like the others, and with it she carefully tapped the calf on its back. She didn't want to hurt the animal, but he did have to go in the right direction. Finally all the calves were in their meadow and the gate was closed. "Now for the cows," Noortje cried. That was going to be even more fun.

"Yes, yes," Everingen said. "But we're in no great rush. A cup of coffee first."

Noortje didn't understand. Why didn't they just untie the cows and let them walk out? Or perhaps something else was supposed to happen?

"Where are the cows going, Evert?"

"To the Ijssel, of course."

"To the river? But why there?"

"Where else do you think they should go?"

Noortje didn't want to say what she'd thought the cows would do: stay near the house. Now she realized that there wasn't enough grass in that meadow for thirteen big, fat milk cows. She had to laugh at herself when she looked out over the field, with its many black mounds of dirt dug out by groundhogs. The grass wouldn't last the animals for even a day.

Alongside the Ijssel, between the dikes, was the best pasture land. There the red-and-white cows could graze all summer long and far into autumn. They not only found the best grass there, but also waybread and leek, buttercups, and even daisies. Maybe that was why they gave such good fat milk during the summer.

The doors of the barn were shut again, and the cows untied one by one. The rope with which they'd been hitched was looped into a knot and placed between the horns, so they had a nice decoration of twisted rope atop their heads. The poles of their stanchions were too close to each other, so they couldn't go forward through them. They had to turn around and step over the drainage ditch behind them.

It was quite an operation to get those big, clumsy animals, so impatient to be outside, to step over that drainage ditch full of their droppings. At the far end of the stalls was a small door, through which they had to pass to get outside. Farmer Everingen held the front cow by a rope.

As soon as they got outside they began to low and stamp on the ground and sniff the short grass with their noses. The cows wanted to start eating right away, but that was not allowed. They had to walk in single file, and calmly too. Wolthuis and Evert and Mr. Vanderhook went alongside the procession of cows, to make sure that none of them went off the road. Henk and Noortje brought up the rear, prodding stragglers. Everingen was in front, leading the cow with the rope.

When they reached the meadow, the animals went downhill in a trot; they calmed down a bit by the time they got to Beech Lane. Often one would stop to get a bite of some tough weeds growing between the trees. Suddenly one of the cows ran off into the woods. She stamped her hooves among the trees so that the brown beech leaves leaped up all around. Mr. Vanderhook walked after her quickly and drove her back.

Noortje felt glad to be walking in the rear. All those red-brown-and-white spotted backs rolling up and down, with speckles of sunlight playing on them, were such a wonderful sight. Sometimes they lowed a few times, happy and excited, and now and then one of them became a bit wild. She would jump on the back of the cow walking ahead and let herself be pulled along a little way. But as soon as she got a tap with the stick she dropped down on her own four legs again.

It was a long walk across the heath and through the Deep Ditch to the main road. They all halted there. There was a lot of traffic that day, and they had to cross calmly and carefully. Trucks full of soldiers rode past, and motorbikes with sidecars roared by at a terrific speed. They had to wait on the bicycle path till there was an opening in the long stream of traffic.

"They're going in the right direction; they're moving

north," Mr. Vanderhook said. "Now the war will really be over soon."

And Henk added, "As far as I'm concerned, they can take all their guns and gear and never come back!"

"We can cross now!" Everingen said. "Calmly now," he warned.

He went and stood in the middle of the road with the cow on the rope, so that the others wouldn't have to worry about the traffic. All thirteen cows started quietly walking toward the other side. But before they reached it, yet another column of trucks approached, with an armored car that made a heavy droning sound leading the way. Everingen waved his stick, and the armored car stopped.

Inside in the back of the truck, soldiers were sitting in two rows facing each other, their heads with the gray-green helmets all turned. Noortje thought, They're looking at us. Maybe they're jealous because we're having such a good time traveling with our cows. When the cows had reached the other side safely, the armored car and the trucks drove on again.

They walked them around the village to the water meadows, and there they finally put the cows to pasture. But they had to cross some land belonging to other farmers before they reached their own part. Evert had to open many a gate and wait till all went through before he closed it again. At last they were there.

"Well, that's done," Everingen said.

The final gate was now shut too, and they all leaned on it, looking at the cows in the field. Immediately they began to graze. Sometimes one would become all wild and frolicsome, leaping around as if she were still a young cow.

"Tomorrow you'll notice the difference in the milk

already," Henk said. For the last couple of weeks you could really taste that the cows were getting more beets than hay. Ugh! That beet milk was hard to take!

"No, not by tomorrow," said Everingen, "but by the end of the week you'll taste it and start to see that their milk will be yellow with cream again. And the wife will be able to make us some cheese."

They stood chatting for a while, eating the bread they'd brought along from home. It was near dinner time now, and they still had quite a walk ahead of them.

On the way back Evert didn't have to open any gates. The men simply climbed up over them, just as he did.

20
Soldiers

For a whole week life at Klaphek seemed almost normal. Every day it got a little warmer and brighter, and sometimes the sun shone through the clouds.

Now that the cow stalls were empty, they had to be cleaned. First the manure had to be removed in a wheelbarrow. Then the walls and partitioning were scrubbed clean with hard brushes. For two whole days the men were at work. The stalls had to be spotless. When it was all finished, the cowshed was so clean that you could eat off the floor. The children now had a wonderful big space for playing in whenever it rained.

In the very early morning and at four in the afternoon the men went milking. They would ride out to the meadow near the Ijssel on the milk wagon. Evert and Noortje went too in the afternoon. While the milking was going on they had just enough time to walk to the bakery and fetch some bread. And when everyone rode back, the two of them ran on ahead of the wagon to open and close the gates. If there was still a supply of bread at Klaphek, Evert and Noortje helped drive the cows together and tether them.

The milking hour was the best of the day. The meadow smelled so nice from the animals and the wet clay soil. The curious smell of the milk cans and buckets was part of it. Even the wagon and its two big wheels had taken on that vaguely acrid aroma, mixed with the much stronger smell of horses and horse manure.

Often it was raining, and the ground got very soggy. Near the river the silence was so deep that the few sounds you did hear seemed louder than anywhere else: a cow pulling its leg out of the clay with a sucking sound, the splattering when one of the cows let go with droppings, the lowing in the meadow far away, or the singing of a lark, high up in the air.

It wasn't easy to find the lark, a gray dot against the sky, blurred by small trembling wings. The sky here was so high and wide all around, so gray and dense with moisture, that people and animals looked very small on the flat earth.

One day Aunt Janna came down from the attic with a little cart, a two-wheeler made of wood with a long stick attached to it. You could pull it or push it with that stick.

"Noortje," she said, "would you do me a favor, and please take Baby Sis outside? The poor thing has been inside the house all winter." She dressed Sissy in a thick sweater and tied a scarf around her neck.

Sissy was put into the cart, which stood outside near the front door. Gerrit and Noortje each took one side of the handle and started pulling Sissy. There she sat, going bangedy-bang over the grass. Sissy even looked a little happy now, but somehow she also managed to look frightened at the same time, her hands clutching the sides of the wagon tightly. "Chirr, chirr, chirr," she cried, sounding like a lively little bird. Aunt Janna stood in the doorway watching. She smiled because the little girl seemed so glad, but she didn't wave at her. She knew too well that Sis would never wave back. While she was looking at her little daughter, Aunt Janna's face was less happy though not quite sad.

That day Granny sat out in front of the house for the first time, and next to her sat Sarah's basket on two kitchen chairs. The baby lay sleeping quietly. Sparrows chirped in the hawthorn hedge and were flying to and fro, carrying twigs and blades of grass in their bills. Granny had taken her knitting outside with her, but she wasn't working much at it. Time and again she'd let the knitting rest in her lap, gazing in the direction of Beech Lane with bleared eyes. The war wouldn't last much longer, she thought, and then she would leave Klaphek along that lane, back to her house in the city.

Theo was also walking around outside. He sat down near the Calves' Meadow against the slope that ran along the edge of the wood and looked at the hazy greenness that hung from the trees. He let the sun shine on his pale cheeks and daydreamed that the war was over and he was getting strong and healthy again.

Whistling while he worked, Mr. Vanderhook prepared the day's supply of wood. Then he took a book outside with him and sat down next to Theo. Lying back in the grass, they talked about how the world would look different once the war was over. For no matter how bad these dreadful years had been, they said to each other, people had learned a good deal from it all, and therefore nothing like this could ever happen again. Mr. Vanderhook was amazed he could have such a good discussion with such a young fellow. And Theo was thinking it was great that you could actually talk to a man so much older. And then both of them fell silent for a long time, feeling quite at ease.

Suddenly Noortje came running up, fear in her face. She stood in front of the two men and said, "The Germans are coming, lots of them. What are we going to do?"

"Oh, don't worry," Theo said. "I'll disappear into the woods for a while and come back when the coast is clear."

But the coast didn't clear, and that night Theo had to slink back to his room in the dark via the side entrance.

Four trucks had pulled up in the yard. Soldiers jumped off, letting their knapsacks fall to the ground first. Baskets and crates were lifted out of the truck. The soldiers were wearing the gray-green uniform of the *Wehrmacht.* Three officers stood to one side, screaming orders.

Quickly Aunt Janna hid Sarah's basket up in the alcove. They couldn't do any more now. They had to wait and see what would happen. The officers told Everingen he had to give quarters to the soldiers. The company needed shelter for the night and possibly the next few nights as well. There was no point in discussing it, and they couldn't tell exactly how long the stay might last.

The soldiers marched into the barn and to the shed. There was quite a hustle and bustle, but they all seemed to know very well what they must do. Evert and Noortje stood in the midst of it. They didn't want to miss a thing. And, meanwhile, the grown-ups sat together in the kitchen looking devastated.

The soldiers took sheaves of straw off the great heap and spread them out in the clean cowshed. A dozen or so of the men stood bare-chested around the pump to wash themselves. They laughed loudly as they let the cold rush of water splatter down each other's backs. Evert watched them with an angry face.

"Will you just look at that mess they're making?" he said. "We only empty that tub a few times a year, but if they go on this way it will be all filled up in a day."

"Your father should say something about it."

Evert was right, really. They just let the dirty, soapy water spill over the edge, and it got all messy around the tub. The floor of the shed was made of hard clay, and the water turned it into wet mud. But it did smell nice there near the pump, for the soldiers were using real soap.

When they'd all finished washing themselves, Noortje

pretended she was going to the door of the corridor and took a careful look around her. Maybe one of them had left his soap lying there. Sure enough, on top of the pump handle lay a big, yellow bar of soap, still wet and foamy. Noortje pocketed it quickly and walked to the kitchen.

"Here you are," she said, putting the piece of soap down in front of Aunt Janna.

The people sitting there had to laugh despite their gloom, and so then Noortje said, "Do you know what those soldiers are doing? They're pumping and splashing water all over the place, making a terrible mess."

Maybe she shouldn't have mentioned it. Now everyone looked angry again, and Aunt Janna said, "If it gets out of hand, Chris, you'll have to say something about it."

Everingen nodded.

"Yes, yes," he muttered.

The soldiers had laid down their beds of straw in the shed. They rolled out their gray blankets and placed their bags on top. The poles to which the cows had been tied before now served as something to hang their belts, cartridge belts, and helmets on. Rifles leaned against the wall behind the drainage ditch.

One soldier had at least twenty hand grenades lying on top of his bed. Evert took a tiny step closer, hesitantly. He wouldn't mind at all having one such shiny hand grenade in his collection, but he didn't dare ask for it. The soldier noticed Evert's curiosity and smiled at him. He was a big, strong fellow with a red face and short-cropped brown hair. When he laughed, you saw lots of straight, white teeth. He held a grenade in his outstretched hand, as if offering it to Evert. Luckily, Noortje was coming back just at that moment.

"No, Evert," she said firmly, "are you crazy?" And she pulled him back.

"You're a real pain," Evert said. "He wants to give me one. Don't worry, I won't do anything with it."

The soldier had gotten up and came toward him now with the grenade. He kept on laughing, holding the thing right under Evert's nose teasingly. Then he made a gesture as if he were going to throw it and asked, "Yes?"

Evert nodded. The soldier walked to the big doors. Only the upper half of them was open. The children stayed right behind him. Then the soldier made a circling motion above his head and threw the grenade in an arc in the direction of the barn. As soon as it hit the ground the thing exploded with a loud bang. Just in time, the German had slammed the upper part of the door shut. A rain of splinters and clumps of mud thumped against the wood.

Noortje was startled, but Evert laughed and the soldier laughed too. He found the explosion a wonderfully funny joke. At that point another soldier called out something to him teasingly, and he joined his comrades again.

There was lots more to look at and take in that day. They were already getting almost used to the sound of German voices. By the end of the afternoon, there was no water coming out of the pump; the Germans had used it all.

"You'd better go pumping again," Everingen said to Evert. "There's absolutely nothing we can do about it. If they don't leave by tomorrow, though, I'll have to talk to them."

That evening Evert and Noortje walked behind the Fox on the circular pavement in the dark, attending to the water supply. They saw Theo coming out of the woods and rushed to check the side entrance to see if the way to his room was clear. They didn't say much while doing their pumping chore. A lot had happened that day, and they were tired. The Fox seemed tired too, for he didn't want to keep up much of a pace. He was probably thinking, What nonsense, pumping three times in one day! I've never had to do that before in my whole life.

At last they were finished, and together they took the Fox to the back of the house. It had grown quite dark now. Noortje helped Evert unharness the horse, and she stroked the Fox's nose, which was nice and soft. When he stood next to Browny again in the stall, they brought him some oats. The soldiers were sitting on their straw beds eating, their legs dangling in the fodder trough. They had brought their own lamps, and you could see everything very clearly in the shed. For a while the children watched the soldiers spoon their thick brown mush out of mess tins. It didn't smell very good. They ate hunks of gray bread with it.

Noortje tried to count the soldiers, but she kept losing track of the number. There were more of them in the barn, and altogether there must have been at least sixty. Most of them were tired; she could see that. They just sat there chewing their bread, half dozing off. But there also were soldiers who apparently never got tired, yelling and laughing and singing songs. They had mugs of coffee, and some jokers raised them high as if holding up glasses of beer and cried, "Gesundheit!"

"Come, let's go," Noortje said. Finally she'd seen enough.

When they got outside Noortje and Evert saw a fire glowing in front of the barn. More soldiers. And there must be something special about them for sure, since they weren't with the others. Noortje and Evert went over to that fire to have a look. A heap of small pieces of wood lay burning upon some bricks. Five men were squatting down around the fire. They were wearing German uniforms and yet they didn't look at all like the other soldiers in the shed. They were short and dark, with wrinkled faces. They weren't speaking German to each other, but a strange sort of language the children couldn't understand at all. It sounded like, *grr, uttuh prrr.* The children stood behind the men, looking.

One of them stuck a fork into the glowing ashes and took a large brown potato out. He lifted the forked potato up toward Noortje, nodding at her kindly and motioning her to take it. Tentatively she reached out her hand. The potato was burning hot, and she could hardly hold it. Another soldier stuck his fork into the ashes and got a potato out for Evert also.

They squatted down between the soldiers. Carefully they peeled their potatoes. The skin came off easily. The potatoes were roasted and all soft inside. The children took little bites. They tasted good.

The strange soldiers were watching them, their eyes black in their red faces. They were speaking among themselves and gently laughing at the children. One of them got up, placed a cup on the ground in front of them, and pointed at it. First they didn't understand what he meant.

Evert picked up the cup. There was salt in it, and he put some on his potato. It tasted even better that way.

The officers slept in the barn that first night. But they didn't seem very pleased about it. The next morning they knocked on the scullery door.

Aunt Janna didn't want to let the Germans into her kitchen. Evert went to get his father, and Mr. Vanderhook had to come too because he spoke German well. They stood talking in front of the house. The officers asked if there was a room available for them inside the house.

"No," said Everingen very firmly.

But they had already looked in through the windows and pointed at the parlor. That room wasn't being used, they said, and they had to have it. The scullery too, so their cook could prepare meals there for the men.

They couldn't do anything to stop them. Nothing they said made the slightest impression. It did no good to point out that there was very little space in the kitchen for all of their people and that, therefore, they sat in the parlor at night. Or that Mr. Vanderhook slept in the closet bed there. Or, least of all, that it was the parlor, the best room, which held their finest furniture, and it was where the beautiful dinner service was kept inside the cupboard. Or that the old clock with the copper pendulum hung there, the one that had belonged to Evert's grandmother.

The officers said they didn't mind if the dinner plates were removed, for they didn't need them, but they insisted the three of them had to use the room.

"Ah, woman!" one cried out. "It won't be for very long anyway!"

Well, that was to be hoped. Everingen started talking about the water problem. He told them his son had to pump a whole extra time the day before and that the soldiers had used a great deal of water. If they weren't more careful, the well would dry up. And he also said that the men splashed and spilled and were making a general mess of things near the pump in the shed.

That was scandalous, the officers agreed, and they promised it wouldn't happen again. There had to be order and neatness; that's exactly what they themselves always insisted upon. The guilty ones would be punished. And if the farmer lent them his horse, the men would pump up water twice a day from now on. After all, the farmer could understand that soldiers needed water too, couldn't he?

From that day on life at Klaphek became quite different.

There were always soldiers walking around the house. The men were forbidden to come near the front house and they paid strict heed to that order. The three officers held them tightly in rein. But the cook and his assistant were busy in the scullery, and they could smell the soldiers' food in the kitchen. Mr. Vanderhook had to vacate the small summerhouse with his saw and trestle, and now he was sawing the wood outside in front of the house. He already had to sleep on a couple of chairs in the kitchen, and now had lost his beautiful sawing shed too.

The soldiers who'd been eating potatoes the night before were Hungarian prisoners of war. The Germans set up one of the Hungarians in the summerhouse with boots and belts and bags and pieces of leather. Using a large, bent needle and rope, he repaired every leather thing that needed fixing. It was nice to watch him at work, but they couldn't talk with him. Each time he looked up at the children he laughed. He was a kind, jolly man.

Since they'd lost the parlor they all crowded around the kitchen table in the evenings again, and they went to bed early.

At first, Noortje had been terribly worried that the Germans would see little Sarah. She didn't want Aunt Janna to put her outside anymore, and she gave her the bottle in the alcove. Actually, she wished Sarah never, ever needed to leave that small bedroom. There wasn't much space for the baby in the kitchen anyway. Sarah cried a lot inside that half-dark little room. She could set up a cry so piercing and loud that it went right through you. It could be heard in the scullery, and sometimes even in the shed. Things couldn't go on like that.

"You'll just make them suspicious this way," Noortje's father said. "They're hearing a child, but they don't see it. We'd do better to act as if it's quite normal that we have a child living here."

"Those young chaps aren't interested in babies anyway, Henk said.

"But if they know who she is. . . ."

"But they don't know. And they won't find out either. Who would tell them?" Aunt Janna said. "Really, child, it's best for her."

And so Sarah reappeared after a few days. Everybody knew what to say if one of the Germans asked who the little girl was. She'd been sick the last few days, which was why they hadn't seen her and only heard her. Now whenever the weather was good Sarah went outside in her basket again. And Granny sat next to her, keeping an eye on her. When it rained or when it was windy, the basket was lifted onto the big bed or set in the Wolthuis family's room.

The officers clomped through the corridor with their heavy boots and slammed the front door loudly. They let the latch come down with such a bang that the ring on the other side of the door kept rattling. Once in a while one of them bent over the cradle and tickled Sarah under the chin. "Kootchie-kootchie, koo! Such a pretty little girl."

When Noortje saw that, she felt as if her heart would stop. She blushed deep red and was afraid her color would betray her anger. That man, with his fat crooked fingers, he'd better leave her baby alone! When he strode off, she quickly went over to Sarah to console her.

"It's all right," she said, "you needn't cry. We won't let him do anything bad to you." But Sarah wasn't crying at all. She laughed to everyone who came near her cradle.

One day they were making a mess with the water again near the pump, and then something awful happened. The soldier who had done it the most was beaten on his back with a belt by an officer. Noortje couldn't watch. "Come on," she said, pulling Evert away with her to the kitchen.

They told Aunt Janna what they'd seen, and Aunt Janna told her husband about it a little later. At dinner they were all talking of it.

"I guess I won't complain anymore when they're sloppy. I should have foreseen this," Everingen said.

Wolthuis got mad. "What do you care? They're cruel to others, and so they are cruel to each other."

Granny wiped a few tears out of her eyes.

"Ah, Granny, do you have to go blubbering about that too?" Ma Wolthuis said.

"N-n-no," she stammered, "it's my eyes. They tear so badly. Because of my rheumatics."

Alie began to laugh.

Aunt Janna took Baby Sis on her lap, gently rocking her, humming a song. Her eyes were gazing out the window past the apple tree, past the hawthorn hedge and the woods into the distance.

21
A Car With a Red Cross

It was impossible to understand where all those birds came from; as soon as the sun gave off some warmth they began to whistle and sing like musicians gone crazy. The wood was full of their song, their twittering, chirping, and warbling sounded all over. The birds were glad that winter was over. They were getting their nests in order so they could lay their eggs in them later, just as usual, just as if there wasn't a war going on anywhere and the heavens, which should have been theirs alone anyway, weren't full of the dronings of bombers and fighter planes.

At Klaphek there was only one person who couldn't enjoy the warm rays of the sun, who was even afraid to sit in front of the open window, as he had done so often when it was still bitterly cold. Whenever a German uniform was visible in the neighborhood, Theo always had to hide. And now Klaphek was crawling with German uniforms, in and around the farm.

Before, either Evert or Noortje would bring him his dinner. But now they did so together. They went around the outside of the house with his dish, and before they turned the corner and walked to the side entrance, they first checked to see if all was clear. There never yet had been a German at the side entrance or on the stairs. But how long would it be till they would start wondering about that little window way up high in the wall? It must belong to a room too, and someone must be living in it. Who?

Theo kept to his bed and felt sicker than ever. He was a prisoner and his own sentinel. And how about going to the toilet? He had to do that outside during the night, for the real toilet was in the shed, and he couldn't show himself there. When it got dark, he crept past the back of the summerhouse, cursing to himself if he should bump into the crooked piece of the V-1, and then he ran like a shadow with a pale ring around its neck to the hedge surrounding the vegetable garden. As soon as he got behind it he dared breathe again. Sometimes he was startled by the whoo-whooing of an owl swooping right behind him across the field.

One evening Theo said to Evert and Noortje, "I have to get out of here. I'm endangering you all by staying."

"Oh, no, Theo," Evert said. "We don't mind. We're used to your being here."

Theo smiled. "But still, it's true," he said. "And you two must help me. You can't tell anyone about it, though, not even your father and mother, Evert. I've got a letter all ready and want you to take it to someone in Zemst for me."

"All right. Who do we have to give it to?"

"I'll explain in a minute where it is exactly. When you get there you have to ring the bell three times. And you must ask whoever opens the door if you can speak to Nico. If the man or woman says no one named Nico is living there, you come back home right away.

"If he *is* there, be sure to put the letter into his own hands. You must not give it to anybody else. Only to Nico. If they say, You can give it to me, I'll see to it that Nico gets it, you mustn't let go of the letter."

"And when Nico does get the letter?"

"Then you don't ask anything, but you wait to hear what he'll say. Probably he'll send you back with some kind of message. But you'd better not ask for one. And when you've done it you come back home at once. Don't do anything else on the way! Understand? Have you got it all straight, Evert? Now you tell me what you two are supposed to do."

Evert repeated what Theo had said, and then Theo let Noortje say it once again, until he was convinced they had it all clearly imprinted in their minds. It wasn't too difficult to memorize. They had to go to a house on Station Road—33 Station Road. Evert knew where it was.

The following morning the children told no one what they were going to do. They got on their bikes and slowly pedaled toward the gate, as if they were just off for fun. They were actually not supposed to go out biking with all those Germans around, but nobody noticed them, and as soon as they were through the gate they pedaled briskly over the slippery path to the side of the wagon ruts. It was a beautiful day and very quiet on the heath. They didn't see a soul going through the Klinger Woods, and soon they reached Zemst.

"Number 33," Evert said. "This must be it."

It was a small house with a yard in front. They slowly walked up to the door. All the window curtains were drawn. There was no way of guessing what sort of people lived in the house. There wasn't even a little window in the door to look through. The bell gleamed as if it were gold, and there were flowering crocuses in front of the house, both purple and yellow ones.

"OK, let's do it," Noortje said. "Who's going to do the talking?"

"Why don't you?"

They didn't have to wait very long after they rang the bell. The door swung open and on the threshold stood a big woman with a flowery apron and rolled-up sleeves. Her hands and massive arms were bright red. She must have been laundering.

"Well, what do you want?" she asked, looking at them searchingly. "There's nothing to buy here!"

Noortje had to clear her throat a few times before she could get the words out. Her voice still sounded hoarse when she asked, "Ma'am, is someone named Nico living here?"

"Ha! So!" the woman cried out. "Someone by the name of Nico! And what is it you want from him?"

"We're looking for someone named Nico. We thought perhaps . . . maybe he lives here."

"So. Now you listen to me, kid. If you don't know where your friends are living, how should I?" said the woman. "And are you going to ring the bells of all the houses now? I find that a little peculiar, you know. You can't bother people in times like these. Why don't you ask him yourself? I think it's rather dumb of you two. Really, you can't do that sort of thing, you know.

"Someone called Nico . . . let me see . . . actually, I've heard that name before. Yes, a friend of my nephew's, my sister's son that is, yes, I think he's called Nico. But where, for heavens' sake, would he live? No, I don't have a clue. Of course, I might ask my sister. . . . What does that Nico of yours look like?"

The woman spoke quickly and so loudly that they were afraid she could be heard all the way down the street. Apparently, she thought they were looking for another kid. Well, Nico did not live in this house; that much was clear. Theo must have made a mistake. Or were they in the wrong street perhaps?

"This is Station Road, isn't it?" Noortje asked. "We've heard he lives on Station Road, Number 33."

"This is Station Road all right! But no, you must have remembered wrongly, for I do know most all of the children here. In fact, there aren't many of them on this street. And I do get along quite well with children, if I say so myself. No, I've never had trouble with that. And they've always liked me too, you know? Yes, well, you know the way it is. . . . Before, when everything was so much better than it is now, well, if a child came to the door with a message or something, yes, that did happen, for my husband. . . . My husband, well, he's in Germany now, and so one lives with nothing to show for it but fear and trouble. But what was it I wanted to say again? Oh, yes, what I wanted to say was, that when a child came to the door here I'd always give him something, whatever there was in the house, you see. A cookie or an apple. But you two must understand I can't give you anything now, for I hardly have anything left for myself, hardly anything at all. So I can't help you or anyone else either.

"They told you it had to be on Station Road? And at Number 33. . . . Yes, this is 33 . . . 33A of course. Next door is 33B, but I'm sure there aren't any children living there, Funny, huh? Well, to tell you the truth I think it's crazy. Don't you?"

They were relieved when the woman finally stopped and both looked at the number to the side of her door. The plate was hidden by the branches of a wild ivy vine, and spaced a little bit away from the 33 they saw the *A*, in luminous paint. Maybe this house used to be part of the house next to it, and it was turned into two houses later. That *A* was definitely added later.

"Well, thank you very much. I guess we'll be on our way now," Evert said.

They waved good-bye and walked down the flagstone path to their bikes. The woman with the bare red arms stood looking after them, and so Evert and Noortje got onto their bikes immediately and pedaled out of sight. At the end of the street, near the railroad crossing, they got off and started laughing nervously.

"What a chatterbox, huh?" Noortje said.

"Yeah, she's really something."

"What do we do now?"

"To 33B of course!"

"Yes, but she mustn't see us. Otherwise, she'll get suspicious."

"I've already thought of that. That's why we went this way, so we wouldn't have to pass her house again."

"How clever you are!"

"Yeah, once in a while."

The curtains in the other house were also pulled shut. It looked somehow as if it weren't being lived in. The grass in the yard probably hadn't been cut once the summer before. Long brown blades were growing wildly all over in thick clumps, on the path too. Here there were no flowering crocuses, and a few thorny bushes grew up against the door. They rang the bell and waited. The hollow echoing of the bell was clearly audible outside.

"Try it again," Evert said.

"Oh, my! We were supposed to ring three times!" Noortje said, so now she rang the bell three times in a row. It made quite a din inside the house.

"Did you ring three times in the other place?"

"No, I forgot. You think he might be living there after all?"

"No, I don't think so, and we'll. . . ."

Evert snapped his mouth shut. The door was very slowly being opened, just a crack. A young girl looked at them, not saying anything.

Noortje said nothing either. Suddenly she got scared she might do it all wrong. Evert was poking her in the back. She turned around and nodded at him angrily.

"Now you do it," she whispered.

So Evert said, "Miss, we've come for Nico!" The girl

still didn't say a thing. She looked them both over intently once more and shut the door.

"Hey! What's up?" Noortje said.

"Shh! Let's wait," Evert decided.

And so they did. Not long after the door opened again. A young man was standing there. He was tall and thin, and he had an earnest and yet friendly face. Noortje thought he was probably the same age as Theo, maybe a little older.

Evert asked, "Are you Nico?"

The man nodded. "Yes," he said. "You better come in for a second."

He let them into the hallway. A glass door with a curtain behind it remained shut, so they could see nothing of the rest of the house. There they stood looking at each other. The man smiled.

"OK, let's have it," he said.

"Are you really Nico?" Evert asked again.

"Yes, certainly."

"We have a letter for you from Theo."

Evert pulled the letter out of his pocket and gave it to the man called Nico. The man read the letter a few times very intently. Then he stuffed it into the pocket of his jacket and remained standing there, sunk in thought for a while. The children began to worry that he'd forgotten they were there.

Finally, after a long time, Nico said, "Listen carefully. I'll give you a message for Theo. I don't want to write it down. Remember you should only tell Theo what I'm telling you now.

"Tell him that it may take a while, but that we'll come to get him as soon as we can. One morning a car will drive up to the farm with a red cross painted on its roof. Only a car with a red cross, understand? He mustn't trust any other car. As soon as that car approaches, he should walk up to it and get in. That's all."

"Do you know the way to Klaphek?" Noortje asked.

"Theo has explained it to me in his letter. You needn't worry about that. So, remember carefully: only a car with a red cross painted on it."

"Are you sure it will come in the morning?"

"Why do you ask?"

"Because Theo can't be on the lookout himself. His room is on the other side of the house. So Noortje and I have to be the ones to see the car coming. And we aren't always around in the afternoons. We have to go milking and fetch bread."

"Very well. I'll promise the car will come in the morning. And now you better go, and give my greetings to Theo. Good-bye!"

When he opened the door for them, he shook both their hands. The door was already shut by the time they got to their bikes.

Theo brightened up when they brought him the message from Nico. And then the waiting began.

Keeping an eye on Beech Lane the whole morning wasn't all that simple. They had to do so many other things, and they realized for the first time how busy they actually were. When Evert had to pump water, Noortje could no longer join him going around on the pavement with Browny; she had to stay in front of the house, watching. She helped her father with the two-handed saw but took little rests to gaze out at Beech Lane after every couple of strokes through the moist birchwood.

"What's the matter with you?" Mr. Vanderhook asked. "I'm better off doing it all by myself. Why don't you go find something to do in the kitchen?"

"No," Noortje said.

Her father looked at her, worried. He thought the work was making her tired far too quickly.

"Shall I split some logs?" she asked. That was fine with him, and Noortje set to work with the axe. She swung it high above her head and split the thick logs with one blow right down the middle. Well, now, thought her father, she's quite strong really! Perhaps she just wasn't in the mood for sawing.

But Noortje's problem was that she couldn't keep a good lookout for the car while sawing, whereas now, every time she lifted the axe high above her head, she could take one fast look down the lane.

She was also quite willing to help carry buckets of water to the kitchen and didn't mind at all sitting in front of the kitchen window with Sarah on her lap or playing with Sissy, as long as she could keep taking peeks outside. And when they had to peel potatoes she quarreled with Dinie to get the place near the window.

"My, how restless you are, child," Ma Wolthuis said. "You've got ants in your pants. 'Cause it's spring, I guess."

Noortje had lots of chores in the kitchen that kept her away from the window. She had to give Sarah her bottle, sitting on the farmer's chair near the stove, or she had to change a diaper, which had to be done in the alcove. When it was really necessary she warned Evert it was his turn to stand watch. Evert instantly dropped whatever he was doing, even if his father grumbled about it.

"You lazy kid," Everingen kept saying these days, "you haven't been much use at all lately."

Five days passed that way. But of course, Nico had said it could take a while. But how long was a while? It wasn't easy to get hold of a car; they both knew that very well. And even if one of Theo's friends had one, they still had to find gasoline somewhere.

The sixth day was a Sunday. It was late afternoon and the men had just returned from milking. Henk was still busy with the horse and the milk cans. Everingen came into the kitchen, his head and hair dripping with water. First he dried his face with the towel hung over the stove, and then he grabbed the communal comb off the mantelpiece to comb his wet black-and-gray hair straight back. He hung his cap on the arm of his wicker chair, sat down on the knitted pillow, and said, "Noortje, will you hand Sissy to me?"

The German cook walked past the window outside, whistling a song totally out of tune. They heard him puttering in the scullery with his pans and spoons. Moments later they heard someone else enter the scullery. Both Germans were speaking in loud voices.

The table was already set for their simple supper. Granny and the girls sat waiting in their customary places.

Aunt Janna said, "Noortje can't lift Sissy, Chris. You should do that yourself."

"Ah, but we know she's a strong girl!" said Everingen.

"Oh, yes, I can do it," Noortje said.

She went over to Sissy and put her hands under her arms to pull her up. Sissy was very heavy, much heavier than you would have thought for such a little girl. That was not only because she was so fat, but because she was unwieldy. She hung all her weight upon your arms when you tried to carry her. Still, Noortje managed to lift her out of her crib.

Sissy looked very content, as only Sissy could. She blew a large bubble of spit out of her mouth. And with her wrinkly little hand she grabbed Noortje's cheek, squeezing it, while Noortje held her firmly and carried her over to her father.

Just as she turned toward Everingen she glanced outside. The sun stood low, making the distant trees look golden. They were very beautiful. She heard Rachel barking. Then she saw something near the gate.

Somebody opened the gate. She couldn't see who. It was already dark under the beech trees. Pressing Sissy against her, she lingered in front of the window, taking one more look. A woman in a white dress with a white thing on her head was walking a little way into the meadow.

"How about it?" Everingen asked impatiently. "Don't just stand there, child. Bring Sissy over here!"

Noortje turned around, startled. Without a word she deposited Sissy on her father's knee, soaking wet pants and all, and ran out of the kitchen. She opened the front door, and there she saw very clearly a small car slowly moving through the gate into the meadow. A red cross was painted on its roof. The car made a turn, till it stood facing its front to the lane again. The motor was sputtering. It could be heard quite clearly in the still late afternoon air.

Evert was calmly walking around and around behind the Fox on the pavement near the well. He hadn't noticed anything, of course.

"They're here!" Noortje whispered.

"Who?" he asked, puzzled.

"The car, stupid!"

"Oh!"

He let the horse go on by itself and ran tiptoe to the corner of the house to take a look at the car. Noortje had already gone in through the side entrance. Theo lay on top of his bed, rolled up in a blanket.

"They're here!" she said.

In one jump he was on the floor and without a word he pushed her down the stairs ahead of him. So they emerged. Evert had already checked the front and the back of the house to see if it was safe and clear. He motioned that Theo could come.

"The other side," Noortje whispered. "Go look at the other side, near the pigsty."

And off Evert went, walking in his stocking feet past the front of the house, past the scullery and its open door. He looked beyond the straw pile, checking out the back yard, and waved his arm.

Theo squeezed Noortje's shoulder briefly, very hard. Then, with a few big steps, he was past the woodshed, with the Hungarian still busy at work inside, and swung his thin legs over the wooden gate near the apple tree. He ran through the meadow to the car, which had been waiting all that time near Beech Lane, with its motor sputtering. The nurse had already gotten in. One door of the car was wide open.

Noortje held her breath. Theo could still run fast! Yes, he'd made it. The door slammed shut. The car began to move. They saw it go bouncing up and down over the cart ruts at a good speed. It all had taken no more than five minutes.

As Noortje returned to the kitchen and Evert walked back to the horse, they met each other. But they said nothing. They walked on and both were smiling.

▪22▪ Hide-and-Seek

It was evening. Slowly a car drove up the yard and stopped at the back of the house.

A German officer stepped out. He had a high-peaked cap and was wearing a long raincoat that flapped against his legs in the wind. The driver remained at the wheel. The officer's boots were of smooth black leather. They shone like polished stovepipes. Around his sleeve was a wide band with a swastika on it. And on his nose he wore glasses without rims. Everything about him looked as neat and clean as could be, like his red, smoothly shaven cheeks.

There he stood in the muddy yard, tall and thin. Then suddenly he turned with an abrupt, angular movement toward the other officers. They rushed to greet him, saluting respectfully with deferential faces. Without any expression at all on his face, the strange German saluted back in the Nazi way.

Evert and Noortje had just locked the hens up for the night and collected the eggs that had been laid when the car came around the house. They stood watching in the shadow of the barn.

"See that?" Evert whispered. "He must be a big shot. A general maybe."

"A general? What would he be doing here?"

One of the officers held open the shed door, and the general went in.

"Come on," Evert said, "I want to know what's up." They walked through the front house to the shed and hid behind the wooden partition of the cow shed. If the Germans saw them and didn't want them to watch, they could just pretend they were going to the toilet.

Kerosene lamps were hanging from the beams, spreading a yellowish light, and every little corner of the shed was clearly visible. The soldiers were standing in a row in front of their sleeping places. Everything was spic and span, there was no rubbish lying around anywhere, and the floor had been swept spotless. The men had rolled up their blankets and placed them neatly at the head end of the straw beds; their knapsacks lay at the foot end. They had oiled their boots with black grease that afternoon, and now those boots all shone in the lamplight. They'd also polished the rifles and hung them up on the leather belts, gleaming barrels pointed upward.

The soldiers stared straight ahead, with tightly set faces. All the muscles in their bodies seemed tensed. Noortje and Evert could clearly see the ones standing nearest to them. They saw their Adam's apple go up and down underneath their skin, as if they had a thick ball in their throats that they couldn't swallow.

"What are they going to do now?" Noortje whispered.

"Shh, shut up!"

The officers stood talking to each other in low voices. Suddenly the general wheeled around, and, striding stiffly to the middle of the shed, he let his eye run along a row of waiting soldiers. The officers stood behind him. The general stretched his right arm forward and up at a slant. "*Heil* Hitler!" he barked.

The officers too called out, "*Heil* Hitler!"

As if they were puppets in a puppet theater and their limbs were moved by strings, the arms of those soldiers went up precisely and simultaneously and together in one big voice they said, "*Heil* Hitler!" And *flop*, the arms dropped down again.

Afterward the general began to speak. First his voice was calm and low, and the children couldn't hear what he was saying. Then he got more and more excited, as if he found it marvelous, whatever he had to say to those men. His voice went up and up, and he began to yell louder and louder. His face was turning red. He sweated so much he had to take his cap off and hold his glasses in his hand.

No matter how loudly that general screamed, the children couldn't figure out what he said. It was not only because the words were in German, for they could understand quite a bit of that already, but because his voice was so distorted by his own loud yelling. He worked himself up to such a pitch that his eyes almost popped out. And the veins in his neck were thick and swollen. Abruptly the voice stopped. He clacked his heels together like a pistol shot, set the cap back on his head and the glasses on his nose, raised the right arm again, and cried, "*Sieg Heil!*"

"*Sieg Heil!*" they all shouted back, and still the soldiers stood as stiff as puppets. It had become dead quiet in the shed. *Click clack, click clack* sounded the steps of the general. And the officers, who all that time had been staring ahead with dim, dumb faces, hurried outside after him. A little later they could hear the starting of a motor, and the general's car drove off. The officers strode back in again.

The shed still was very quiet. The soldiers had sat down on the straw. An officer picked out several of them to help carry something.

"What are they up to now?" Noortje asked.

"How should I know?" Evert said. "Wait and see."

They didn't have to wait long to get an idea of what was happening next. Crates of bottles were being carried in and put down in front of the soldiers' sleeping places. It was almost unbelievable how fast those soldiers could drink. They drank as if there were water in those bottles and they were men dying of thirst. Each one took big swigs and passed the bottles around to the man sitting next to him. The bottles were emptied quickly, but more were brought in right away.

The drinking hadn't been going on for more than ten minutes, before the men began shouting and talking all at the same time. One started to sing a song, and others joined in. Soon many were roaring along together. The officers weren't doing any drinking. They just sat on some of the crates, watching.

"They're all getting drunk," Evert said.

"Yes. What do you think is in those bottles?"

"Gin or something . . . brandy, maybe."

"Or wine perhaps?"

"No, wine doesn't get you drunk as fast as that."

"Why do you think they're doing it?"

"Don't know."

They could talk out loud freely now, for the soldiers were making so much noise among themselves that they couldn't hear anything else anyway. But Mr. Vanderhook heard them. He'd already been watching awhile, standing behind the beet-cutting machine. Then he noticed Noortje and Evert hiding in their dark little nook and was angry.

"Are you both out of your minds?" he hissed softly. "What are you doing here? What is happening there is none of your business."

"But . . . what *is* happening?" asked Noortje.

"Off, you two! To the kitchen."

But later that night they had to come to the shed again, for that's where the toilet was. Then they saw all the soldiers were dead drunk. Bottles in hand, one or two still sat singing. But most were just lying there open-mouthed, snoring, and in the strangest postures. There was a foul, acrid smell, for a few had thrown up on their straw beds, and now they lay sleeping face down in their own vomit. One soldier seemed to have gone totally out of his senses. He had placed a tin basin filled with water on the floor and now lay on his stomach with his face in the water. He moved his head from side to side, making strange burbling noises.

Now and then one started crying out in his sleep or singing. There was also a soldier crawling around on all fours, crawling over the other men, and he kept yelling, "*Sieg Heil! Sieg Heil!*" At the far end of the stalls another one was singing the same tune over and over, "And we'll go all the way . . . to England."

The three officers were still sitting on their crates, watching the drunken men. Their faces seemed even more troubled than before.

"Come on, hurry up," said Mr. Vanderhook. "This is not something to be seen by children."

"Oh, but we've already seen it all, and what's so special about a bunch of drunken guys, anyway?"

That night the children slept soundly, but the grown-ups lay awake listening to the noises. What were all those drunken men in the house going to do? Drunken enemy soldiers, and only three officers sober enough to control them! Everingen and Henk had gone to bed with their clothes on. Their clogs stood ready to be slipped into. Aunt Janna lay listening the whole night through, open-eyed, staring into the darkness. She smiled when she heard the peaceful, regular breathing of her husband beside her. Chris is having a good sleep, she thought. Well, it didn't matter. If something happened, she could wake him fast enough.

In the early morning, just before the sun came up, she did hear something. Cautiously climbing out of bed, she went to the kitchen. Mr. Vanderhook was up also, dressed and sitting in front of the window looking out. He'd opened the shutters, but it still was dark in the kitchen. Outside they could hear a soft droning that was coming closer. A few trucks, their headlights dead, drove into the yard and stopped right in the middle.

"What is it?" Aunt Janna whispered.

"Trucks." Mr. Vanderhook nodded. "Is Farmer Everingen asleep?"

"Yes. Let him go on sleeping. As long as nothing is happening."

They saw dark shadows walking in single file, helmeted soldiers, the barrels of their rifles sticking up above their heads. The soldiers climbed into those trucks. Again they heard the droning of the motors, and one after the other the trucks disappeared along Beech Lane.

"The bastards," Aunt Janna said, when it had become silent again. "First they fill them up and get them drunk. Then . . . poor boys!"

"They're off to the front now," Mr. Vanderhook said. "That's what the general was screaming about in his speech."

"Did you hear it all?"

"Yes, I was standing next to the pump and could hear everything. And then later I found Noortje and Evert hiding behind the partition. Those two kids are getting quite an education, aren't they?"

"Yes, they're old and wise for their age," Aunt Janna said.

They stayed at the window, sitting in silence. The birds were singing already in the apple trees. Very slowly the sky turned a light purplish color. It was time to wake up Everingen and Henk.

Evert and Noortje and Gerrit spent that whole morning in the shed. Everingen was removing the dirty straw, and Henk wheeled it away to the muck heap. The children poked around in all the nooks and crannies, searching for things the soldiers might have left behind. The Germans may have been blind drunk, but they didn't miss much in packing up their gear. There was hardly anything to be found. A brown basin, a few spoons, a tin of boot grease, and that was all . . . if you didn't count the many cartridges that all three children soon had their bulging pockets stuffed with. They found them in the weirdest spots: small cracks in the walls, in between the boards above the stalls, and even in the hayracks of the horses. And there was also a stack of beautifully shiny blue paper, which they'd used to cover the upper partitioning to black out light coming through it.

"Nice," Noortje said. "We'll make beautiful things out of this paper later."

"Aw, can't we make some beautiful things now, Noor?" asked Gerrit.

"No, later. Or, do you know what? I'll fold a blue Napoleon hat for each of us." A few minutes later the three of them were walking around each crowned with a blue three-cornered hat.

"How classy you all look," Henk said. "Are you going to the queen's birthday party perhaps?"

Evert felt a little childish with his paper hat on, and so he gave it to Gerrit, who slapped it right on top of his other hat and so had two. Evert was disappointed. He'd thought he would find some new weapons for his collection. "C'mon, let's take a look near their latrines too."

"Ugh, no!"

"Don't be such a baby. There's a good chance they lost something there, maybe something super."

The three children went off to the latrines. The German soldiers had not been allowed to use the Klaphek toilet, and in the wood next to the Calves' Meadow they'd dug a deep, rectangular hole. From a few young trees they'd built a sort of platform to sit on. Two long trees with a little space between them, and one a little higher than the other, ran at each side of the hole. They were attached to upright little poles. The children looked into the pit.

"Ugh, how filthy. It stinks here," Gerrit said.

Yes, it did, and how could it help but stink. There were also lots of flies.

"Well, I must say, they really lost something 'super' here." Noortje laughed.

"Do you dare sit on it?" Evert asked.

"Are you crazy? Forget it. Imagine falling in!"

"Why? The Krauts didn't fall in."

Sometimes they had actually peeked at the soldiers when they were sitting there. None of them seemed bothered by a few small children watching. Sometimes they were seated four in a row, their pants down, smoking a cigarette and talking to each other. Evert decided not to try it out after all. They searched all around the pit, between the thin, tough grass and the blackberry bushes, but they found nothing. No knife, no helmet, no bullets. What a pity!

It was a lovely, quiet day. The farm was just as peaceful as before the Germans had come and been quartered there. Once in a while some visitor came to the door to buy some milk. There was a cold wind blowing, and that was good in a way, because now the soggy, trampled-on earth of the yard had a chance to dry up some. All the marching around the house the past few weeks had changed the thawing fields into a muddy mess.

"Shall we play hide-and-seek in the woods this afternoon?" Noortje suggested. "Evert, you mark a trail, and Gerrit and I will track you down."

"You'd better not tell anyone," Evert warned. "They probably wouldn't allow it."

"But you'll come?"

"It's OK with me."

They hadn't played hide-and-seek for ages, not once during the whole winter. In autumn, when Noortje had just arrived at Klaphek, they'd played it almost every day.

Evert went off in the afternoon with a piece of blue paper in his pocket. On the way he tore off strips, which he stuck onto the branches. A few times he drew a large arrow in the sand. Noortje set out fifteen minutes later. They could see the bits of blue paper easily, even from a distance. Evert hadn't made the trail too hard, and soon Noortje and Gerrit came to the edge of the heath.

"Is this the right way, Noor?" Gerrit asked.

"Oh, yes, this is right."

"Do you think Evert went all the way to Zemst?"

"Ah, no, dummy, we're staying close to the woods."

They walked over the heath, following the edge of the wood, but now there were no more arrows or pieces of paper.

"Someone's coming, a man on a bike," Gerrit said.

The man came closer, and they saw he was Munkie. He swerved wildly from side to side while doing his best to keep his balance on the bike. The path was very narrow, and there were lots of holes in it. Many of them were full of water, and the path was slick and slippery. Munkie had a burlap sack hanging on the handlebars. He was probably out looking for food again. There weren't many people who wanted to help him. His bike made a rattling noise as if something was loose, for there were no tires around the wheel rims. And he had no place behind his seat for putting things.

"Hi!" he said.

"Hi, Munkie!" Gerrit cried. "Did you see Evert, maybe?"

Munkie got off and looked at them questioningly.

"Evert," said Noortje loudly, "have you seen Evert?"

"Brudder?" Munkie asked.

Gerrit and Noortje nodded, and Munkie pointed behind him across the heath.

"Brudder dere," he said.

"Thanks a lot," Noortje said, and she took Gerrit by the hand, marching on with great determination. They found no more clues. Gerrit removed his hand and started wandering all over the heath, picking up pieces of silver paper that were lying on the bushes. He thought they must be clues also, but Noortje told him that the silver paper was dropped by English planes to disrupt radio messages.

"That's nice of the English, right?" said Gerrit. "They're on our side. Remember, Noor, when we made those beautiful silver balls out of this stuff for the Christmas tree?"

Noortje nodded silently. Even Christmas seemed a long time ago now, more like years instead of a few months.

"Yes, Gerrit, the English are good to us. They are coming to chase away the Germans," she said.

Noortje felt uneasy walking across the heath all alone

with Gerrit. You could see a great distance, true, but you also could be seen from all sides. Walking out in the open this way wasn't very smart. She grabbed Gerrit's fat, warm, little hand and pulled him. "Come on, we're going back in the woods. I'm sure Evert stayed in there."

For a long time they walked behind each other along the narrow, winding paths, staring at the ground, looking for arrows in the sand. This wood was like the Eighth Wood. Here too there were all sorts of different kinds of trees, with bushes between them and a thick layer of dead leaves and dead branches covering the ground. Gerrit began to get tired. He kept stumbling, or he would lose one of his clogs, and then she had to wait for him.

"Phew! That's what I call a real walk," Gerrit said.

Noortje thought, He talks just like a little old man. Boys are sometimes totally nutty. Sarah will never be like that. Suddenly they came to the edge of the wood. The path stopped, and before them was a deep, dry ditch with heather bushes growing in it. They let themselves slide to the bottom and climbed up the other side. There they saw a wide valley. In the distance, on top of the hills, was the churchyard, and more toward the south they could see the spire of the church in Zemst sticking out above the trees of the Klinger Wood. A bit farther up on the hill was an enormous oak tree standing at the edge of the ditch. It was so very thick that it must have been hundreds of years old.

"Take a good look at what a fat giant this one is, Gerrit. I can't even put my arms all the way around it," Noortje said, as she pressed herself against the rough wrinkled trunk and embraced it. Gerrit clambered up the slippery side of the ditch and also spread his little arms out. They could almost touch hands.

From above them, they heard a laugh. They looked up and there was Evert, sitting on a thick branch.

"You were lost," he cried. "I saw you two, all the way out on the heath. I've won, I've won! Who were you talking to out there?"

"Munkie. He said he'd seen you. Hey! Watch out!"

The same instant she called out Noortje dropped down into the ditch and pulled Gerrit with her onto the ground.

There were airplanes, airplanes flying so low over the wood it seemed they were touching the treetops. Evert slid down out of the tree and without saying a word crept up next to them. They pressed down flat against the ticklish heather.

Sometimes you get the oddest thoughts in your head at the strangest moments. While she was lying there Noortje thought, What a sweet smell heather has, and how beautiful it is here. I must be crazy to be thinking that now!

Cautiously they stuck their heads up above the rim of the ditch. There were four planes flying so low over the heath that they could see the pilots sitting inside in their glass bubbles. They also saw the propellers turning, and the motors were making a terrific noise. Letters were painted on the bellies of the planes.

"English," whispered Evert.

When the planes were over Zemst, they dove down even further, and it looked as if they started to fly more slowly. Then, very clearly, they saw a door opening in the bottom of the plane. Bombs came dropping out, a string of bombs connected to each other by chains. They were big, black things, and came down slowly in a slanted, uneven line. As soon as the bombs were out, the door snapped shut again; the planes zoomed off, noses pointed upward, and disappeared into the distance. The whole attack hadn't lasted more than a few minutes.

They heard a thundering, and a black cloud of smoke rose up, somewhere beyond the Klinger woods. Only then did the sirens of the air-raid alarm start wailing.

"Will they come back?" Gerrit asked.

"Don't know. We'd better wait a while longer," Evert decided.

They stayed in the ditch for quite a while, looking out over the heath; they were sheltered from the wind there, and the earth was dry. The branches of the old tree above them were moving from one side to the other, creaking. Behind them in the woods, birds were singing. The airplanes did not come back. They heard the sirens one more time: the all-clear signal telling them it was safe to come out.

"That was a beautiful sight, wasn't it?" Evert said, getting up and scratching his head. "Ai, it itches! All that sand in my hair."

Noortje looked at him. "Yes," she said, "it was a beautiful sight. But it was terrible too, Evert. How can it be both?"

"Oh, Noor, there are so many terrible things. Come on, we'll take the short way home."

No one had been looking for them at Klaphek. The grown-ups were sitting together looking very distraught again when Evert and Noortje and Gerrit entered.

"Let's go, and you two come along," Everingen said in an angry voice. "You've got to go milking. Hurry up, it's late already."

"What's going on?" Noortje asked, looking from one to the next.

"Nothing, child, finish your milk quickly. Farmer Everingen is waiting for you."

"Will you see to Sarah for me?"

"Yes, I will."

And yet there was something wrong; she could feel it. "Has something happened?" she asked, between two sips of milk.

"There are Germans in the shed again. That's all."

"Again?"

"Yes, and even more of them than before. You'll see them soon enough. Off you go now." The trip to the meadow on the Ijssel river was made in total silence.

▪23▪ The Boy Soldiers

What kind of soldiers were these? They hardly seemed much older than Evert! What a sight, those boys in their uniforms and their much-too-heavy boots! They must have had special trousers and coats made for them back in their own country. True, some were already as tall as grown men, but how spindly they were, with gangly legs and arms. And the short ones among them were a little fat. Their round, childish faces above the stiff collars took in the world with set, earnest expressions. They looked at the farm, the people, and the animals, and it seemed as if they didn't see anything at all and they didn't care where they were. These soldiers were not noisy; they didn't yell and they didn't sing. Very quietly they sat on top of their knapsacks, eating their hunks of dark bread.

This time there were five accompanying officers, and they brought all sorts of strange stuff into the parlor room. They set up field beds and radios and transmitters there. All night long the farm people could hear their voices talking into the microphone. Wolthuis and Mr. Vanderhook sat with their ears pressed against the door, listening.

"I think that somewhere around here there's a lookout station, at a high point," Mr. Vanderhook whispered. "They're relaying messages."

"Listen, do you hear? Now he's reading something," Wolthuis muttered. "Twenty-five tanks, he says, forty-three armored cars, twelve cannons, eighty trucks. . . . What could that mean?"

"You know what I think?" Mr. Vanderhook said. "I think their contacts at the lookout station must be able to see the Allies approaching. Maybe they're already very close, on the other side of the Ijssel."

The next morning the milkers discovered the lookout post. As the first rays of the sun colored the heath a pinkish rose, they drove over the hard gravel road that ran past Dassen Mountain. And there, on top, where the white-colored paths met and where all winter long beehives had stood underneath the birch trees, they saw busy dark figures with large binoculars. And someone up there was sitting on a crate doing something with a piece of equipment.

"Those Krauts over there are in touch with the Krauts in our house," Henk said. "They can't be too far off now."

"Yes," Everingen said, "yes, but in order to get to us they'll have to cross Ijssel!"

That morning all the young soldiers were sent out with shovels in their hands. They were scattered all over the yard and the meadow, up to the gate, and began to dig. Each soldier dug a round hole as wide as a potato basket. They threw up the yellow clumps of earth, forming a wall around the hole. Toward noon most of them had already gotten so far they could stand in their holes up to the waist.

"There goes our meadow, Mother," Everingen said. "When all this is over, we'll have to sow it anew."

"Still, I wonder what the meaning of this can be," Ma Wolthuis put in. "Did you see what boys they are? They're children, mere children! It's a shame, that's what it is."

"Poor monkeys," Granny said. But it wasn't certain if she had quite understood which children they were talking about, and no one took the trouble to explain to her.

Alie and Dinie sat around the kitchen all day. They were afraid of the new officers, who were much older than the officers they had in their house the first time. Somehow, they thought, these were much fiercer looking. When the radio in the parlor was silent, the officers went outside and sat in front of the open window. They would try to strike up a conversation with whomever came by then. But they didn't get much of a chance. No one felt like socializing.

Noortje went looking for Evert. She was at loose ends that day. The atmosphere in the house seemed strange, outside it was even more so, and she didn't know what to do with herself. There was something in the air, as if something important were about to happen soon. She saw Evert and Henk next to the straw pile, talking to one of the soldiers who was busy digging his hole deeper and deeper.

"Henk," she asked, "why are they digging those holes?"

Henk gave no answer. Shaking his head, with pity in his face, he said to the soldier, "Ah, young fellow, it won't last much longer now. Do you understand me?"

The youngster had plump, rosy cheeks, and there were drops of sweat on his nose because of the heavy work.

"Me is afraid," he said, and it was very strange to hear a soldier speak with the voice of a child. "Me is very terrible afraid. The English so near close . . . we all go to die. . . ."

"Oh, no," Henk said, "no, no, you needn't! It will all soon be over now. Then you can go home. You go home then . . . you understand?"

The young soldier sniveled like a child and wiped his nose with the back of his hand. A few big tears went rolling down his cheeks.

"My mama. . . ." he stammered.

"How old are you?" Henk asked kindly.

"I sixteen, one month ago I sixteen."

Henk kept shaking his head. He didn't know what else to say to the boy. Therefore, he only said, "Courage, keep it up!" and he turned around and walked away. Evert and Noortje left too.

"How odd, for such a big boy to stand there crying like a little kid," Noortje said. In her eyes a boy of sixteen was as good as grown-up.

"Well, and how would you like it if you knew you were going to be shot at soon?" Evert asked angrily.

"Oh, come on, he shouldn't stay here then. Why doesn't he run away, like Munkie?"

"Sometimes, Noor, you can say very stupid things."

Noortje looked at Evert, astonished. She'd never heard him talk like that before. Suddenly she saw that Evert had rosy-red cheeks just like the crying soldier's. Evert would be thirteen in a month. Sixteen or thirteen, she thought, what's the difference really? How would it be if Evert had to dig such a hole somewhere, far away from home while nearby a big army was approaching with guns and tanks?

"Evert, why are they digging those holes in the ground?"

"That boy told us. They call them foxholes. When the English come, they all have to sit in their own hole and empty their guns at the enemy."

"And then? What happens when their guns are empty?"

"Mmm, well, I guess. . . . How should I know?"

Evert seemed to be a little angry with her still. Noortje went back to the kitchen. No one was there, and the trapdoor to the cellar stood open.

"Aunt Janna, are you in there?" she called.

No answer. She sat down on a chair in front of the window and looked at Baby Sis. Sissy lay on her back, sleeping very quietly. The sun was touching her nose, but it didn't wake her. She had round, ruddy little cheeks, and under her eyes were small bluish rings. Noortje noticed them for the first time.

Poor little Sissy, she thought. Actually, Sarah was much better off, even though her father and mother and her little brothers would never come back. Sarah could still have a really nice life later; she was so pretty and so sweet and so sunny. But Sissy always cried, every single day. She was only happy when she sat on her father's or mother's lap, or when Evert played with her. Sometimes Evert could be very sweet to Sissy, playing with her hands and her feet as if she were a normal little child.

Sissy was already seven . . . you could hardly believe it. Oh, what a bad smell there was again around her bed, Noortje thought. Why was it that Sissy's diapers smelled so very awful, while Sarah's weren't so bad at all? Ah, yes, that was probably because her number ones and twos weren't so big yet. Till now the only thing she took in was milk or porridge. When Sarah was as big as Sissy, she would have been toilet-trained long ago and never wet her pants.

The door swung open, and Ma Wolthuis entered with her arms full of pillows and blankets. Alie and Dinie followed after, dragging a large straw bag between them. They could hardly get through the door with it.

"Just let it drop down the stairs," Ma Wolthuis said. "I'll go and fix it up down below. Hurry up, the rest too!"

The girls rolled the mattress down the cellar stairs and started to leave the kitchen again.

"What are you doing?" Noortje asked.

"None of your business," they answered.

Noortje decided not to say anything. That's how it always went, but sooner or later she always found out anyhow what was going on. She just sat there quietly, watching the Wolthuis family carry all their belongings to the cellar. Granny came in too, with the large bag in which she kept her things. She sat down next to Noortje, taking a little rest.

"Granny, what are you all doing?" Noortje asked.

"We're going to sleep in the cellar tonight."

"Why? Is everyone going into the cellar tonight? Us too?"

"Well, child, I don't know what your father's plans are. But if he has any sense left at all, he'll join us in the cellar too. And you should definitely go, you and your baby."

"But why? Because of the V-1's?"

"Yes, those V-1's. They've been terrible again lately. I haven't closed an eye for a single solitary night."

"But the V-1's have been going all winter."

"Haven't you noticed them getting worse and worse, night after night? And one never can tell what else is going to happen. . . ." Granny talked on, whispering, as if afraid the Germans might hear what she was saying. "There are so many Krauts in the house, and they are expecting the end too. Wolthuis has heard it himself. Maybe they're going to fight for this very house, maybe this very night. . . ."

Before it got too dark in the cellar to do anything, Aunt Janna had made some beds on the floor there for Evert and Gerrit and for Noortje and herself. Everingen and Henk carried Sissy's crib down. The crib was placed against the wall behind the cellar stairs.

"That's right," Aunt Janna said, satisfied. "That's a safe spot for our little girlie. Oh, yes, it's the best spot in the house, don't you worry. And even if a bomb were to fall right into the kitchen, nothing bad can happen to you here. . . ."

After Theo left, Mr. Vanderhook had taken over the maid's room. He was very glad to be in a real bed again, no longer having to sleep on a couple of chairs in the kitchen. At supper Granny asked, "Mr. Vanderhook, are you going to sleep in the cellar tonight too?"

"No," said Noortje's father, "I wouldn't dream of it. As long as there's no actual fighting going on here, I don't want to. I'm not afraid of the V-1's; I've grown used to them by now."

"You won't see me in the cellar either!" Everingen said. "I won't let myself be chased down into my own cellar, not by anyone. Not by the Germans, and not by the English either!"

"Ah, but Chris. . . ." Aunt Janna started. But Everingen didn't want to say another word about it.

And so they slept in the cellar that night for the first time: the Wolthuis family and Granny, Aunt Janna and the children. Sarah's basket stood on the floor next to Sissy's crib. They didn't hear a single sound in the cellar the whole night long. It was a quiet night, and yet no one slept very well. So many people were packed together in a small space that no one could turn over without waking one of the others. Wolthuis grumbled and gave off heavy sighs all the time, and Granny and Ma Wolthuis seemed to be having a snoring contest. When they got up early next morning, none of them felt very rested.

"Well, did you all have a nice, long sleep?" Mr. Vanderhook asked mockingly. No one answered him.

The following evening Noortje said to Aunt Janna, "As long as Sarah is safe with you in the cellar, I don't really care. There's so little space for us all that I'm going to sleep with my father tonight."

"If he agrees to it, Noor, it's up to you," Aunt Janna said.

Noortje climbed the stairs to Theo's room that evening and lay next to her father in the big bed. Now she had lots more space than down below in the cellar. That was more like it. Nice and cozy. Only just the two of them in a room. It was almost as if everything were normal again, like the old days.

"Nice, huh, us lying here?" she said.

"Yes, dear," her father said. "I'm glad you are so brave and dared come up here. Those Wolthuis people are an odd bunch, really."

Outside the window they saw the clear, starry sky. And then they heard the sound of a V-1 in the distance.

"You're not afraid of the V-1 either, right?" Noortje asked.

"No, I'm not. Chances are very small that one of them would land here, on this house of all places. And since we've already had one hit nearby, those chances have become even smaller."

"But how can you know that?"

"You can't know for sure. But there is such a thing as the theory of probability; it's possible to figure out mathematically the degree of risk we run."

"And did you figure it out?"

She heard her father laugh softly. Meanwhile, the V-1 had come closer. She saw its fiery trail go through the dark night sky. It was far away and held no danger. But a long time passed before the sound died in the distance.

"I can't figure it out," her father said. "I'm not a mathematician. But I do know it's possible, for I've worked with an insurance company all my life. In our office, they compute all sorts of things very precisely. How much chance someone has of getting sick, for example. You can insure yourself against such things, even against the chances of rain during your holidays."

Noortje thought it was funny that her father could talk so calmly about things that had absolutely nothing to do with the war, as if nothing special were going on, even now, when just the two of them were alone in this room, away from all the others in the house.

They heard another V-1 coming, this one really far off, but they couldn't even see its light.

"Did Farmer Everingen figure it out too?" she asked. "Is that why he doesn't sleep in the cellar?"

"Now with Everingen it's something else entirely. He believes in God. He thinks it's a sin to be afraid, when all things are in God's hand."

"I don't understand. Such terrible things happen in a war, bombs falling and everything."

"Certainly, and yet Everingen believes everything that happens is God's will."

"Well, God's will isn't much fun these days."

Noortje's father had nothing to say to that. Perhaps he didn't quite understand it himself, she thought.

"And Aunt Janna?" she asked. "She believes in God too, doesn't she? She prays even longer than Mr. Everingen before dinner."

"It's different with Aunt Janna," her father said. "I don't think she's afraid for herself. But she is worried about the children, especially Sissy."

Noortje suddenly had to yawn tremendously. "I wouldn't feel very peaceful here either, if Sarah weren't in the cellar."

They were quiet for a long time. The window gleamed against the dark night. There wasn't a single sound in the house, till Noortje's father started talking again, "Perhaps you think I'm forgetting your birthday, Noor," he said. "But that's not the case. The day after tomorrow you'll be twelve. I'm very frustrated that I can't give you a present."

"Ah, don't be silly. I don't mind!"

"Yes, well, we're not much in the mood for parties now, I guess," her father continued. "I could give you money, of course, for I still have some. But what use would that be to you? Why don't you just keep in mind that as soon as the war is over, and everything is more or less back to normal, you'll be getting a real birthday party. And a wonderful present. What would you like to have?"

"How should I know now? Let's just wait and see, huh?"

Noortje's eyes had closed, and a little later she was in a deep sleep.

▪24▪
In the Cellar

And yet Noortje did get a birthday present after all on the morning of April ninth, the day she became twelve.

The table was set for breakfast. The soup plates were on the brown oilcloth. A pan of steaming porridge made of rye flour stood on the stove. The whole kitchen smelled of it, a dry, hearty smell. Next to Noortje's plate on a small dish lay freshly picked green leaves and little yellow flowers, and atop that cheerful little bed of crowfoot was a huge egg.

"For your birthday, Noortje," Aunt Janna said. "You can eat the whole egg. It's for you."

"What a big egg! Is it real?" Noortje asked in amazement.

"It's a goose egg," said Aunt Janna. "The geese are laying now. And so I thought that we may as well eat a few, for there'll be plenty left for hatching."

"Happy birthday, Noortje!" said Everingen, taking his seat, and Evert and Gerrit both shook her hand, somewhat shyly.

Henk came in, cheerfully calling out, "Happy birthday, princess of the pea! Oh, no, princess of the egg, I should say!"

It was a splendid day. The dandelions were already flowering in the meadow, and the hawthorn hedge had put out its curly leaves. The old plum tree in the middle of the Calves' Meadow grew pink blossoms on its naked black branches. The buds on the beech tree were open.

After breakfast, Noortje sat down in the grass with her egg. She had already finished a whole plateful of porridge, and after a few bites of the egg she felt as if she were going to explode. It was a good thing Gerrit came by to help her eat it.

The goat had been tethered in front of the house on a long rope. Her stomach was all round and swollen up, and the young ones could be born any day now.

Even the hens and geese seemed to be enjoying spring. They made a lot more of a fuss than usual. Two cocks were fighting. They jumped on each other's necks while the hens cackled with excitement, each one thinking the cocks were fighting for her. The soil wasn't so hard anymore, so now they could work at pulling out fat worms from between the grass blades. The hens had set to laying eggs again, and the last few days Evert carried dishes full of eggs into the kitchen.

There was no wind, and the sun warmed the earth. The sparrows carried on their noisy business as if they were the only ones in the world. The boy-soldiers had nothing to do. They were bored and sat in small groups, talking. Their faces no longer showed the anxious fear of the first few days.

That's how it was at Klaphek, the morning of Noortje's birthday.

But in the evening everything changed. Evert came back from the hen house emptyhanded. There were no eggs in the nests.

"The Krauts must have done it," he said. "I'll go over and ask."

"You won't do anything of the sort," his father said.

It was already dark when someone knocked on the kitchen door. Everingen went out. A few minutes later he came back with a worried face.

"Mother," he said, "prepare some food for me. I have to ride for them."

"Even now? That too!" Aunt Janna cried, frightened.

"Yes, and I've got to hurry. They're in a big rush. Henk, give me a hand. I'll take the flat wagon."

"Why don't you let me go?" Henk said.

"You stay here. There's got to be a man in the house."

That didn't flatter Mr. Vanderhook and Mr. Wolthuis, but neither of them said anything.

Everingen did not return home that night. The children were quietly asleep in the cellar. The Wolthuis family slept too. Mr. Vanderhook and Noortje were asleep in Theo's room. But Aunt Janna couldn't sleep.

Long before it got light outside she was up and opening the entrance to the cellar without disturbing anyone. Quietly she poked up the fire in the stove. She opened the shutters, then sat down on a chair near the window.

And there she waited. The night was unnaturally still. There were no airplanes, and not a single V-1 came flying over. She was so used to hearing sounds from the sky that this silence oppressed her.

Yes, but now she did hear something. It sounded far away, a low rumbling like a storm in the distance. It was like hearing the thunder coming on a hot summer night.

A thunderstorm? she thought, at this time of the year? And so she went outside to check the weather. The night air was fresh, and the sky dry and clear. An owl flew by, low to the ground, searching for its prey. A small animal made a rustling noise close to the house. A weasel, maybe. Aunt Janna didn't care where that sound was coming from; it probably was a mouse. She stood still, listening.

And again she heard that strange, distant rumble. All of a sudden, there, above where the Ijssel flowed, the sky was lit up by two searchlights, huge beams crossing one another and then disappearing. Now it seemed even darker, and the rumbling became more clearly audible.

No, it definitely was not a thunderstorm. This sound rose and subsided in waves but never entirely stopped. And the longer she stood outside, the more clearly she heard it.

Aunt Janna shivered with cold and went back inside again to sit at the window. She sat until it got light and the day's work began. Evert had to go join Henk that morning at milking the cows. Farmer Everingen still had not returned. One by one the people brought their sleepy faces into the kitchen. Aunt Janna said nothing as she calmly did her work at the stove. She let the girls go fetch water and gave Noortje the bottle to feed Sarah.

"What is that noise I hear?" Ma Wolthuis asked. She was the first to notice that strange sound.

"Something rumbling in the distance," Aunt Janna said. "It began long before sunrise."

All were quiet for a moment, listening. It sounded much louder now than during the night. "Cannons!" Wolthuis cried. "They're coming closer!"

At that moment Mr. Vanderhook stepped into the kitchen. "Good morning, everyone," he said in his usual voice, which was always a trifle solemn. But now even Mr. Vanderhook looked quite excited.

"Have you heard it too?" he asked. "Cannons and grenades. The front is advancing. It's very close."

Wolthuis and his wife gave no answer. Aunt Janna had glanced at him only briefly. Now Mr. Vanderhook turned inquisitively to her. He saw that something was bothering her.

"Anything wrong?" he asked.

"Farmer Everingen hasn't returned yet," she said softly. And then she lifted the steaming hot pan of porridge onto the table and started dishing it out with the ladle.

"I could have told you that!" Wolthuis cried out. "It

was the stupidest thing he could have done, going himself. Hah! Why couldn't he let Henk go?"

"Will you please, for just this once, keep your big trap shut?" Mr. Vanderhook said. "Everingen is the one who makes the decisions around here."

Wolthuis's face twisted with anger. He strode out of the kitchen and slammed the door shut behind him with a loud bang. Mr. Vanderhook turned to Aunt Janna again.

"I wouldn't be too worried yet," he said. "There could be many explanations for why he's late. As long as we don't know anything, there's no reason to be anxious."

Aunt Janna smiled. She said nothing.

The morning went by very slowly. Coffee time had passed, and the pot with their midday dinner was already on the fire. And Everingen still had not come back. Life went on as if nothing was wrong. The sound of the cannons was still there to be heard, but by now they were all so worried they forgot to listen.

They were sitting eating their potato hash in silence when the door opened. They hadn't heard a sound in the passageway. It was Farmer Everingen. As usual, he'd padded over the stone floor in his socks.

"Oh, my, what a night!" he said, flopping down in his own chair. He nodded at his wife, took his cap off, folded his hands underneath the cap, and shut his eyes.

The others sat waiting in silence until he had finished saying his prayers. Then Aunt Janna dished him out a big plateful, and still not a word was said. They let him eat quietly first. And while Everingen was having his meal, Aunt Janna read a page from the Bible. Then he told them what had happened.

The Germans had ordered him to take a wagonload of their things to a station somewhere in the woods near Beekbergen. They'd gone over Heuven Hill. Although it was dark already, he saw the artillery positioned there and thought he could also make out tents. The trip through the woods had been without any incidents. He hadn't exchanged a single word with the German soldiers who rode with him, not a one during all those hours. But on the way back something happened to him that he wouldn't have imagined possible. There, in the Unholy Woods, he'd gotten lost! For hours he'd driven around with his horse and wagon, perhaps going in a small circle all that time. Not one single tree seemed familiar, not a single clearing in the woods. That had been most strange, for he thought he knew those woods better than anyone. He didn't find his way back till it began to get light. And then it turned out he was right back near the spot where he'd dropped off the Germans!

"But you know, it's very beautiful there in the woods at night," he said, laughing. "Only I kept hearing the rumblings of a thunderstorm in the distance. And that was very strange, for the sky was clear. First I thought I only imagined it or that I was losing some of my marbles. But I'm positive I heard it. Now I'm going to take a nap for half an hour."

Every day the roar of the guns came a little closer. Sometimes it was completely silent for a few hours; then they would listen anxiously to see if it had started again. And sometimes it seemed as if the distance was increasing again. "It's not getting anywhere," they said to one another. "It's not really moving! How long is this going to last?"

The milkers were bringing back good news. They saw an almost continuous stream of German armored cars on the main road going north—trucks with soldiers, troops of horses, and marching columns slowly trudging onward in silence with heavy packs.

A few days later the shooting sounded awfully close, right across the Ijssel. Evert and Noortje weren't allowed to go out in the milk wagon anymore. Everingen and Henk went by themselves, every morning and every evening. No matter what was going on the cows had to be milked.

A few more days passed. They were all sitting in the cellar one evening, except for Everingen. He was in his own bed asleep, or perhaps he was only pretending to be sleeping.

The shooting was continuous. No silences now. The English were aiming at the German position on Heuven Hill. Sissy and Gerrit and Sarah were quiet.

"Those are grenades," Wolthuis said. Nobody answered.

They could hear the guns booming very clearly. How close they were now! There was a whistling sound as a grenade skimmed over the roof, and right afterward a loud bang. The house was shaking and trembling. Another grenade . . . the whistling . . . then boom! The shuddering impact. The terrible noises followed one another faster and faster. Aunt Janna stood listening at the bottom of the stairs.

"Get away from there, woman," Ma Wolthuis said. "They're shooting at the house. If one of them hits, that's the least safe spot."

Aunt Janna didn't say anything. She looked up the stairs, to where her husband lay in his bed in the alcove. Suddenly the cellar door was yanked open. A pair of booted legs stumbled down the steps. A strange German soldier without a helmet stood among them, without a gun or a rifle, looking wildly around.

"I'm not going back anymore!" he screamed. "I'm not! I'm not!"

He was still very young, a young soldier scared to death.

They'd never seen him before. He couldn't belong to the soldiers who had been in the shed. Leaning against the wall, he slid down to the floor, put his arms on his knees, and with his face pressed into his sleeve started sobbing.

"Oh, my, the poor boy," Granny said, and she sat down on the floor next to the soldier. "Don't you worry. You don't have to be afraid," she whispered. "You can stay here."

The soldier looked around, frightened. "Five bullets they gave me," he cried. "Five bullets and a rifle! Nothing else! And then a tank came right up to me. What can five bullets do against a tank?"

"A tank?" Wolthuis whispered, as if to himself. "A tank, right near here?" And he asked the soldier, "Where was that?"

"Where?" the soldier answered. "I don't know . . . exactly. Around Zemst. I was in the forest. Then suddenly there was the tank . . . an English one!"

"Don't worry, boy. It's all right," Granny said.

The soldier started laughing, a strange, loud laugh. Wolthuis cried out all excited, "Then they're already in the Klinger Woods! They're coming!"

The soldier said, "I shot into the air, and then I ran away. And I didn't keep my rifle anymore either."

Suddenly he jumped up again, grabbed his fly, and gestured he had to go very urgently. As fast as she could, Granny got up and took the chamber pot out from underneath the stairs.

"Here you are, my boy," she said. To the others, she added, "The poor thing's so scared that he's peeing in his pants."

Because the trapdoor was still open, the wick in the oil glass that stood among the empty preserve jars on the shelf was moving wildly back and forth, and the flame created strange, huge shadows on the walls. The soldier had turned around, and with his back to them he urinated in the chamber pot. Then he sank down into a squat again, dozing off, his head leaning back.

Moments later his eyes opened wide, and glaring he cried, "Let them send Hitler to the front! I'm not going anymore!" And lolling his head from side to side against the wall, half-asleep, he muttered, "Let him go, let him find out for himself what it's like . . . no more for me . . . I'm not . . . going."

Everingen had left his bed. He looked in through the opening to the cellar. "What's all this racket?" Can't a man ever get a good night's rest?" he asked.

"Ah, Chris," Aunt Janna said. "Come down here, please."

They couldn't hear his answer as a grenade exploded very close by. Not much farther away than Beech Lane.

"Who's down there?" Everingen asked, when they could hear him again.

"A German, a fugitive. Now will you come down?"

"I won't let myself be locked up in my own cellar because of the Krauts, even a hundred thousand of them. You know that very well, Mother," he grumbled.

"But don't you hear how close they are?"

"Don't you worry about me, Janna. Our lives are in the hands of the Lord."

They heard him stumble back into bed above. Henk let the trapdoor fall shut. It was better this way, for the smashings of the grenades sounded less loud now. The soldier got up a few more times to use the chamber pot.

"The poor boy, he's all strung out," Granny explained once more.

Henk sat dozing on the steps. His eyes were shut, and he was breathing deeply. Noortje sat down close to him.

That was a good spot, she thought. Now she could see into Sarah's basket. Look at the little thing, quietly sleeping through all this uproar!

"Henk, are you asleep?" Noortje whispered.

"Huh, uh? What'd you say?" said Henk, pretending she had startled him out of his sleep. He stretched and yawned. "Why did you wake me up?" he asked. "I was just having the most wonderful dream."

"What was it about?"

"I dreamed . . . of a very beautiful princess!"

Noortje laughed. Things weren't as bad as they seemed after all, even though there was such a dreadful clamor going on outside. And she lay down in the space between Gerrit and Sarah's basket and tried to get some sleep. But sleep was out of the question. The grenades flew over the house faster and faster, and the antiaircraft guns on Heuven Hill responded to the shooting.

A few hours past midnight the trapdoor was yanked up again. A German officer came down some of the steps and looked inside. He saw the soldier, sitting there asleep with his mouth open, leaning against Granny. "Ah, there he is!" he cried. "I heard that one of them had gone in here. He has to come with me!"

Perhaps that frightened boy reminded Granny of one of her own who had left her house so long ago. She was so concerned about him, as if he were the only thing she cared about. Very carefully, and without waking the boy, she got up and said to the officer pleadingly, "Ah, sir, let the poor youngster be. We don't mind his being here. He's all right. And the war is almost over anyway, isn't it?"

The officer didn't understand her, and yet he knew what she meant.

"Yes, but it's impossible," he said, looking a little bit

embarrassed. The soldier had awakened and jumped to attention.

"You, out! Move!" the officer shouted sternly. "Hiding down here, huh? Up!" And he stuck out his hand to pull him up. Stumbling, legs shaking, the boy walked up the stairs.

"But he's got no weapons!" Granny said. "How can you send him out against tanks?"

Somebody else must have been waiting up in the kitchen, for the officer paid no attention to the soldier anymore. He bent back down and in a friendly voice said to the people in the cellar, while Mr. Vanderhook quickly translated the words, "None of us have any weapons left. We're on the run. And if we don't move out fast, we'll be taken prisoner. Don't worry yourself so. We'll take care of him. *Auf Wiedersehen*!"

He tipped his cap and clicked to attention. You could only see the bottom half of his body. They heard him cry, "*Heil* Hitler!" And then he disappeared.

The roaring and howling whistle of the grenades went on through that whole night. Toward morning it got still. The antiaircraft guns on Heuven Hill were heard no more. After a while the English stopped their shooting too.

The Germans were gone.

▪25▪
It Is Over

The sky was radiant and beautiful again the following morning. A lark hovered high in the air, singing joyfully. The earth was so warm that it seemed to breathe. There were even a few insects flying around already.

The shooting had stopped entirely. The German soldiers retreated overnight, and no one had seen them go. Everyone stood outside now and said to each other, "How still it is! Quiet at last." But they didn't quite dare to believe yet that the war was over.

Everingen was busy in the back of the house, harnessing one of the horses to the milk wagon. And then, reins in hand, he went riding past the pigsty and halted in front of the house.

"Come on, Henk, how about it? Animals can't be kept waiting," he called out. Cows simply have to be milked, and they were an hour late already.

There was something, a feeling in the air, as if a miracle had happened. It was the stillness, the peaceful, deep quiet, that was what it was.

"Are you coming?" Evert asked Noortje.

"Where to?"

"To look!"

Yes, they had to go and see. Noortje ran after Evert. "Where?" she cried.

Evert was walking toward Second Beech Lane.

"Let's go to the village," Noortje said, "to the main road. Maybe we'll see the English then."

"Yes, we'll do that too. But first I want to take a look on the heath."

They came to the sand path at the bottom of the lane. There was nothing to see, nothing to hear. Only the few early bees that had survived the winter buzzed around their ears. Evert walked among the low brushwood shrubs that grew alongside the road. The heath lay before them, like a brown, wavy blanket on a very large bed, hills and valleys covered by heath as far as they could see. Narrow paths of white sand went winding their way between dry bushes. Rabbit droppings were all over the place. They breathed in the fragrant, warm air, which smelled of wood and earth.

They walked straight across the heath, first down a steep slope, and then up a hill. Before they were all the way to the top they saw something moving.

"Lie flat," whispered Evert.

Strange soldiers were coming close—five men walking behind one another. Crouching, each one holding a rifle in both hands, ready to shoot. They were not Germans, for these soldiers were wearing strange uniforms, jackets reaching only to their waists and trousers tight at the ankles. Those uniforms were a funny light-brown color, and the soldiers had flat helmets on, covered with knotted nets. They looked tensely to the left, and then to the right.

"What are they doing?" whispered Noortje.

"Looking for Krauts," Evert whispered back. "They don't know for sure if they've all actually left."

"Shall we tell them?"

"No. Maybe some Krauts stayed behind in the woods. Keep down. If they see something moving, they might shoot."

The strange soldiers had come very close now. They stopped for a second and looked out over the hills farther on. The one in front was the leader; he said something to the others in a language the children had never heard before. It must have been English. Then they walked on across the heath. They hadn't even noticed Noortje and Evert.

Later that day they went to the main road to look at the Allied army. Tanks and armored cars were parked between the trees. Trucks were driving back and forth. It was terribly noisy with all those roaring motors and rolling wheels and clanking caterpillar treads. Noortje and Evert had to shout to make themselves heard and soon gave up trying. They just looked.

Soldiers were sleeping in the grass beside the tanks. Soldiers were lying on top of the tanks, too, basking in the sun. You could tell they had fought hard the last weeks, for they all looked dirty and tired. And you could tell from their dark, sunburned faces they had come from the south. The soldiers who weren't sleeping looked around gaily and laughed at lot. They shouted jokes to each other in their strange language and waved at the people from the village. It definitely was a lot nicer belonging to the winning army than to the one on the run.

Evert and Noortje walked slowly on the bicycle path. The road had changed so much that they hardly recognized it. There were deep ruts in the surface and on the shoulders alongside, where the cannons had gone on their heavy caterpillar tracks. Wherever a truck had been stopped, blocking the bicycle path, they had to walk around it. They looked at the soldiers who lay resting on the grass between the trees, and they just stepped over them. The men who weren't asleep glanced up at the children and laughed. Some cars had a maple leaf painted on them and others a polar bear. Later they discovered that the maple leaf belonged to the Canadians, and the white bear was English.

One soldier, who stood leaning against a tank, stuck something out at them. A small packet wrapped in shiny green paper.

"Do you think he wants us to take it?" Noortje asked Evert.

Evert shrugged his shoulders and kept standing there, looking with a blank face, his hands in his pocket. Noortje was curious, and she came a few steps closer. The soldier laughed at her and held out the packet. Hesitantly she took it. There were a few flat things in it wrapped in silver paper. What in the world was she supposed to do with them? The soldier just kept laughing; he pointed to his mouth and made chewing motions with his jaws. Oh, it was something to eat!

They each opened one of those flat, tiny packets. There was a strange gray thing inside. Well, they thought, they might as well try it. It tasted rather nice at first, but soon it didn't taste like anything at all, and you couldn't swallow it either. The stuff just wouldn't go away once you had it in your mouth. It stuck to your teeth.

"Ugh!" Noortje said. "What junk!" And she spat out what was left of it.

Later Mr. Vanderhook explained that the strange stuff was called chewing gum and that the Americans and Canadians like chewing gum a lot.

After the liberation everything was different. That year the spring was the most beautiful you could imagine. The days got longer and the sun shone on the gay yellow buttercups, the purple bugle, and whitish meadowsweet all blooming alongside the roads. Life at Klaphek was becoming good again.

Two young goats were born. Noortje felt that nothing was more fun than lying on her back in the grass and letting those two white kids walk all over her. Their hard little hooves didn't hurt her. The goats liked sucking on anything, sniffing at everything. And lying there, she could look at the stretches of blue sky between the clouds as they slowly drifted by way up high.

After they'd been to the meadow near the Ijssel for the milking, they stopped at the milk factory on their way home. They delivered the full milk cans, taking only a few quarts of their own milk home, only what they needed for themselves. No one came to their doors asking for milk anymore, not even Munkie.

What had become of Munkie? They didn't know. On Liberation Day someone had seen him, hanging around the tanks and the troops. He had pinned an orange ribbon to his coat. Probably he'd become a prisoner of war, for they didn't hear anything more about Munkie.

After a week the Wolthuis family decided to return to their house in the city, and Granny went with them. Henk took them there on the milk wagon. And then the house was suddenly very quiet.

Mr. Vanderhook received a message telling him he could get a ride in a car going to Amsterdam, where the main office of his insurance firm was located.

"I want to get back to work as soon as possible," he said before he left. "And when I come to Klaphek again, we'll soon return to our own house. Or maybe to a different house somewhere. We'll just wait and see where."

That really startled Noortje! So they were going away, away from Klaphek, and soon too! Noortje ran around the house, looked inside the barn, walked by herself up and down Beech Lane a few times. . . . She didn't know what to do with herself, and she didn't want to talk to anyone.

The war was over, and she could go away from Klaphek. Of course, she'd always known that she would. She knew she did not belong to Klaphek. But Noortje had been there so long that she had gotten the feeling the war would go on forever. She'd rather not think about the fact that the world was so much bigger than this house, this yard, the woods, and the heath around. All those months she hadn't once thought that there would come a time when she wouldn't be there anymore. No longer with Aunt Janna and Farmer Everingen, with Evert and Henk and Gerrit and Sissy. And with little Sarah.

The city was far away. What did she care about the city! And their own house there. She didn't long for their house at all. If only a bomb had dropped on it, she thought, then it wouldn't be there anymore. For wasn't Klaphek the most wonderful house in the whole world? Wasn't it? And would she have to go back to school again, too? But surely that was impossible! How would she ever find the time to go to school? However had she managed that before? But, of course, she hadn't been living here before.

Now that it was springtime, they were very busy! Noortje's father was going to be away more than three weeks, and Noortje helped Aunt Janna almost the whole day long. That's how, little by little, the angry and sad feeling began to fade into the background and finally disappear.

The vegetable patches in the garden were being put in order. Noortje drew neat, straight lines in the black earth following a string that had been attached to two small sticks. Aunt Janna put those sticks in the ground so the rope would be taut above the groove where they wanted to sow. They had crumbled the remaining clumps of earth with their fingers, the soil had dried nicely, and now the sowing could begin. Sowing was a very precise little job. With an earnest face Noortje dropped each tiny black seed into the groove. In a few months those tiny seeds would grow into big carrots. They also sowed parsley, cabbage, and leeks, and lettuce. And then she and Aunt Janna planted the beans and scallions.

There was a lot to be done inside the house as well. Each room got a thorough cleaning, and now everyone could sleep in his own bed again. Sissy and Sarah each had her own crib now, in the bedroom of Aunt Janna and Farmer Everingen.

Oh, that Sarah! She'd grown so big that she didn't fit into the basket anymore. And she was gay and strong, too. She could turn herself onto her stomach whenever she wanted to. And when she wasn't asleep, she was laughing or talking in her own funny baby language. Her dark-brown hair was longer and soft as silk.

The parlor was the parlor again. They needed to go in there only once a week, to wind up the clock. In the evenings they just sat around in the kitchen, and it was much cozier there now. After dinner, when the dishes were done, Aunt Janna put a nice soft cover, with beautiful patterns over the brown oilcloth of the table. It gave Noortje a rich feeling to sit at the table with her bare arms on that cover, so that the thick short pile could stroke against her skin. One evening the large kerosene lamp was lit, for now they could get oil again.

Yes, there were many changes at Klaphek. Every little thing told you that the war was over—even the forks and spoons in the drawer of the kitchen table. They'd always been all jumbled together in there. Dinie and Alie would just throw them in when they had washed up, and Noortje had been guilty of that too. One morning she saw that somebody had put all the spoons together, so they fit snugly into each other. The forks were all together like that too, and next to the forks lay the knives in a neat row. It looked really elegant.

"Oh, how beautiful, Aunt Janna!" Noortje cried.

"What is, child?"

"The spoons and the forks!"

Aunt Janna had to laugh and said, "But that's how it should be, isn't it?" So even the cutlery said that the war was over.

Noortje still fed Sarah. You had to be rather strong for that now, for Sarah was also a little stronger every day. She could already eat vegetables and porridge with a little spoon. Noortje sat with her in Everingen's chair, and Sarah kicked her legs and grabbed at the spoon. Noortje had to hold both her hands tightly. But she ate a lot, and she grew fast, and every day she got a little prettier and wiser.

When Sarah had finished eating she had to go to sleep, and Noortje sat down on the floor by the side of the crib. Sarah looked at her and laughed. She waved her arms and kicked off the blanket. She was always so happy when she saw Noortje.

"My sweet little Sarah," Noor whispered one time. "You know, I'll never leave you. I won't go back to the city. . . ."

She remained sitting there for a long time, leaning her chin on the edge of the crib. There was a dull, heavy feeling inside her head, and her throat was dry. She knew very well that soon everything would be different, but she was trying not to think of that.

Little blossoms were floating down from the trees. The sun touched Sarah's face. She had to sneeze and got a funny wrinkle in her nose.

"It must always stay like this, always," Noortje said softly. "It must. I want it to."

▪26▪ Sissy's Death

Then suddenly Sissy was dead. It happened very fast.

One day she was sick. She had a high fever and difficulty in breathing. And she lay there crying softly.

The doctor came and said she must be taken to the hospital immediately. And he told them all they must come to the hospital also, where their throats were swabbed to see if they'd gotten the disease too. Sissy had diphtheria, which was dangerously contagious.

A week later Sissy was dead. Evert and Noortje walked with Aunt Janna across the heath to the hospital in Zemst.

"Oh, you've come to look at Wilhelmina," one of the nurses said. After all, that was Sissy's real name: Wilhelmina Everingen.

Sissy lay in a large bed. The children stood there silently, looking in wonder at the dead child. They could see it was Sissy all right, and yet it wasn't Sissy really. She had become Wilhelmina. Now that she was dead, Sissy had a beautiful, smooth face. You could see very clearly that she was Gerrit's sister. She looked like him. Strangely, after her death Sissy looked like a normal child: pretty and sweet.

"That's how she really was, right, Aunt Janna?" whispered Noortje.

Aunt Janna could not say anything. She looked at her little daughter, and a tear slowly glided down past her mouth to the chin.

* * *

Many people were at the funeral. The Wolthuis family was there, and Noortje's father came over from Amsterdam. There was a letter from Theo. He was in Switzerland in a sanatorium, where he had hopes of recovering completely. There were also relatives from the Betuwe region, Aunt Janna's sisters, who also lived on farms, and their husbands. They all drank coffee in the parlor and talked about the war that was over now and about their farms. Alie and Dinie sat stiff and straight on their chairs, for now they were at Klaphek as visitors.

The house was rather solemn. The men wore black suits and had plaid caps on, and their clogs were scrubbed so clean that they were white. Even in the corridor you could smell their cigars, which they held carefully in stiff, crooked fingers, while puffing out little blue clouds of smoke. A funeral was a sad event, to be sure, but these were the first cigars they had smoked since the war. So they should enjoy them, shouldn't they.

Evert stayed in the parlor the whole afternoon, listening to the men talking. Noortje soon found she didn't like it there, and she went to the kitchen to help out a little. There was a lot of washing up to do. A couple of fat women she'd never seen before were already busy putting the dirty cups in the sink. One of them was pouring hot water into the basin and said, "It's a good thing the child has died. She was such a heavy burden for Janna."

"Ah, those, they never get to be very old usually. And it's just as well. It's really too much, taking care of them," the other woman said.

Noortje walked out of the house. Not long after, the guests said good-bye, and Henk was already busy harnessing Browny to the milk wagon. He had his old clothes on again, but he still held a piece of cigar clenched between his teeth. Evert, wearing his old work clothes again also, placed the empty milk cans in the wagon. No one asked Noortje if she felt like joining them, so she slowly walked back to the kitchen. The strange women would probably have gone by now.

The kitchen was very still, oddly still. Flies buzzed around the lamp. Noortje's father was sitting there also, and Noortje thought she saw that he was about to say something to Aunt Janna just as she came in. But he didn't.

Aunt Janna was feeding Sarah and didn't say anything either. At each spoonful she put into Sarah's mouth, Aunt Janna's chin went up and down briefly; and between spoonfuls, while Sarah had to chew and swallow, she rocked the baby on her lap.

Sissy's crib had been removed as soon as she'd been taken to the hospital. But today, for the first time, Noortje noticed how empty and quiet it had become in the kitchen without Sissy. The sounds she was always making, the howling and screaming, they had gone away forever. And also that unpleasant smell of wet diapers had disappeared.

"Yes, yes," said Mr. Vanderhook, "that's the way things are." And he was drumming away with his fingers on the oilcloth. He must be feeling that awful stillness too.

Aunt Janna wiped Sarah's mouth. "So you've had enough now," she said.

She let Sarah grab her finger and swing it up and down, and then Aunt Janna started humming a tune to that motion as if there were nothing unusual about this particular day.

She looked at Noortje and smiled. "What a nice, chubby little child she is, huh, Noortje?" she said. "Yes, you're a nice little thing." And she cuddled Sarah, and Sarah crowed with pleasure.

Aunt Janna sat up straight and looked at Mr. Vanderhook. "Well, then, that's agreed. You're so much closer than we are. If we have to wait for news it could take a long time. Those people have so much to do these days."

"Ah, but of course," said Noortje's father. "The Red Cross will be best. They've assured me that all the names are coming in to them. As soon as they know or hear something, I'll be informed. But, in the meantime, I'll keep checking with them myself."

"What about the Red Cross?" Noortje asked.

"We've asked Red Cross if they have any information concerning Sarah's parents—if they're still alive, or if there are any other relatives, in case they are not," her father told her.

"But," Noortje said, "if they're not living anymore, isn't Sarah ours then?"

"Ours?" Aunt Janna asked. "How do you mean that, girl?"

"Well, yours, Klaphek's, ours, all of us, of course. . . ."

"Noortje, Sarah isn't ours in any event," her father said. "I still very much hope that her father and mother and two brothers will return. But I'm afraid that won't happen, for so far there hasn't been any news of them. However, that doesn't mean we can just do as we please with this baby. Anyway, we ourselves won't be staying here much longer either. You know that, don't you? I'd wanted to talk these things over with you tonight quietly, just the two of us. But we might as well go into it now, with Aunt Janna here too. Much better, actually."

Noortje looked from one to the other, with big, questioning eyes. Was this it? Was it really coming, the day everything would change?

Her father said, "Listen, dear. I've been given work in Amsterdam, and as soon as I have a place for us, we're both going to live there. But first I'll have to leave you here for a few more weeks. You don't mind that, do you?"

"But," Noortje said, "if no one comes for Sarah, what happens then?"

"We'll have to wait and see," her father said. "Whatever is best for her, we must let happen. Don't you agree?"

And Aunt Janna said, "No child is ever ours, Noortje. Sissy wasn't ours either. It was given to us to take care of her. The Lord has given, the Lord has taken away!"

"Yes, Sissy!" Noortje said. "But Sarah isn't. . . ."

She wanted to say, But Sarah isn't dead! And she looked at the child, kicking with her sturdy, brown little legs in Aunt Janna's lap.

"We have taken care of Sarah together," said Aunt Janna. "And you have done that very well, dear. We're proud of you!"

The next morning Noortje's father left again.

Less than two weeks later someone came to Klaphek. He came in a car, and Mr. Vanderhook had traveled with him. The man told them that he was a brother of Mrs. Meyer's. He had received their address from the Red Cross, after Noortje's father had reported the whereabouts of Sarah.

Mr. and Mrs. Meyer never came back. Nor did their two little boys. After they were found by the Germans, they were immediately sent to a concentration camp, where they were killed in the gas chambers.

The man came for Sarah. He was going to the United States, he told them. He had relatives there. He could leave in a week by boat. And he wanted to take Sarah with him to the Meyer relatives.

The man drove off in his car, and Sarah's basket, with Sarah in it, sat on the back seat. Aunt Janna had tied up her clothes and diapers in a blanket. Sarah was really already too big for the basket, but still it was the best way for her to make the long journey.

When the car had disappeared from sight, Noortje ran off. She hid in the old rubbish spot behind the barn where once, very long ago, she and Evert had smoked some of Henk's tobacco together. She wasn't thinking of that now.

Noortje cried. She cried as she had never cried before. Her whole body shook. Tears streamed down her cheeks, and they kept coming. The waves of grief were so bad that her stomach hurt. Now that Sarah's own father and mother and her two little brothers were no longer alive she should stay with her, with her, Noortje, and with Aunt Janna! It was too much, and wasn't it ridiculous that all of a sudden everyone was going away to live in a different place in the world!

Crying makes you tired. Without realizing it, Noortje fell asleep, just like that, on the dusty floor of the junk shed. And there her father found her.

He had been searching all over. Father took Noortje to the stone cistern next to the well house. He washed her face with his handkerchief.

There they sat for a long time, on the edge of the cistern together. The sun was shining, and yet Noortje felt cold. She had goose pimples all over, and she felt that her eyes were red and burning. They sat there quite awhile without talking. Noortje was glad her father didn't say anything and that he stayed with her until she was calm again. Finally Father got up; he took Noortje's hand and led her inside for supper.

The next morning they were to get a ride in a car going to Amsterdam. Since gasoline was so scarce, the owner of the car didn't want to drive all the way to Klaphek. He was going to wait for them in Dieren. Henk offered to take them there.

Noortje's clothes were packed in a bag. It was a hot day, and she wore a thin blouse and a very short skirt. The blouse was tight around her, and the buttons kept popping open.

"You've grown," her father said, laughing. "I'm bringing a big daughter back to Amsterdam!" Yes, Noortje had grown, and the few clothes she owned were much too small for her. But that wasn't important at all.

It was much more important that they were riding away now, over the meadow to the gate. And that Aunt Janna and Farmer Everingen stood in front of the house waving to them. Gerrit had already gone off to play behind the barn, forgetting that they were leaving. Suddenly Evert was running after them on his clogs. He closed the gate behind the milk wagon.

"Henk, I'm coming too!" he yelled.

"Jump on then," Henk said.

Evert sat in his dirty overalls on the bench opposite Noortje, grinning. "It's such a nice trip that I wanted to go too!" he said. "And Dad said I could come."

"Right you are," Mr. Vanderhook said. "Now Henk won't be so lonely on the way back."

"No," Henk said, "and we can console each other after our princess is gone."

When they got to the main road, the horse went into a trot. His hooves clattered gaily, and now and then Henk cracked his whip.

Noortje's father looked at the sky, and blinking his eyes he said, "I bet it's going to be a beautiful summer. After a severe winter, a hot summer. You often get that."

All at once, Noortje knew that what was happening

was inevitable. Once something began to happen, it just had to be like that. In a little while all they had to do was say good-bye to Henk and Evert, and that would be it.

But later, much later, when Noortje had been living in Amsterdam a long time and was back in school, she sometimes found it difficult to pay attention in class. She wouldn't hear what the teacher was saying and didn't see the blackboard at the front of the classroom or the heads of the other students sitting at their desks in front of her. For Noortje was dreaming of Klaphek.

She needn't even close her eyes to see the thick trees of Beech Lane. She heard the wind rustling in their tall branches, and she also heard the sound the latch made when she opened the kitchen door.

She smelled a wonderful smell: burning wood and rye-flour porridge. Then she smiled to herself and saw it all before her, everything as it had been in that kitchen. The tiles behind the cooking stove, the cookie tin with the nickels and dimes on the mantelpiece, the farmer's chair with the knitted cushion. She heard Sissy screaming, and she saw the tiny, warm feet of Sarah kicking.

And when she sat dreaming to herself like that, she would be scolded by the teacher for being inattentive. But she hardly even noticed. It only made her angry, because she was pulled away out of that warm kitchen into a classroom full of strange people.

About the Author

Els Pelgrom was born in 1934, in Arnhem, a provincial town in the Netherlands, where an important battle was fought in 1944. The author experienced the consequences of the Battle of Arnhem firsthand, and her memories of those final days of World War II form the basis of *The Winter When Time Was Frozen.* The novel, published in the Netherlands as *De Kinderen van het Achtste Woud,* gained wide recognition and in 1978 was awarded the Dutch literary prize for the best children's book of the year.

Mother of three children, Ms. Pelgrom currently lives in Amsterdam, where she works as a full-time writer.